THE OFFICIAL MOVIE NOVELIZATION

UBISOFT

625 3rd St, San Francisco,
CA 94107, U.S.A.

Published by Ubisoft.
The publisher does not have any control over and does not assume any responsibility for author or third-party websites or their content.

Special thanks:
Yves Guillemot, Laurent Detoc, Alain Core, Geoffroy Sardin, Yannis Mallat, Gérard Guillemot, Stephanie Simard, Etienne Allonier, Aymar Azaïzia, Antoine Ceszynski, Anouk Bachman, Maxime Durand, Richard Farrese, Joshua Meyer, Virginie Gringarten, Marc Muraccini, Cécile Russeil, Faceout Studio, Paul Nielsen, Derek Thornton, Torrey Sharp, Michael Beadle, Heather Pond, Joanie Simms, Megan Beatie, Andrien Gbinigie, Stephanie Pecaoco, Sain Sain Thao, Michael Kwan, Hector Rodriguez, Clémence Deleuze, François Tallec.

ISBN 978-1-945210-05-1

10 9 8 7 6 5 4 3 2 1   16 17 18 19 20

First printing 2016. Printed in the U.S.A.

Book design by Faceout Studio, Derek Thornton and Paul Nielsen.

ASSASSIN'S CREED®

THE OFFICIAL MOVIE NOVELIZATION

WRITTEN BY
CHRISTIE GOLDEN

BASED ON THE SCREENPLAY BY
MICHAEL LESSLIE
AND ADAM COOPER &
BILL COLLAGE

BASED ON THE
ASSASSIN'S CREED®
GAME SERIES

This book is dedicated to all those
who have played and loved the Assassin's
Creed games, but especially to Ryan Puckett,
who has always demonstrated kindness and
generosity far beyond his years.

For centuries, the Order of the Knights Templar have searched for the mythical Apple of Eden.

They believe it contains not only the seeds of man's first disobedience, but the key to free will itself.

If they find the relic and decode its secrets, they will have the power to control all human thought.

Only a brotherhood called the Assassins stands in their way. . . .

PROLOGUE

The sky was golden fire, gilding all it touched; the rocky facets of the jutting mountains, the city spread out below them, and the red tile roof of the Moorish fortress, which offered up fire of its own in the open courtyard.

The eagle soared through the whipping wind, winging its way toward its evening resting place before the gold gave way to the cooler lavender hues of an encroaching night. Below, those who labored tending the forge and shaping blades paid neither the eagle, nor the wind, nor the sky any heed.

Their faces were swathed in shadow, hidden by the hoods they all wore as they worked; sharpening fresh blades, pouring molten metal to form new ones, and hammering red steel into gray obedience. No one spoke. The silence was broken only by the scraping and clanging of their task.

Outside the entrance of the great fortress stood a single figure. Tall, well-formed, and sleek with muscle, he was both somber and impatient. While he wore a hood like the others, he was not truly one of them.

Not yet.

It was in his blood; that much was undeniable. His parents had been part of the Brotherhood he was about to pledge his life to protect. When he had been but a child, his parents had taught him how to fight, how to hide, how to leap and climb, all in the guise of play or adventure.

He had been too young, too innocent, to understand the brutal reality behind the lessons he was learning. And then, when he was older, his parents had told him who they were, and what they served. He had not liked the idea that he was not the master of his own fate, and had been reluctant to follow in their footsteps.

It had cost them all.

The great enemy had sniffed them out.

Had observed their behavior, their habits. Like predators, the ancient foe had culled his parents from the herd, from their brothers and sisters, and descended in numbers too great to resist.

And the age-old enemy had slain them.

Not cleanly, with respect, in a fair fight, oh no. Not this enemy. This enemy had bound them with chains to a stake. Had placed bundles of wood at their feet, doused the bundles—and them—with oil, and set them afire while crowds cheered the horrific spectacle.

He had not been there, when they were taken. He had wondered then, and still wondered now, as he shifted his weight from one foot to the other, if he had been, could he have turned the tide? The members of the Brotherhood, who had come too late, assured him that no, he could not have. Not without training.

The murderers had made no effort to hide their deed, but had rather boasted of capturing "infidels." Tall, with a chest broader than a barrel, cold-eyed and colder-hearted, this man—Ojeda—had led the attack. And he had stood beside Father Tomás de Torquemada as the monster had condemned, then burned, Aguilar's family.

It had been too late to save them. But it was not too late to save himself.

The Brotherhood had turned him away at first, questioning his motives. But Maria had seen in him more than a desire for revenge. She had broken through his raw grief and instinctive, impulsive anger to the man inside, to someone who could see beyond taking revenge on the man who had killed his family.

To the man who knew there was more in this world that mattered than those he had loved—there was the Creed. Something that would outlive all of them, and could be passed on to generations yet to come.

To the children of Assassins—like he had been.

And so, he had been trained. Some of it was easy, and he blessed his parents for their nurturance of such "play." Some of it was harder, and he bore scars as testament to the times when he had been slow or inattentive or simply too weary.

He learned the history of his lineage, and the courage that drove what must seem like mad recklessness to those who stood on the outside, whose pulses did not quicken as those of the Brotherhood did.

Through it all, was Maria.

Quick to laugh, quicker with her blades, she seemed to thrum with intensity with every breath. She pushed him mercilessly when he flagged, praised him when he succeeded, and now, she was inside, helping with the rite that would move him to stand where the spirits of his murdered family would have him be.

He snapped out of his reverie when several of the hooded forms appeared at the door, beckoning him to follow. In silence he obeyed, his heart racing with anticipation, but cultivating calmness as he walked down the stairs into the open area. The sound of chanting reached his ears: *"Laa shay'a waqi'un moutlaq bale koulon moumkine."*

The other hooded figures stood in a loose circle around a rectangular table in the center. At one end stood someone close to the initiate; Benedicto, the Mentor, with whom he had trained and fought beside. He was a kind man, free with laughter and praise, but the light of the candles on the table and the torches flickering in their sconces revealed a face currently devoid of lighter emotions.

It had been Benedicto, along with Maria, who had reached out to the bereft young man. He had not pretended he could replace the father that had been snatched away from a broken son, but Benedicto had done what he could. He had earned the respect of everyone in attendance —including the initiate.

When he spoke, his voice was strong, and he addressed all present.

"The Inquisition has finally delivered Spain to the Templars. Sultan Muhammad and his people still hold out in Granada. But if his son, the prince, is captured, he will surrender the city and the Apple of Eden."

The tattooed faces, many of them sporting scars, remained largely impassive, but Aguilar could feel the tension rise in the room at the news. Benedicto looked at them, and seemed to be pleased with what he saw.

His dark gaze finally alighted on the initiate. It was time.

"Do you, Aguilar de Nerha, swear to honor our Brotherhood in the fight for freedom? To defend mankind against the Templars' tyranny, and preserve free will?"

Aguilar answered without hesitation. "I swear."

Benedicto continued, his voice intense.

"If the Apple falls into their hands, the Templars will destroy everything that stands in their way. Protest, dissent... our right to think for ourselves. Swear to me that you will sacrifice your life and the lives of everyone here to keep it from them."

Aguilar sensed that this was not part of the standard ritual, that Benedicto wanted to make certain beyond a shadow of a doubt that in this most dangerous of times, the initiate fully understood all that might be asked of him.

But Aguilar had no hesitation. "Yes, Mentor."

The Mentor's brown eyes searched his, then he nodded, moving to step beside Aguilar. He reached for the younger man's right hand, wrapped with bandages in anticipation of the required sacrifice, bringing it down not ungently to rest upon a block of carved wood banded with decorated metal.

There were other, darker decorations on the wood as well; stains the hue of old rust.

Benedicto took care to place Aguilar's hand just so, and settled a two-pronged instrument over the younger man's ring finger. Aguilar knew the Mentor felt him tense, despite himself.

"Our own lives are nothing," Benedicto reminded him, his gaze boring into Aguilar's. "The Apple is everything. The spirit of the Eagle will watch over the future."

His mother and father had left behind a legacy of fierce love, and a history Aguilar now ached to follow. They had also left *him* behind. He had thought he was alone, but in a moment, he would not be. In a moment, he would have a vast family—a brotherhood.

Benedicto shoved the instrument down, severing the finger.

The pain was exquisite. But Aguilar steeled himself and did not cry out, nor jerk back instinctively. Blood gushed, swiftly drenching the bandages that soaked it up greedily as he breathed deeply, his survival instincts vying with the discipline instilled in his training.

The blade has been honed to perfect sharpness, he told himself. *The cut is clean. It will heal.*

And I, too, will heal.

Maria walked toward him, holding out an ornate gauntlet crafted of metal and leather. Aguilar slipped his arm in carefully, gritting his teeth so he would not wince as his fresh wound scraped against the gauntlet's edge. He would not look at it, would look only at Maria, into the depths of her warm blue-green eyes rimmed with dark kohl, her beauty enhanced by the tattoos that kissed her on forehead, chin, and beneath both eyes.

Maria, who had come to him first in the role of a kind sister, but who over time had become so much more. He knew all of her; her laughter, her scent, the soft puff of her breath against his skin as she slept in his arms. He knew the curve of her thigh, and the strength of her arms as she playfully pinned him before rewarding him with the heat of her mouth.

But there was no playfulness in this moment. Maria was many things to him, but Aguilar well knew that should he stumble here, her blade would be the first to find his throat.

Before all else, she was an Assassin, and before all ties, she was bound to the Creed.

As he would be.

Her voice, sweet and strong, spoke the ritual words. "Where other men blindly follow the truth, remember..."

"... nothing is true," said the rest in unison.

"Where other men are limited by morality or law, remember..."

"... everything is permitted."

Aguilar held her gaze a moment longer, then made the slight movement of his wrist, as he had been taught. With a bright metallic sound, as if joyful it had been freed, the blade on the underside of his arm sprang forward to fill the gap left by the severed ring finger.

Aguilar's voice trembled with intensity when he spoke. "We work in the dark to serve the

Light."

He took a breath.

"We are... *Assassins*."

And above them, an eagle's cry sounded, as if the spirit was pleased.

CHAPTER 1

BAJA, CALIFORNIA

1988

Cal Lynch looked up at the sound of the eagle's cry, squinting against the sunlight. He couldn't see it clearly, silhouetted against the sky as it was, but he grinned at it as he flipped the hood of his gray sweatshirt over his dark blond hair and prepared himself.

He, too, was going to fly.

He'd been wanting to do this... well, *forever*, since his parents had first moved here a few months ago. They moved a lot; it was something Cal simply took for granted about his family. Dad and Mom got odd jobs wherever they could, they stayed for a while, and then moved on.

19

Because of this, Cal had never really had the chance to make friends. So it was that today, the day he was finally going to do it, he had no audience. It didn't particularly bother him, and in fact, it was just as well—he was definitely *not* supposed to be doing this in the first place.

He'd dragged his bike all the way up to the roof of one of the vacant, dilapidated old buildings. Once his foot had gone right through one of the rusted-out steps, slicing through his jeans to bite at his leg. It was cool; he'd gotten a tetanus shot from the low-cost clinic a year ago.

He was used to rooftops. At night, when his parents thought him safely inside his room, he would crawl out his bedroom window and onto the roofs, scampering off into the coolness and secrecy of the night—and into many misadventures of which his parents were blissfully ignorant.

Cal's destination today was a large shipping container, set slightly lower than the roof upon which Cal and his bike were perched. The gulf between them was twenty feet or so—no big deal.

Except his heart fluttered in his chest as he sat, one foot on a pedal, one foot on the building's roof.

He closed his eyes, breathing slowly through his nostrils to calm his racing heart and shallow breath.

You're already there, he told himself. *It's already done. See every inch of the journey. See the wheels landing perfectly, how you're going to bring the bike around right away so you don't shoot off the other side.*

Oh, that wasn't a good image, and he immediately tried to scrub it from his brain. But it was like the old joke—"don't think of a pink elephant," and boom, suddenly that was all you could see.

Cal redirected his attention, seeing himself pedaling, soaring, landing—victorious.

In his mind's eye, he flew. Like the eagle.

He could do it.

Slowly, calmly, Cal opened his eyes and tightened his grasp on the handlebars.

Now.

He threw himself into it, pedaling furiously, his eyes fixed not on the rapidly decreasing length of roof or on the pile of junk that lay between it and the shipping container, but on his destination. Faster, faster, and then, there was nothing below his tires as he pulled the front wheel of his bike up hard.

He sailed over the trash below, his face spreading in a grin of absolute perfect, pure joy. Yes! He was going to make it—

The first wheel cleared it.

The second didn't.

So quickly he didn't even have time to be frightened, Cal and the bike landed hard on the pile of old mattresses, trash, and other detritus he had laboriously dragged to the spot over several weeks. He moved experimentally, but nothing appeared to be broken. Cal was bleeding from a scrape on his face and his whole body ached, but he was okay.

The bicycle wasn't in the best shape, either, and it was seeing the damage to it more than anything else that brought his failure home hard.

"Shit," he swore, then dragged himself and the bike out of the trash heap. He was *not* looking forward to explaining his injuries to his parents.

He took a few moments to inspect himself. A few cuts and bruises on his face and body, nothing too bad; even the cut on his leg had stopped bleeding. The bike, too, had some cosmetic dings here and there, but was still rideable.

Good. Cal looked up, squinting, and smiled as he saw the small dot that was the eagle.

Well... Mom and Dad didn't have to know everything right away.

Cal set off to follow the eagle for a while.

* * *

Shadows were starting to lengthen by the time Cal returned to the rundown tenement community he called home.

His bike stirred up yellow dust from the dirt road. Everything here was covered with the pale, drifting gold, and a few decorative strands of colored pennants strung across the road provided the only splashes of color.

Cal's usual good mood had returned. He was already analyzing what he had done wrong, and how to make the jump successful the next time. After all, this *was* only the first attempt. Callum Lynch was not a quitter. He'd try again tomorrow—or, he amended, being realistic, as soon as his parents let him have the bike back.

It was only after Cal was well within the town's limits that he noticed that something was off. People were out of their houses, a few sitting in chairs with drinks, but most standing around, just... staring.

And they were staring at *him*.

Their faces were carefully neutral, but Cal's stomach clenched.

Something was wrong.

He increased his pace, dropping the bike outside his door, and cast one more glance behind him at his silent, solemn neighbors.

Cal's heart sped up slightly, though he didn't understand why. He reached for the porch doorknob, and his hand froze.

The door was standing wide open.

His parents *always* closed it.

Cal swallowed, then stepped forward into the small enclosed porch, pausing, listening, moving slowly, like a stranger, in this so-familiar place. The door to the main part of the house was open, too. One small hand extended, parting the long strands of amber-colored beads that provided a token barrier between most of the rooms in the house.

There was no conversation or laughter, no smell of supper on the stove, no rattle or clink of dishes. The only sound of normalcy was Patsy Cline's voice, tinny and faint, coming from the old beige radio, and the drone of the television in the background—some kind of news show.

"Today, we have Dr. Alan Rikkin, CEO of Abstergo Industries," the host was saying. "Alan, it seems the world is on the precipice."

"It does, doesn't it?" The speaker had an upper-crust English accent. Cal caught a brief glimpse of a man in his late thirties, well-dressed, elegant, with dark eyes and sharp features.

"It seems mankind is intent upon destroying itself with this continuous and widespread violence. I believe unless we address the root causes of our aggressive nature, civilization as we know it will be lost. But we at Abstergo Industries are working towards isolating the key component—"

He droned on. Cal wasn't paying attention as he continued to move forward. It was dark inside, but that wasn't unusual; summers were hot here, and darkness kept things cool. But it wasn't a friendly darkness, and Cal realized his hands were clammy.

As he stepped into the family room, he could see his mother seated in the kitchen, a silhouette against the windows. Relieved, and unsure why, Cal started to call out to her. But the words died in his throat. He realized now that she sat at a strange angle, leaning against the back of the char, her arms hanging down to either side.

And she was still. So, so still.

Cal froze, staring at her, his brain trying to work out what was wrong. Motion caught his eye—a slow drip of something on the floor, falling from her hand.

Drops falling into a spreading red puddle. This, the cruel sunlight caught.

Cal's eyes were transfixed by the movement. Then they slowly traveled upward to follow the path of red.

The crimson droplets fell languidly from a silver pendant Cal remembered seeing every day around his mother's long, slender throat. An eight-sided star with a diamond shape in the center. Etched on it in black was a symbol that looked almost like the letter A, if that letter's lines had been made from stylized, slightly curved blades.

The chain was tangled around her hand now, and its silver links were bathed in scarlet.

Every instinct in him screamed to him to tear his gaze away, to flee and never look back. Instead, Cal stood, rooted to the spot.

Her hand was covered in blood. The left sleeve of her white peasant blouse was saturated with it.

And her throat....

"Mom?" he murmured, even though the hole in her throat meant she was dead.

"Laa shay'a waqi'un moutlaq bale kouloun moumkine."

The whisper seized Cal's attention, and he realized with a shock that he and his mother were not alone in the room.

Her killer was here, too.

He stood beside the television, a large man topping six feet, his back to Cal, staring out the window. A hood was over his head.

But once again, Cal's eye was drawn to movement, to the same ghastly red fluid, dripping, dripping to the cheap linoleum floor, his mother's blood flowing from the tip of a blade that extended beneath her murderer's wrist.

"Dad," he whispered, his world shattering as his body threatened to vomit, to collapse, to curl into a fetal position and never move again. It couldn't be true.

Slowly the hooded figure turned, and Cal's heart spasmed with grief and terror as he realized he had been right. The figure was his father.

Joseph Lynch's eyes were haunted, as if he, too, was grieving, but how could that be? Why? He was the one who had—

"Your blood is not your own, Cal," his father said, his voice, with its trace of Irish brogue that years in the United States had never been able to completely erode, heavy and aching. "They found us."

Cal stared, uncomprehending any of it, all of it. And then, his father faced him fully, and began to walk toward him. The footfalls echoed loudly in this house of horror, a sound that ought to be normal and wasn't drowning out the chatter on the television and Patsy Cline singing that she was crazy.

Crazy. I'm crazy. That's what's happening.

And yet, somewhat to his surprise, of their own volition, Cal's feet were doing something not crazy at all. They seemed to move of their own volition, backing away from his father, his *dad*, who had just stuck a knife in his wife's neck.

On the hooded man came, slowly, inexorably, as inescapable as death itself. Cal's retreating feet suddenly stopped.

He didn't want to live in a world where his father had killed his mother. He wanted to be with her.

Joseph Lynch stopped, too, his arms hanging limply, almost helplessly, at his sides, blood still dripping from the blade he had plunged into his wife's delicate throat.

"They want what's inside you, Cal. Live in the shadows," his father said, as if his heart were breaking at the words.

Cal stared at him, his own heart slamming against his chest. He couldn't move, couldn't think—

The screeching sound of tires and the shadow of cars outside broke the deadly spell. The killer looked up, over his son's head, at the cars now fishtailing to a stop outside his door.

"Go!" he screamed at his son. "Go! *Now!*"

Galvanized into action, Cal bolted for the stairs. His once-frozen limbs now propelled him up them two at a time, and he exploded out of the window onto the rooftops, the secret path of freedom his parents had never known about now turning into an acrobat's escape route.

He ran as he had never run in his life, jumping without hesitation to one level above or below the long, low rooftops, rolling as he struck, leaping to his feet and running again. Out of the corner of his eye, Cal saw what seemed like dozens of black SUVs pouring like a flood down the dusty streets.

At one point, Cal ducked out of sight for a moment to catch his breath and risked a glance down.

In the passenger side of one car, he caught a glimpse of a pale, angular-featured man with dark hair, dark clothes, and dark sunglasses. It almost looked like the man he had just seen on the TV, but of course it couldn't be.

Could it? For no reason he could fathom, a chill went through the boy.

The second the SUV turned, Cal ran again, jumping off the roof into a pile of debris, and pelting down the road that led away from the cluster of tenement buildings, away from his dead mother and murderous father, away from everything it meant to be Callum Lynch.

CHAPTER 2

Frank Kimmler, forty-seven, had been a guard at the Huntsville Department of Criminal Justice for seventeen years. In that time, he had seen some of the worst things a person could do to another person. Yet somehow, he was always surprised by the darkness that dogged his days, and after a bad one he always came home promising his wife he'd quit, get something a little calmer, safer. Something he could tell his girls about when he came home at night. Yet the next day, Kimmler was always back at work.

On this evening of October 21, as surveillance screens played out beside and behind him, a bologna and cheese sandwich and a Coke sat untouched as he sat watching a different screen entirely and talking on the phone to his wife, Janice.

"Breaking news of what appears to be three assassinations in Houston, Texas today," the television reporter said somberly into the camera. "The head of the IMF Cassiane Lacroix, Texan oil billionaire Luther Wiley, and Chinese media mogul Bolin Chang, were all killed at the Four Seasons Hotel in broad daylight."

"Yes, honey, I'm watching it on the news right now," Kimmler was saying. "Three in one go. In broad daylight. I know, I know, it's awful. Where are *you*?"

"I just pulled into the driveway," Janice said. Her voice was shaking. "They blocked off some of the roads. Police cars everywhere. It was so backed up it took me three hours to get home! Frank... I wish you weren't working there."

He wished it, too, but he couldn't say that. Instead, he said, "Oh, honey, I'm safer than anybody right where I am. It's all my girls I worry about. Are they home with you?"

His eyes wandered back to the images of the three victims plastered on the TV screen as Janice told him that Suzanne was home upstairs doing her homework, but Patricia had called saying she'd be late. That got his attention.

"What do you mean she's not home yet? It's a school night!"

"She called, says she's with her friends at the mall and Debbie's mother is picking them all up as soon as she can get there. She's fine."

There was a long pause, then Janice said, "Will... will you be able to come home? I'm going to make pot pie. I think we could all use some comfort food."

He glanced at his bologna sandwich and sighed longingly. "I'll have to heat some up when I got home, babe. I'm stuck here. He goes under at six, so I'll be home at nine."

He waved at the familiar face approaching his desk. "I gotta go. Father Raymond is here."

Frank hung up and turned to the priest, giving him a friendly smile. Father Raymond had been coming here for the last four years, and Frank had gotten fond of the skinny, soft-spoken younger man. He was fairly new to the cloth; he told Frank once that he'd been an English professor at some east coast university before finding his true calling. Frank could easily imagine him in the halls of academia, talking about Shakespeare or Dickens or somebody.

"Always on time, Father. How is that? The city's on lockdown after what happened today. My wife took three hours to get home."

"I'm glad she's safe," Father Raymond replied, looking relieved. "How are the girls?"

"One's home, the other's stuck at the mall with some friends. I try to keep tabs on them, but...."

Frank sighed and scratched the back of his head. A few years ago, his hair had started falling out. Last time Father Raymond had come, he'd teased Frank that he could have become a tonsured monk.

"I'm kind of scared for them, y'know. The way things are in the world today... it's not a happy place."

Father Raymond nodded sympathetically. "And... how is our man?"

"Quiet. All he does is draw. All day. It's against regulations, but what are you gonna do? It's the guy's birthday. Turns out his father killed his mother. It's gotta mess you up."

Frank looked up at the priest with doleful brown eyes. "I don't know, Father. He kills a pimp, we kill him. Doesn't make sense...."

"The ways of God—" Father Raymond began.

"—are not our ways." Frank sighed.

The priest produced a handkerchief and wiped at his palm, smiling self-deprecatingly at Frank. "You never get used to this part of the job," he said.

"Nope," Frank replied. "And I don't think that's a bad thing."

Father Raymond tucked the handkerchief away and nodded as another guard stepped up, ready to escort him back.

"Give my regards to Janice and the girls. Tell them I'll keep them in my prayers."

* * *

The inmate in cell 304 was not a particularly gifted artist, Father Raymond thought. But he was prolific, and he threw himself into his task with an almost furious singlemindedness of purpose.

Pieces of rectangular, cream-colored manila paper with drawings that ranged from the haunting to the grotesque adorned the wall as high as a man could reach. On the other three walls, thick felt-tip markers in shades of black, green, and blue had left their marks in the form of gibberish graffiti, or in strange symbols that perhaps even the creator of the nightmarish gallery could not interpret.

Father Raymond observed the prisoner in his late thirties as he sat on the floor, scribbling with a piece of charcoal. The inmate paused, rubbing a spot with his thumb to smooth the harsh black lines into a softer, misty form. He only looked up from his work as the door was opened to admit the priest. He got to his feet, then sat quietly on his cot, looking up at Father Raymond with an expression of mild boredom.

Keys rattled as the door was locked behind the man of God, who regarded the unsettling images intently, with no hint of distaste, only compassion. He had certainly seen cruder things before in the cells of men about to die.

Father Raymond perused them with seriousness and thought: charcoal sketches of men with bizarre headpieces, lumpy, barely-formed shapes that were only vaguely human embracing or killing one another, skulls embedded in flowers, a cavernous mouth open in a scream, a hand brandishing a cross, a figure engulfed in flame, a nearly-skeletal horse neighing in terror.

One in particular gave the priest pause: it was the crude, almost cartoonish shape of an old-fashioned executioner, with a black hood pulled over his head.

Then he turned to the prisoner.

He had a name, of course; all men had names. Father Raymond made sure he used them. At the hours of their deaths, of all times, it was important that they know that others understood that.

"You're Callum Lynch," the priest said, his voice calm and kind. "I'm Father Raymond."

Callum Lynch's hands were covered in charcoal dust, his reddish-blond hair cropped short, and there was something blazing in the depth of his blue eyes that told the priest that Lynch's veneer of calm control was exactly that—a veneer, one perhaps paper-thin.

"Are you here to save my soul?" the prisoner asked, his voice husky from disuse.

"Something like that."

Father Raymond hesitated, wondering if should mention what Frank told him, then decided to go ahead. "I, uh... understand it's your birthday."

Lynch laughed slightly at the words. "Yeah," he said. "The party's just getting started."

Father Raymond was at a loss. He was supposed to be the one offering comfort at this time, as a man looked death in the face. Most of those he went to were emotional—frightened, angry; regretful, some of them. But now the priest stood, looking at a man who seemed completely calm, and Father Raymond wasn't sure what to do next.

"Sit down," Lynch said, adding, "you're making me nervous." He did not look in the least bit nervous, but Father Raymond took a seat on a small bench facing the prisoner and opened his Bible. He had a few favorite passages that had, over the years, seemed to offer comfort to the condemned men.

He turned to one of them now and began to read. "'And he said, O Lord, wash away my sin, and I will be clean. Let me hear the sounds of love and gladness, and though You have crushed me and broken me, I will be whole once again.'"

Father Raymond glanced up at the prisoner, who was clearly disinterested. The priest had discovered that how a man reacted to death was as unique as the individual. Some wept, seeing a promise that God would forgive them, and grant them admission into heaven if they were truly repentant. Some were angry, justifiably so, and had nothing but crude, vicious, violent words. Some men just sat and sobbed quietly, and never said a word. All deserved to be respected.

As did Callum Lynch and his polite boredom. "You're not much for the Bible, are you?"

Father Raymond asked, knowing it to be a rhetorical question.

Cal shook his head absently.

"Is there anything I could say that might bring you comfort?"

Father Raymond was not expecting an answer, but to his surprise, Cal said, "There's a poem my mother used to read to me. 'After Apple-Picking.'"

The priest was pleased that his prior career now enabled him to accommodate a man's last request. God was good. Nodding, he said, "I know it. Robert Frost," and began to speak.

Not nearly as familiar to most as some of Frost's other poems, such as "Stopping by Woods on a Snowy Evening" or "Fire and Ice," this poem was one that Father Raymond himself was fond of. It was, curiously and sadly, appropriate for Cal today.

The priest spoke the lines in a soft, gentle voice. The ladder of the poem, seemingly pointing to heaven, and an empty apple barrel the narrator did not have a chance to fill made Father Raymond think of a life cut short.

Like the victim's had been; like Callum Lynch's was about to be.

Keys rattled as the priest paused to take a breath. The door opened.

It was time.

If this had been an ordinary visit, the priest would have asked for a chance to finish reciting the poem. But it wasn't. Death was on a time-table here, and men, even men of God, were forced to yield the stage.

Cal got to his feet. Father Raymond rose, too, and stood beside him. At least he would walk with Cal to the chamber, and would stand there until his soul left his body.

Where it went after that, Father Raymond could not pretend to know.

***

Chains were placed on his ankles and feet, clinking as Cal walked the seemingly intermi-nable, but somehow too-brief hallway to the room where his life would end.

The priest hadn't finished the poem, but that was all right. Cal knew it by heart and finished it himself, in silence, thinking of how the poem evoked the smell of the harvested fruit, and the echoes of approaching winter.

His mind was not on the gurney to which they strapped him, but elsewhere; in a safe and peaceful place, with light the color of honey streaming in from the window. In that timeless place, he was seven years old, and *she* was still alive, her voice sweet and soft, her body warm as he lay trustingly against her, the faint scent of her lavender soap teasing his nostrils. Drowsiness was in that memory, as in the poem.

Straps were fastened over his legs, across his chest.

The image of drowsiness and peace was an illusion. Any safety had been an illusion, forever sliced to ribbons by the same bloodied blade that had ended an innocent life.

The poem spoke of winter's sleep, of hibernation, of retreating to dream until spring. But it was no such sleep that he faced now. Cal was in the death chamber.

They tapped his arm, getting the vein to rise. He'd been in his share of hospitals, and had watched IVs drip before. But this time poison, not medicine, would soon flow through his body with every last, numbered beat of his rapidly accelerating heart.

The gallery windows opened. Cal squinted, trying to see them, but the warden stepped in front of him.

The warden's voice was to-the-point, devoid of emotion; almost bored. And why shouldn't it be, Cal thought bitterly. The warden had said these words often enough. There'd been a dozen or more executed in the state so far this year.

"Be it known that Callum Lynch has been found guilty of capital murder and is sentenced to die on this day, October 21, 2016. Does the prisoner wish to make a final statement?"

Happy goddamned birthday.

For a beautiful, perfect moment, hatred and anger chased away the fear of the coming darkness, leaving defiant, if illusionary, courage in its wake.

"Tell my father I'll see him in hell."

Perhaps then, he could get some answers.

The gurney tilted, slowly, and Cal stared up at the ceiling. The motion, mechanical, impartial, slow and steady, suddenly did what the priest, and the walk, and the warden's statement hadn't managed to do.

It had made this real.

He broke out in sweat, rank and clammy. His breath was coming quickly now, and he could not resist the macabre desire to turn his head and watch the clear liquid death creeping up through the tube into his arm.

It was cold as it hit his system, and each beat of his heart as it slammed against his chest pushed death through his body that much faster.

My own body is killing me, he thought.

The anger that had fueled him but a moment

ago evaporated before the stark realization, come too late for him to change his actions on that day, too late to pull a punch or not grab the knife, too late to just get up and walk out, too late for anything but scalding regret and the five words that pounded through him:

I don't want to die.

He raised his head, to see the shapes of those in the gallery, watching a human being dying right in front of them. Stern, cold faces; older, wrinkles chiseled into faces as stony as if they had been carved from rock.

Most of them were, at least... but one was not.

Cal's body ceased to obey him as paralysis took hold. He could not move his head, nor close his eyes as they leaked tears.

So it was that the last thing Callum Lynch saw before blackness descended was the oval shape of a woman's face swathed in shadow, and he could not help but wonder if he beheld the angel of death herself.

CHAPTER 3

I'm dead, Cal thought. *I'm dead, and hell is a wasteland of white.*

Through a veil of lashes against the brightness, he looked around carefully, his vision blurry and his eyes burning and aching, like twin coals stuck in his head. His body felt cold, all except for his hand, which was warm, as if someone had been holding it. Flashes: honey-hued light, giggles, the arms of his mother around him, whispered words about apple-picking.

A shape hovered in front of him, fading in and out. Maybe it was the angel he'd seen when he died.

He faded back into darkness again, then

again into consciousness. There was a sort of clinical smell, clean, but cold, as cold as the whiteness of the walls, of the lights.

He doubted Heaven smelled like antiseptics. *Hospital*, his mind said.

Maybe something had gone wrong—or right. Maybe the governor had called in with a pardon, and they'd stopped the IV drip before all the poison had reached his heart. His eyes tracked around to white pieces of equipment with colorful, small lights, and then met the impossibly blue gaze of the angel who had watched him die.

The oval of her large-eyed face was framed with short black hair, and her skin was like porcelain. Its smooth perfection was not marred, but rather enhanced, by a small mole on her forehead. She was clad in white, and her red lips curved in a gentle smile. Disbelieving, he reached out to touch her cheek, to see if she was real.

Gently, she caught his hand before he could do so, and he felt warm, strong fingers against his own.

"My name is Dr. Sofia Rikkin," she said in a musical voice that was softly accented.

He tried to place it. French? English? It added to her otherworldliness. But she was still speaking, and her next words seized and held his full attention.

"At six P.M. yesterday evening, you were executed and pronounced dead. And, so far as anyone in the world knows or cares, you no longer exist."

His heart surged in his chest. *I'm alive. But I'm still trapped.*

I have to get out of here.

Cal's body was disobedient, sluggish, but he forced it to obey his will, clumsily ripping out the IV in his right arm, kicking and flailing and grunting as he tried to get out of the reclining chair-bed.

The angel—Dr. Sofia Rikkin—made no move to stop him, though she watched him with concern in those large, soft eyes.

"It's better that you sit," she advised. "You're still processing the toxin."

Cal blinked, trying to focus, but vision hurt. "My eyes..." he groaned, rubbing his heels into them.

"What you're feeling right now is normal, if uncomfortable," she said. "The tetrodotoxin is very potent, but it's the only thing we can get past the prison doctors."

She said the words slowly, emphasizing the logical, as if she understood that right now he still felt like Alice falling down the rabbit hole. Cal blinked, angry at his uncooperative eyes, trying to force them to see clearly.

Sofia Rikkin leaned down, her face close to his, her voice soothing. "Cal."

He turned toward her at the sound of his name. She was so beautiful that he still couldn't help but wonder if this was a dream— or a nightmare—before the final sleep; a last attempt by his brain screaming that he existed, he mattered.

"I'm here to help you, Cal." How many had said that before to him, he wondered. But she looked as though she believed every word. "And you're here to help me."

For a moment, he wanted to. But then more memories returned. No. No, she wasn't an angel; he was lucid enough to know that now. She was a doctor, and she had kidnapped him, and he had to escape.

He could dimly make out two metal bars that looked like door handles, and he lunged toward them. To his astonishment they opened immediately and he hit the clean white floor hard, the wind knocked out of him.

Two figures clad in white approached from his left, striding briskly. Cal turned to his right, still unable to rise, crawling, pulling himself along with his lower arms like an animal, gradually feeling movement in his lower limbs. Behind him, he heard Sofia's voice saying, "Let him go."

* * *

In a room solely devoted to interior surveillance, multiple screens were regarded by multiple observers. McGowen, Head of Security, stood a solid six feet tall, with close-cropped hair and beard, and heavily-lidded eyes that missed nothing as he watched Callum Lynch, dead man, crawl and hobble in a fruitless attempt at escape.

* * *

In another room, an office where antique weaponry vied with a beautiful grand piano and the finest liquor and bar set, an elegant man dressed in a casual cashmere sweater and black trousers, his gray hair and lined face making him look dashing rather than aged, also watched Cal struggle toward an illusory freedom.

* * *

Cal clenched his teeth, growling in his frustration with his recently-paralyzed body as he clambered to his feet and lurched through doors, stumbled past orderlies and technicians and cold, metallic walls and stone. Veins of artificial light flowed along the walls, and what little natural illumination there was filtered in from high up.

Cal pressed on, tripping and falling and stubbornly clambering to his feet, moving like a drunken man past tree trunks—*tree trunks*—that stretched upward, a bizarre sight so deep indoors, but no stranger than anything else he'd encountered here.

Step by step, though, his eyes adjusted, his body came under his control, and he picked up speed. He shambled past a guard in black with a gun at his hip, who did not stop him as he flung himself up the stairs. "Don't touch him," he heard Sofia say. She was behind him, following him, and her voice gave him renewed energy. Angelic she might appear, but she was his jailer.

He raced across a metallic ramp, his feet making an echoing clang, and emerged into bright sunlight. Flinging up an arm to stave off the still-painful illumination, Cal realized that, somehow, he was in a garden.

Maybe he *was* dead after all. He didn't have the imagination to make this all up.

There were pathways and grass, benches and small trees, and birdsong. Slitting his eyes, Cal slowed, looking around. He was not alone in this strange garden. There were orderlies, and... patients? Prisoners? He did not know what to call them. They wore matching gray pullover tunics, white shirts, and pants.

A uniform. Cal did not like uniforms.

Some regarded him strangely, but others simply moved about, muttering to themselves, disinterested in his sudden, chaotic appearance. He moved forward, his eyes at last adjusting, to the low wall, stepping on top of it.

To one side, Cal saw helicopters: shiny, sleek, and doubtless expensive. But they did not command his attention. Far, far below, a city sprawled. But this was not an American city. This one had skyscrapers, yes, but Cal could also see ancient cathedrals, mosques, towers. *You're not in Kansas anymore*, Cal thought, and something inside him shattered.

What a fool he was. Idiocy to hope that, somehow, he could escape. He was alive, he accepted that now, but, once again, he was a captive.

This time, though, he was not in a prison. He was in a goddamned fortress.

As he stood on the wall, despairing and swaying slightly, a middle-aged black man, his neatly trimmed beard white and his pate bald, stepped up beside him on his right.

"Go ahead," he urged. "Do it."

Cal stared down at his feet, encased in soft-soled white shoes that closed with Velcro straps. The shoes—and he—were halfway off the ledge.

"Jump."

And the man grinned.

Cal felt the gazes of others now turning toward him, but he did not dare spare them a glance. He was trembling, knowing his limbs still were not entirely his own, wondering if he would step down, jump of his own free will— or simply fall.

The idea of jumping was tempting. To end his life on his own terms, to never again be anyone's prisoner. But then Cal remembered the sudden revelation he had experienced as the clear, liquid death had flowed into his veins at his execution: that despite everything, he did not want to die.

Another voice came from his opposite side; Sofia's. *Devil on one shoulder, angel on another,* he thought.

"You're not a prisoner here, Cal."

At that, he turned to look at her, his eyes narrowed with suspicion. "Doesn't look that way to me," he said.

"I'm here to protect you," Sofia continued, her bearing erect and her mien calm. "If you listen to me, everything is going to make sense. You'll learn nothing if you step off that ledge right now. But you need to trust me."

Trust? Absurd. She had kidnapped him, for God's sake. No matter what she said, he was a prisoner, and here she stood, asking him to *trust* her.

But... he was alive.

"Where am I?" He made no move to step down.

"You're in the rehabilitation wing of the Abstergo Foundation in Madrid."

Cal's eyes widened for a moment. Abstergo? He knew the name, of course. Everyone knew about Abstergo Industries—everything from cough syrup to cereal was produced by them. Hell, they probably manufactured the pentobarbital used to execute prisoners and the tissues their loved ones sobbed into afterward.

Then he grinned and started to laugh softly. Undaunted, Sofia continued.

"This is a private organization dedicated to the perfection of humankind."

He laughed harder at the crazy, delicious irony. He and anything remotely resembling the perfection of humankind had never gotten within spitting distance of one another.

Have you got the wrong guy, he thought.

But the angel wasn't done. "With your help, Cal, we can pioneer new ways to eradicate violence."

Eradicate violence.

His mirth faded. Violence had been as much a part of his life as breathing. It was efficient, casual, off-handed, and came so easily. It always had.

Except that wasn't true. It hadn't been like that when he was a child. He'd been a handful, he knew that; a daredevil, brimming with too much energy, but never cruel, never abusive, never... *violent*. Like an unwelcome houseguest that refused to leave, violence had come into his life the day his mother's life had been ended by it, and not before.

What if she could really do it? And what if he could help her?

What if some kid somewhere never had to worry about waking up one day to discover his mother had bled out in the kitchen on a perfectly ordinary afternoon? To discover his father standing there, with a strange knife dripping blood?

Sofia Rikkin held his gaze for a long moment. Her ethereal, calm certainty was compelling. His eyes still locked with hers, Cal set one foot down and then the other, and stepped away from the edge.

Her serene expression didn't change, but her eyes looked... happy. Joyful, almost. Damned if she still didn't look like an angel to him, even if the drug had worn off.

There was a sharp, stinging sound. A small dart abruptly appeared in Cal's neck, and he collapsed soundlessly to the ground.

CHAPTER 4

Anger welled up in Sofia. Mindful of her audience, she squelched it quickly. She turned to see the large shape of McGowen regarding her unapologetically.

Of course it would be McGowen. None of the other guards would dare to intervene after she had expressly told them to leave Cal alone.

"I had this," she said icily.

"Your father wants him in," McGowen said by way of explanation.

Of course. Father speaks, everyone listens. She had begun to grow tired of it years ago. Now it was becoming more than a nuisance and an implied lack of faith in her ability; it was actively interfering with her ability to obtain the results they both wanted so badly.

"He's *my* patient. This is *my* program."

Sofia held the security chief's gaze a moment longer. She did not fool herself into believing that this was anything less than a classic pack dynamic, and she refused to surrender her position as alpha over McGowen.

And he wasn't alone in observing. It was unwise of him to have challenged her in front of the patients. Most of them didn't care, but the few who did were all present... and paying very close attention.

Moussa, as was his wont, was trying to make the situation worse, egging Cal on like that. Sofia had seen Lin here, too. The Chinese woman knew English, but she tended to be as silent and taciturn as Moussa was garrulous and extroverted. The temperate Emir was bearing silent witness to the confrontation, and so was Nathan, remaining unexpectedly calm as well.

Sofia was well aware that her father was watching from the screens in his office. He was always watching when he was on the premises. She loved her father, and respected his opinion. But she wished that he would demonstrate that he felt similarly.

Cal had undergone an extreme ordeal and

had revived just a short while ago. He was not only mentally unprepared for what lay ahead of him, he wasn't even *physically* ready for it. He was still recovering from the effects of the toxin that had brought him sufficiently close to death to allow him to be smuggled out of prison.

Sofia's plan had been to allow the newcomer time to adjust, to learn about the value of the work she was doing here, of its importance not merely to humanity, but to him personally.

Her father, on the other hand, had arrived from London determined to push things into high gear, but he had not yet told her exactly why.

Sofia had wanted Cal to come around willingly to everything, to work *with* them, not simply *for* them, but Alan Rikkin, CEO, had forced her hand.

As always.

McGowen simply stared expressionlessly at her. He knew he would win. And Sofia knew it, too.

Finally, bitterly, she said, "Prepare the Animus."

* * *

Cal drifted in and out of consciousness as he was dragged down the hall, one burly orderly on each side. His head lolled back as he tried to make sense of this new room through a drugged haze. Everything about this place— no, he had a name for it now, the Madrid Abstergo Foundation—was bizarre, incomprehensible, and Cal knew enough to know what was and what wasn't part of the drug's effects.

First the hospital, impossibly sanitary. Then the strange collision of medieval and modern corridors and rooms through which he had stumbled. The rooftop garden and the not-quite-zombies who inhabited it, perched so high above the ground as to be eye to eye with eagles—or angels.

But this...

Church, was the first thing that came to his mind, although he had seldom darkened the door of any. The stone floor was inlaid with beautiful mosaics, and the center was a wide area encircled by arches on the ground level and on a second higher level. The overall effect was that of a honeycombed beehive.

Dimly, Cal glimpsed paintings on the walls, faded by more than his fuzzy vision. Sunlight filtering down from high windows merged with dim artificial blue light, glinting off glass cabinets housing weapons from past eras—swords, bows, knives—glimpsed blearily in passing.

Off to the sides that surrounded the open space in the center, though, everything was cutting edge technology. Cal saw screens alive with strange illustrations, blinking lights, and a sense of focus that dredged up another word to describe the strange scenario: *Laboratory*.

What, then, did that make him?

A third orderly jogged over to join the two who still held Cal tightly by each arm. This one slid a heavy canvas belt around Cal's waist, and he glanced down to see it lock into place with a clink. Was it the meds, or did it look like the buckle formed the letter A?

His self-preservation instinct kicked into panic mode. A chain was a chain, be it of links of metal or a belt with a shiny letter on it, and he looked up frantically to see Sofia regarding him evenly. There was no explanation in those cool blue eyes.

"Are the blades prepared?" she asked. It took Cal a second to realize that she wasn't speaking to him, but to one of her attendants standing over a collection of monitors and keyboards in the alcove area.

"Right here," a young bearded man said. He moved from the twenty-first century back to the fourteenth by stepping from his monitors to one of the display cabinets and handing some-thing off to two orderlies, or lab assistants, or whatever the hell they were.

"And we've confirmed their provenance?" Sofia continued.

"They definitely belonged to Aguilar, recovered from his burial site."

Burial site? Who the hell were these people, grave robbers?

Sofia had told him to trust her, that everything would make sense. And so he'd stepped down from the ledge, literally and figuratively, and for that gesture of trust he'd been shot with a dart like he was some kind of animal and literally dragged into this church-like place where *nothing at all* made *any* kind of sense.

Each of the lab assistants now carried some kind of glove or gauntlet, and the two men gripping Cal's arms tightened their grasp as the leather things were shoved onto Cal's hands.

He looked up at Sofia, groggy, alarmed and seriously out of his depth.

"What are these?" he grunted, trying—futilely—to resist. They were leather, and smelled old, and somehow familiar.

"These relics and your DNA will allow us embodied access to your ancestral lineage," Sofia replied.

"What?" Cal knew all the words, but in combination they made no sense. Sofia resumed speaking to her assistants, but she never took

her eyes from Cal's.

"Assume final preparations. Our regression: Andalusia, 1491. Record everything."

Screens sprang to life, and Cal's darting eyes caught images, blueprints, spidery scrawls of data over in the alcoves. Everything was as far beyond his comprehension as an airplane was beyond a cat's.

"Arm's ready," one of Sofia's assistants told her.

Arm?

Cal heard an ominous hydraulic whirring sound from overhead. The drug had left his system now, and so it was with perfect clarity that he beheld a massive mechanical device, the light from the domed ceiling glittering on its shiny surface. It spiraled downward, humming with deceptive gentleness, undulating and unfolding itself like a robotic snake awakening from slumber, until a U-shaped end was revealed.

It dipped down behind Cal and clicked gracefully into position. *The arm.* Such it was, and its two-pronged hand now gripped Cal firmly about his waist.

Total abject terror surged through him. His bowels clenched, threatening to let loose, but somehow he overruled the crippling fear long enough to gasp, scared but also furious, *"What is this?"*

She looked at him with that angel's face, and then lowered her gaze, unable to meet his eyes. She said with what sounded like genuine regret, "I'm sorry, Cal. This is not how I like to do things."

"Then *don't do it!*"

Something inside him, something deep and primal, told him if she was able to do what she intended to, he would never be the same.

Sofia lifted her blue eyes, regarding him with a mixture of sorrow and implacability. "Insert epidural."

Ten tiny points of metal settled down on Cal's neck, like the legs of some mechanical insect. But before he could jerk away, something sharp, long, and blindingly painful jabbed into the base of his skull.

He screamed.

Cal had fought. He had killed. He had almost *been* killed several times. He had run from police, been shot, stabbed, beaten within an inch of his life.

But never had he felt anything as painful as this.

Not a hospital. Not a lab.

A torture chamber.

And then, as swiftly as it had descended, the pain receded, not entirely, but enough for Cal to gulp in air and gasp, uncomprehending and furious, "What do you want from me?"

Sofia gazed at him, calm, in control. "Your past."

"My past...?"

Bizarrely, he thought of the song that had been playing on the beat-up old radio on that afternoon thirty years ago: Patsy Cline's "Crazy."

I'm going insane, he thought. *Crazy.*

Cal looked down at Sofia, now in pure, primal panic mode. She seemed to sense it, for her voice and manner changed. "Listen to me carefully, Cal. You are about to enter the Animus."

The word jolted him in a way she could not have anticipated. As a teenager, he'd known about expensive software put out by the company that would later be known as Abstergo Entertainment. He'd heard the rumors about how they were developing games based on memories of someone's ancestors, gleaned from lucky Abstergo employees, presumably sitting comfortably in ritzy offices, who spent time in a semi-legendary apparatus called the Animus that looked like a whiz-bang recliner.

When Cal had been in and out of juvie halls and foster homes, he'd mastered the art of stealing the software right out from under the noses of store employees and selling them to kids with too much money and too few real threats in their lives, who got to experience knife fights and violence vicariously rather that getting their own hands and noses bloody.

This was the Animus? This monstrous thing, this grasping, implacable *arm* out of someone's depraved and deeply buried nightmare—*this* was the source of a kid's video game?

Sofia continued, pulling his attention back to her. "What you are about to see, hear, and feel are the memories of someone who has been dead for over five hundred years."

Cal abruptly realized that as she spoke, Sofia had been slowly, deliberately backing away from him. Fresh fear shot though him and he reached out imploringly to her, the only one here who had seemed to truly want to see him as a human being; the one who had put him into this *arm*.

"Wait a minute!" he pleaded, but it was too late. He was suddenly hoisted into the air as if by a giant, as if this whole ordeal was nothing more than some sort of twisted carnival ride. The arm had him, and moved him about with casual, absolute power, and Callum Lynch dangled as helpless as a ragdoll in its implaca-ble metal grip.

"You must understand that you can't change what happens, Cal," Sofia said, raising her voice to be heard above the whirring of the arm. "Try to stay with the images. If you attempt to change anything, or try to break away, this could be dangerous for you. *Stay with the memories.*"

Since that awful day when he had walked in on his mother's still-warm corpse, had watched his father, blood dripping from the blade which had slain her, approach him with the intent of killing him as well, Cal had been determined to never, *ever,* let anyone have control over him. He had even managed to retain some sense of autonomy, a sense of self, in prison.

But here, the *arm*, and the angelic but unreachable woman who manipulated it, had ripped that away from him in seconds. And Cal had a dreadful premonition that somehow, they would be stripping him of more than he even knew he had.

More mechanical whirring. The *arm* maneuvered him about as Sofia called out instructions that meant nothing to him, but would influence everything.

"Engage scanner!" ordered Sofia.

Myriad lenses shoved themselves into his face, one after the other, their "eyes" irising open and closed as they observed—what?

Other devices that looked like things out of a mad scientist's wet dream descended, moving slowly with ominous clicking sounds.

Cal tore his gaze away from the machines, looking down at the humans below and the screens they gazed upon.

"Scanner reading memories," one of them called to Sofia. She stood a good twenty feet below Cal now, her oval face upturned to him.

"Status?" she asked of her team, though her eyes were still locked with Cal's.

"Monitoring blood flow and neural activity... DNA match identified."

Sofia, bathed in blue light, smiled up at Cal. "Stay with it, Cal," she urged again, and despite everything she had allowed to be done to him, Cal felt that she was on his side.

"Scanning DNA chains, searching for time-frame."

The arm moved Cal with surprising gentleness now, languidly lifting and lowering him, turning him to face into one strange piece of equipment, then the other. He was calming down now, growing used to the sensation, though his heart was still racing and his breath came quickly.

"First memory match locked," the assistant announced.

"Ego integrity?" Sofia inquired.

"Optimal." This time, a female voice responded.

"Attempt synchronization," Sofia ordered. She was still gazing up at him, and he saw concern furrow her brow. For him? No, more likely for the project.

"First ancestral link is complete. We've found Aguilar."

Without any intention of doing so, Cal abruptly flicked first one wrist, then the other. Blades hidden inside the gauntlets shot forward. He stared at them, stupidly.

"Ego integrated." The female assistant's voice; floating to his ears, seeming distant, somehow.

He wanted to close his eyes for some reason, though that seemed like the wrong thing to do. A few heartbeats later, he gave in, letting his eyelids flutter closed.

A strange calm descended.

"Synchronization achieved," said the male voice.

Then *her* voice, musical, like a breath of summer air in its peaceful joy. "*There!*"

There, yes. A still point, where there was nothing that had come before, nothing that would come afterward. It was... blissful.

Slowly Cal opened his eyes, as peaceful now as he had been terrified when he closed them.

"Commence regression," said the angel.

"Regression in progress."

And then Cal was dropped.

The stone floor rushed up to meet him, and his stomach churned violently.

The floor suddenly seemed to open up, engulfing him in a fiery, churning tunnel of blinding light. Then, so quickly Cal couldn't even begin to close his eyes against it, the light dimmed, grew dusty, and he was looking down on a great city painted in hues of gold and tan and bronze.

He observed everything—more than he knew his eyes could reasonably take in, and as he moved smoothly over the landscape, he was reminded suddenly, peculiarly, of the eagle that had flown over him on that day so long ago, when he had tried and failed to jump his bike across the gulf, when his biggest worry was how to explain to his parents the damage he'd done to the bike and himself.

When his life had been shattered.

Then that memory, and all that was Callum Lynch, retreated, surrendering to the vastness that was spread out before him, in the vision of the eagle.

CHAPTER 5

SIEGE OF GRANADA, SPAIN
1491

From above, the events of man seemed like nothing at all, certainly nothing compared to the whipping wind and the powerful upthrusts of the Sierra Nevada mountains. But if one dropped closer, diving down as the eagle did, one could see the small, repeated shapes of dwellings, and the uprising of structures that had more of the mountain in them than the hearthfires: a mighty fortress wall, following the silvery curve of the river, and upon its bridges and ramparts and streets was battle and blood and death.

Little things, the breaths of a human life,

but precious to those who took them. They fought by the thousands, with sword and bow and arrows, with daggers and spears, with fire and faith. Smoke rose in grim plumes, and what sunlight penetrated to the streets below caused steel helms to gleam.

Horses and men thundered through the streets while archers desperately tried to pick them off from above. Banners of now-filthy white cloth were torn and tattered, but the red cross embroidered upon it could still be seen.

Below the eagle's wings, too, was the great palace known as the Alhambra. Moorish soldiers fought desperately to protect the palace, while its sultan stared somberly down at the furor below him, then raised his eyes to the mountains beyond, where a great treasure was hidden in a small village, many of its buildings still burning, and where the strangest of protectors stood ready to recover it.

* * *

"Our mission is the boy," Benedicto, the Mentor, had told them a few hours earlier. "We have been betrayed. The Templars may not find his hiding place, but if they do, they'll trade his life for the Apple. Sultan Muhammad will have no choice."

Few words, but enough. No one on this mission was inexperienced, and they all knew the incalculable preciousness of the thing they sought. Aguilar de Nerha, however, suspected that the words were directed at him in particular.

He knew that in the few months since he had formally joined the Assassin Brotherhood, he had performed well. He had followed the orders of the Mentor, and not taken matters into his own hands. He had proven himself trustworthy, developing a calm head to overrule his impulsive heart and brain. The very fact that he was being allowed on this mission was testament to how well he was regarded.

The Assassins were well aware that Master Templar Tomás de Torquemada was behind the Templars' drive to obtain the Apple. And when the short, intense Grand Inquisitor was involved, two things were inevitable. One, innocent people would die horribly to advance the Templar cause under the guise of "religious purity."

And two, at some point, somewhere, the Templar black knight Ojeda would surface.

The scout who had reported the Templars' approach had informed that the company consisted of over two dozen mounted soldiers and a pair of wagons. One carried several barrels; containing what, the scouts could not venture a guess. The other was a large, empty cage.

The meaning was clear. The Templars were intending to present the prince to his father as if he were no more than a trapped animal.

The company was commanded by a familiar face—General Ramirez. Ramirez cut an elegant figure, with his scarred visage, long gray hair, and spear-straight posture. He served the Templars with his considerable military skills and gift for strategy, and Torquemada valued him.

And with Ramirez, the scout reported, his eyes flickering to Benedicto, was Ojeda.

Benedicto had not batted an eye, nor had he said anything to Aguilar. But the younger Assassin knew that the proximity to the monster who had captured his family and given them to Torquemada to burn was bound to trouble the Mentor. It was not unreasonable for Benedicto to fear that Aguilar might be tempted to forget that their mission was one of rescue, not revenge.

Aguilar understood that. He would not forget.

But he also knew that if fate presented him with the opportunity to slay Ojeda with his own hands while the Assassins rescued Prince Ahmed, he would take it in a heartbeat.

They began the long climb down, leaping from crag to crag, finding foot and hand-holds where no others possibly could, moving swiftly toward the village where the enemy was already present and had set fire to some of the outlying buildings as a means of intimidation. Now, the Assassins blended in effortlessly with the throng that stood, frightened and uneasy, awaiting the approach of the Templars. It was one of the tenets of the Creed: *Hide in plain sight*.

The Assassins separated, threading their way in different directions as the company of Templars galloped up. In the vanguard were a cluster of soldiers, hard-eyed men in armor and red cloaks who carried weapons ranging from spears to swords to crossbows.

Some remained atop their horses, watching the crowd with the advantage of height. Others dismounted and took positions among the gathering crowd of villagers, ready to quell any semblance of discontent.

After the soldiers came their commander. The legendary General Ramirez was dressed in an elegant, elaborate red velvet tunic worn over his armor. He cut a dramatic figure, but

Aguilar had no eyes for him. All his attention was on the mountain of a man who waited, his face as expressionless as if its owner had indeed been kin to stone, while the general slid off his mount.

Aguilar understood now why he had gotten the nickname of the "black knight." From his topknot and braided hair to the toes of his boots, everything Ojeda wore was as black as night; as black, Aguilar thought with a surge of anger, as his heart.

The well-tooled leather around Ojeda's thick neck and broad shoulders was battle-marred, the embroidered cloak pale with yellow dust. His broad chest was covered with leather armor, the silver studs and glints of chainmail the only things that caught the light. Ojeda wore not gauntlets but bracers that dwarfed those that encircled Aguilar's lower arms, also of exquisitely tooled black leather.

Even the horse upon which he rode matched his rider. The stallion's black coat was dulled with dust, but the thick mane and tail, powerful build and proud carriage spoke of excellent breeding. Like Ojeda, the beautiful Andalusian horse wore black armor. His head was protected by a second skull of ink-hued plate, and the leather that draped his body was adorned with sharp protruding iron triangles.

Together with a handful of his men, Ramirez strode into a simple stone house. Ojeda remained outside with the bulk of the red-cloaks, not saying a word or making a move, but causing terror with his simple, silent presence. It was no wonder he was so valued by Torquemada. Gray smoke mixed with yellow dust, causing Aguilar's eyes to sting. He blinked, clearing them, ignoring the pain as his training had taught.

But despite that training, Aguilar's heart sped up as he gazed for the first time upon the man who was his parents' killer. He forced himself to call upon his learned discipline and, as his Mentor had ordered, to remember the mission.

The boy—and, through him, recovery of the Apple of Eden—was what mattered. Was all that mattered. Indeed, if by some stroke of luck Ramirez failed to discover that this forgotten, simple village was the hiding place of the sultan's precious heir, the Assassins would not engage him or his men. Aguilar would be forced to watch, unable to lift a finger, let alone a blade, as the hated Templars rode off in safety.

Such, of course, would be the perfect out-come. Ahmed would be safe, and the Apple would be safe, and no Assassin would lose their life today.

But despite this knowledge, Aguilar found himself wishing it were otherwise.

That less-than-noble wish was granted a moment later when there came a shout from inside the house, and one of the soldiers emerged.

"We found him," the soldier announced to the still, massive knight. Ojeda nodded and dismounted with a grace surprising in a man so large.

Aguilar wondered who had betrayed them. He would likely never know. It did not matter. Someone had, out of fear or greed, and now it was the Assassins' task to recover the young Prince Ahmed.

Somehow.

Ojeda strode among the frightened villag-ers like a lion among goats, his narrow-eyed gaze flickering over them. He settled on one of them, seized the woman by her headscarf and wrenched it hard, bringing her to her knees.

"Which family harbored the boy?" he demanded.

Aguilar could see the fear and pain in her

eyes, but the woman refused to answer. Ojeda frowned, twisting his big hand more tightly. The woman hissed.

"I alone," came a voice as one man stepped forward.

It was Diego, who had long been a friend to the Brotherhood. Benedicto had come to him asking for help to hide the young prince, and Diego had bravely agreed. Like the women Ojeda was tormenting, Diego was afraid—any sane person would be—but he held his head high.

Aguilar was well aware that all Diego needed to do in order to have his life spared—and indeed, perhaps even gain riches as a reward—would be to point at any of the hooded figures in the crowd and shout a single word: "Assassins!" But he did not.

Threading his way through the crowd, Aguilar noticed the fleeting look that passed between Diego and the woman. Brief though it was, Ojeda saw it, too. With a grunt the black knight twisted the woman's hair once more before hurling her down to the dust. He turned to regard the man who had stepped forward, over whom he towered by at least a foot.

"Nobody else knew he was there," Diego continued.

Ojeda looked him up and down, then nodded to his generals. "I admire your bravery. For this, I will spare your life."

The man released a breath he likely hadn't been aware he had been holding. Ojeda's lips twitched slightly in what might have been a smile as he added, "Hang his family and make him watch. Burn the whole village. The women first. They reek of pig shit and sin."

And the Templars dare say they are on the side of the angels, Aguilar thought, white-hot rage spurting through him. He forced it away; forced himself to keep moving casually instead of launching himself upon the hated, brutal enemy.

Even now, Diego remained silent, not betraying the Brotherhood. He understood what was at stake, and he knew that while the Assassins yet lived, he and his family still had a chance at survival. Templar soldiers dragged both Diego and the woman—his wife—away.

Aguilar kept his head low, the heavy rust-colored hood shadowing his face. Everything in him cried out to change his position, to thread his way toward Ojeda, so that he could claim the kill. But Fate would have it that he was closer to another target, and Benedicto even now was subtly moving behind the black knight.

Resigned, Aguilar maneuvered his way toward the edge of the crowd and slipped around to the back of the single-story building that had housed the prince, climbing swiftly to the roof and flattening himself against it.

No one noticed. The townspeople were being manhandled to the ground while their prince was hauled forth by a pair of soldiers. Ramirez followed them outside, looking triumphant. He watched, gloating, as the soldiers dragged the child across the dusty earth to a cart in which sat the cage. Roughly, they opened the barred metal door and shoved Ahmed inside.

"Behold the prince of Granada!" shouted Ramirez, his voice dripping scorn. "His father the sultan will surrender his rebellious city— the last safe haven for the infidels! God will punish His people's heresy. Finally, Spain will be under one Templar rule."

The Assassins permitted him half a moment to gloat. Then, as coordinated and precise as if they had choreographed every move, they attacked.

Aguilar sprang from the roof, his hidden blades at the ready. Ramirez saw the Assassin's shadow and turned, too late to draw a weapon, but not too late to stare into Aguilar's eyes as the slender metal pierced his throat.

* * *

Cal stared at his hand, seeing the blade activated, lean and lethal beneath the five digits—no, there were four, *he had only four on his right hand, the ritual—*

"Stay with the memory, Cal."

* * *

Aguilar closed the dead man's eyes, and rose. *"Assassins!"*

The cry went up, and all hell broke loose.

CHAPTER 6

Aguilar's brothers and sisters had sprung into action the moment they saw him leap.

As Aguilar had observed seconds earlier, Benedicto had positioned himself to stand directly behind Ojeda. Somehow, impossibly, the knight seemed to sense the Assassin's presence. Just as Benedicto's axe descended in a blow that surely would have decapitated Ojeda, the Templar ducked and whirled with startling speed.

A grapefruit-sized fist came up, landing squarely in Benedicto's face. The second blow in rapid succession knocked the Assassin mentor to the dusty earth.

Aguilar suddenly understood that the reassurances from the Brotherhood—their words that, even if he had been present, he still could not have saved his parents—were not idle. Aguilar was no unbloodied novice. He had fought with his brothers before now against skilled, trained men such as the Templar general he had just killed. But Ojeda seemed more like a force of nature than a mortal man.

All this was processed in less time than it took his heart to beat.

Out of the corner of his eye, Aguilar saw one of his brothers pull twin swords from his back, smoothly lopping off a Templar soldier's head between their razor-sharp edges. It bounced to the dusty earth, the eyes open and staring in a final expression of surprise.

Another slit a throat from behind. A third snapped a neck.

Still another kicked a soldier to his knees and finished him off with a powerful step to the throat.

But it was Maria who remembered Benedicto's instructions—"Our mission is the boy." While the rest of the Assassins—including Aguilar, who was now being attacked on two sides—were busy taking down the soldiers, she had headed straight for the cart that bore a young prince in a cage.

Each Assassin's blades were unique. Maria

had adjusted the mechanism on one of her gauntlets to enable her to fire her blade as a projectile weapon, turning it into a throwing knife. Her other blade, Aguilar knew, was twin-pronged.

Now, she flicked her left wrist and plunged the two sharp metal points into the belly of the lone red-cloaked Templar soldier standing beside the cart. As he doubled over, Maria snatched the man's own spear, sprang back, whirled it around, and drew the spear's point along the soldier's neck.

He crumpled to the dusty earth. She jumped easily into the seat, slapped the reins sharply across the horses' broad backs, and they obligingly sprang into motion.

Aguilar caught this only fleetingly. He was busy taking down those who might follow her. He punched one red-cloak, who stumbled backward, whirled to slice the throat of another charging soldier behind him, then completed a full circle to seize the red-cloak's head and slam it into the dusty, hard-packed earth.

He looked up for a moment, catching his breath, his eyes on the biggest threat present—Ojeda. The man was not only massive and a cunning warrior, he was intelligent. That was why the Mentor, Benedicto, had selected Ojeda as his own target.

But all of the Mentor's skill, experience, and usually unerring sense of timing had, in the end, proved futile. Three soldiers were now struggling to subdue a fiercely resisting Benedicto.

Aguilar's heart sank, but his grief was replaced by implacable fury.

It should have been me. Benedicto was not fueled by hate, as I am. I would have taken him.

"Aguilar!" Benedicto was screaming, silenced momentarily by a fierce kick to his abdomen.

As Aguilar began to move toward Ojeda, the big man's head whipped around.

He had seen Maria absconding with the prince.

More quickly than a man of his size should be able to move, Ojeda took off for the second wagon the soldiers had brought with them, leaped onto it, and made his way to the front, where he threw one of his own men to the earth and took his place.

"Aguilar!" Benedicto's voice somehow carried over the screams and clash of weapons. "The boy! *The boy!*"

Aguilar gritted his teeth. Every fiber of his

being screamed at him to go after Ojeda. The odds against the Assassins were not good. He was well aware that he might die today. And if he did, he wanted to do so in combat against this monster who had murdered his family, would have murdered everyone in this entire village for their hubris in daring to stand up against the Templars.

Instead, he obeyed his Mentor, changing course in mid-stride toward a mounted red-cloak. He grabbed the skittish horse's reins with one hand and hauled the rider off with the other, flinging himself into the saddle and kicking the beast hard.

Strong, swift, and obedient, the beast hurled itself forward like an arrow shot from a bow. Others of the brethren had also heard their Mentor's order. One by one, they finished off their current adversaries—or fell trying—and took off after the fleeing wagon.

But the Templars, too, had noticed Maria's flight, and were riding as if all the demons of hell were after them.

Ojeda was already closing in, pulling his wagon alongside Maria's. The Assassin favored him with a quick, scornful glance, slapping the reins and crying out to her team to move faster. But it was another Templar soldier who pulled his horse up close to the back of the wagon and leaped from his mount, clinging to the bars of the prince's cage.

Aguilar urged his mount on faster, crouching low over its neck. Maria herself reached the Templar in time. He watched, pleased but not surprised at her skill, as within the space of a heartbeat she had jumped from her seat at the front of the wagon, propelled herself off the rock wall of the gorge, and landed smoothly in the wagon's bed, directly behind her enemy.

Startled, the Templar was slow to draw his sword. It cost him. Maria kicked him in the midsection once, forcing him to drop the weapon, and then once more. He toppled off the wagon to the rocky earth below, but not before Maria had seized his sword.

A second soldier climbed up, ready to resume where his fellow had left off. Maria had brought the sharpened steel of the first Templar's sword across in a wide sweep.

But this one was not as easily taken unawares as the first. He ducked the blow, coming up at her with a foot-long dagger. She danced away, almost effortlessly, whirling like a dervish, and slammed her elbow into his face. Another turn, and her booted foot crushed his throat. He stumbled, gasping, and fell off the wagon.

A third man was galloping up on a horse, but Maria snatched up a crossbow and fired a bolt into the soldier's chest. He, as the other two had done, fell and struck the ground hard. Quickly, Maria sprang atop the cage and scrambled back into the driver's seat, snapping the reins again.

The entire incident had taken a little over a single minute.

Many had joined in the chase on both sides, and the flat road was becoming crowded. Aguilar kneed his horse, urging it to veer to the right, up onto a rockier pathway where he could give the beast its head and pass the Assassins and Templars clogging the path. Ojeda was closing in on Maria and the young prisoner, but Aguilar was closing in on Ojeda.

He kicked the horse, asking just a bit more from it, then, moving swiftly but with exacting precision, stood on his mount's saddle. The extra height of riding along the bank had given him a distinct advantage in achieving his goal.

He balanced for the briefest of instants, timing it just right, and then leaped from the galloping, frothing animal to the bed of Ojeda's wagon. It was not the most graceful of landings, but Aguilar made it, striking the wooden planking hard.

He knew his landing would alert the driver, and even as he got to his feet, Ojeda was climbing over to face him.

For the first time, Aguilar de Nerha was able to look his parents' killer in the face. He was surprised to see that Ojeda had odd-colored eyes—one dark brown, the other a pale, unnatural blue—with a scar that ran from above the brow to down across the cheekbone. But both eyes revealed a cold and cruel nature.

A faint glimmer of recognition flickered in Ojeda's eyes, quickly dismissed. Aguilar understood. He knew his strong jaw was exactly like his father's, and his mother had often commented that her son had her eyes.

Do you see them in me, Ojeda? Do you feel a prickle, as if perhaps you are gazing at ghost?

The two men stood for a heartbeat, eyeing one another, and then, with a guttural cry, Ojeda lunged.

He carried a small but sharp axe, and swung it down, throwing all the strength of his powerful body into the blow. Aguilar's arm came up barely in time, slamming into Ojeda's and knocking the axe from the bigger man's grasp. It went flying. Ojeda didn't waste a second, pummeling Aguilar with such vigor and violence that the Assassin was hard-pressed to even counter, let alone spare a precious instant to activate his hidden blades.

More Templar soldiers were catching up to Maria. At one point, Aguilar lost sight of her. Fear that she had been cast down to be trampled beneath the thundering hooves of the horses stabbed him, but he could not let it affect him, not now, not when Ojeda—

Suddenly the cart lurched violently as it struck a great stone in the road. It was never meant to be driven at such speeds across such rough terrain, and now it had lost the battle. There came an enormous splintering sound and the terrifying, unforgettable scream of horses in agony as the wheel came off and the wagon collapsed, threatening to topple forward. The motion hurled both combatants forward. Aguilar used the momentum to launch himself toward Maria's wagon—

* * *

—the massive mechanical arm abruptly lifted Cal, letting him dangle in the air, only to shove him down hard on the unforgiving stone floor—

* * *

—and he barely missed colliding with the sharp metal corners of Prince Ahmed's cage, landing flat on the wooden bed of the wagon with a grunt.

Aguilar heard the continued sounds of wood groaning and snapping, followed by a smashing sound that told him that the wagon from which he'd just leaped would now be nothing but splinters. He hoped Ojeda was, too; lying bleeding in the road, life ebbing with every breath.

It was a good image. The only grief he felt was for the beautiful, proud horses.

Aguilar's attention was now on what was happening in the front of the wagon, where Maria definitely was not. It appeared as though she had somehow fallen between the rear pair of horses pulling the wagon.

He knew she yet lived, for the Templar soldier was making outraged noises as, oblivious to the Assassin in the wagon behind him, he stabbed down furiously with his sword.

There was no time for Aguilar to climb over the cage. In one swift motion, Aguilar seized the dagger at his hip, aimed, and sent it hurtling through the air, directly over the head of the startled young prisoner. It struck none of the bars, instead embedding itself precisely as Aguilar had intended—in the throat of the Templar, who tumbled helplessly off the seat, now nothing more dangerous than another obstacle in the road.

Aguilar got to his feet and gazed ahead, over the top of the cage. Fresh urgency spurted through his veins as he realized that Maria and her would-be killer had been so intent upon one another, no one had been steering the cart. The horses had simply kept galloping, panicked by the violence and the smell of blood, and they were going to *keep* galloping—right off a cliff and into the massive gorge that loomed ahead.

It was too late to seize the reins and pull the terrified creatures sharply to the left, back onto the road. Aguilar looked down into the wide, frightened eyes of the boy prince, who had not yielded to his terror despite his ordeal.

Even as Aguilar's blade extended and he began to pick the lock with its tip, his heart swelled as he heard a beloved voice from the front of the wagon shouting "Aguilar! The boy!"

Her voice heartened Aguilar. He yanked the door open and hauled forth the prince, who was already reaching out to him. The Assassin knew he shouldn't have been able to. The horses should have already been over the cliff by now. He realized that, somehow, they had made that left turn, veering and thundering to safety—but the wagon was still speeding toward absolute certain destruction.

And he and Ahmed were still in it.

The wagon's wheels devoured earth no longer, and it hurtled forward—and down.

At last, at the end, the prince cried out. But even so, he clung to Aguilar with fingers of steel as the Assassin raised an arm. Instead of a hidden blade shooting forth, a grappling bolt soared out, embedding itself securely as the rope attached to it snapped taut.

Ahmed slipped.

Faster than a snake striking, Aguilar's hand shot out and closed around Ahmed's wrist. The pair swung wildly in mid-air as the motion of their arc brought them around to strike the side of the gorge with teeth-rattling force.

The wagon crashed to the ground far, far below them.

And above them, his wide face stretching wider in a grin of malevolent glee, stood Ojeda.

CHAPTER 7

"**P**ull him!" Sofia shouted. She had hand-picked every member of this team partially for their lightning-fast responses, and she had never been more glad of her constant effort to achieve perfection than now.

The Animus arm struck the floor. Cal sagged in its grasp, unconscious—but alive.

"Commence rehabilitation," she instructed her team. "Run a systems check and log his condition."

Sofia went to the unconscious man, kneeling down beside him. She gazed into his open but unseeing eyes, surprised to find herself having to resist the urge to touch him in a comforting manner. Sofia Rikkin was a scientist, and a good one; scientists could not afford to let themselves grow fond of their lab rats.

But so much hinges on him....

The words left her lips before she realized it. "You did well, Cal." And her voice was warm.

Orderlies came to gather up the limp form. "Be careful with him," she said. "No one enters the room without my permission, no matter what happens. Including my father," she added.

They nodded agreement, and she watched as they bore him off, if not tenderly, at least, as she had requested, with care.

"You did well too," she said to Alex and Samia, two members of her team. "How's he doing?"

"Surprisingly well," Alex replied. "Strong fellow. His stats are good, but as you know, this is going to take it out of him."

"It was an intense simulation, especially for his first," Sofia agreed. Cal would be exhausted, and would sleep for several hours. They would have plenty of time to go through what they had recovered, but Sofia was eager to start.

"Why don't you two grab some lunch?" she suggested. "We can examine it all together once you get back."

Samia and Alex looked at each other knowingly. They understood their boss better than almost anyone, and realized that what Sofia wanted was some time alone to sit and puzzle a few things out herself.

After all, the technology as it manifested now, the great arm in the center of the room and in the earlier versions now in place in various Abstergo facilities around the world, had been developed by Sofia Rikkin.

They nodded and said they'd be back in an hour. The other members of the team left as well, and within a few minutes, Sofia was alone with her creation.

She had been born in 1980, the year that Warren Vidic, the creator of the original Animus, had begun working on it in earnest. Sofia liked to think that she and the Animus had grown up together. In most of its incarnations and until very recently, the Animus had been a sort of chair or table, where the subject could recline, head engulfed in a special helmet that analyzed brain activity and allowed access to ancestral memories through the subject's DNA. Subsequent recordings of the simulation played out on a computer screen.

But Sofia, who grew up with computers as babysitters, had wanted better simulations. Ones that were three-dimensional, life-sized, which allowed observers to experience the event in a manner similar to the way the subjects did. Virtual reality, except on a much more advanced level than anything currently available.

She'd also been the one to want to involve the subject's body, to make reliving the memories an active, rather than a passive, event. Sofia believed the benefits of kinesthetic memory were underrated by most scientists. It would, she firmly believed, create a positive feedback loop. If the subject moved as his ancestors did—his arm drawing back and activating the hidden blades before striking a blow, for example—the memory would seat itself even more deeply in his brain.

"It's so obvious, really," she had said to her father as they dined in Paris one night. She could tell despite his carefully neutral expression that it wasn't obvious at all to him.

Earlier models had featured parts of her sweeping changes. This one was the first to incorporate them all.

Now, Sofia activated a section of the recording, strode to the floor, and watched it again. While she could see what Cal could see, she could not feel what he felt, and she was grateful for that. Sofia had never harbored a desire to enter the Animus herself, though she had heard that the new Director of Historical Research in the London offices was pushing for all high-ranking Templars to do so.

She walked past the recording of Cal kneeling over Ramirez, when he had paused, horrified and uncomprehending. She could have easily lost him then—the first real assassination. But Cal had listened when she called out to him, had stayed with the memory, and oh, what they had gotten. Everything was so clear, especially considering that it was Cal's first experience.

Sofia froze the recording at a different spot and walked around the massive bulk of Ojeda, taking in the exquisite detail of his armor—so much work to make it beautiful, when the leather would inevitably be scarred with marks from blows, and all of it covered with dust and dirt and blood. Remarkable. She could almost reach out and touch the black knight.

For Cal, such a thing was possible. He could experience the memories through all his senses. When he had killed Ramirez, it was as real for him as if he had plunged one of his blades through a living person while standing right here on the floor.

The secret that Sofia Rikkin kept from everyone, including her father, was that most of her great scientific breakthroughs had come not just from focus, a disciplined mind, and a thirst for learning. They had also stemmed from her imagination—that of a lonely girl, too important to the great Alan Rikkin, Grand Master Templar, to be permitted to play with ordinary children, but not important enough for him to notice that play had been precisely what she had desperately craved.

So Sofia Rikkin had created her own stories... and provided her own playmates in the form of "imaginary friends." Because she liked history, they were boys and girls from various historical eras; and because she liked science, they all came to visit her through a time machine.

She had not created a way to *literally* travel back in time, but the Animus offered the closest experience that science could provide. The huge Templar standing frozen in the center of the room was the culmination of an idea conceived when she was five or six. She had given form and voice to that which resided only in the memories of a man long dead.

She looked over again at the frozen hologram of Callum Lynch. They had more in common than he probably would ever have thought.

And, in a way, Sofia envied him.

***

Alan Rikkin, CEO of Abstergo Industries, Grand Master and member of the elite Inner Sanctum of that Order, was a citizen of the world. But he was also an Englishman, and his office in London was his favorite. He'd been there just last evening. He'd arrived in Madrid rather later than he had hoped to, due to wrapping up some unpleasant business there. In fact, he had just received word an hour ago that he was wanted back there again tonight. Alan Rikkin certainly gathered no moss.

He was glad that things seemed to be moving well with Sofia's research. Recently, it had been made clear to him that not every high-ranking Templar's views aligned with his and those of the Elders, and that needed to be nipped in the bud as swiftly as possible.

Rikkin had to admit, the Madrid office of the Abstergo Foundation one ran a close second to the Abstergo Industries' London one.

Most of this was Sofia's world, and he indulged her in it. But this office was his, and it reflected what he thought beautiful and worthy—and befitting his myriad stations in life.

Fine art covered the walls, depicting great moments in Templar history. A map of the world adorned the wall behind him. Small green dots indicated Abstergo offices, and small white ones, sites of particular Templar interest. In some cities, such as London, they overlapped. Above the map was a row of clocks that showed the time in every single major city.

A truly special and rare item, a white flag with the red Templar cross which had been flown by the great Templar Grand Master Robert de Sablé during the Crusades, stood in solitary splendor in its own case.

Fragile, leather-bound books rested in displays safely behind archival glass. Antique weapons rested in others, some—like shields and row of swords bearing Templar crosses—from Rikkin's own history.

Others, like the morningstar, the crossbows, early wheel-lock pistols, arquebuses, and the intricately wrought smokescreen bombs crafted to look like filigreed containers of scented oils, had been wielded by Assassins.

One of Rikkin's favorite bows had ornate carvings along its length, depicting stylized figures of hooded "heroes" using their infamous hidden blades to handily dispatch enemies wearing tabards with square crosses. He reveled in the fact that a weapon so openly anti-Templar was now in the possession of a member of the Inner Sanctum.

The weapons were his, now. Soon, the Assassins themselves, or what remained of them, would be his, too.

And that ought to put the little handful of misguided Templars in their places. He wondered if that was the reason he'd been called back; he had not been told much.

Tonight, with so much running through his mind, he calmed and focused himself by doing two things: running his long fingers over the ivory keys of a grand piano, coaxing forth the soothing sound of Chopin, and watching his recent presentation to a G7 assembly.

"Looking back," said the earnest, miniature version of himself on the large plasma screen, "it's clear that the history of the world is a history of violence. Last year, the economic impact of anti-social behavior was nine trillion dollars. We believe that man today experiences a measure of aggression for which he finds no acceptable outlet."

Rikkin heard a slight whispering sound over his own voice and the soft strains of music, but continued watching the recording.

"Now," his image continued, "imagine if all these costs could be channeled elsewhere—toward education, healthcare, new technology—"

"Do I look old to you?" the current Rikkin interrupted himself, addressing his daughter, who had moved to step beside him. She had changed out of her white doctor's coat and into a simple black dress.

"Yes, Father," Sofia replied, impolitely but accurately. "Because you are."

Rikkin smiled self-deprecatingly. "Well played," he said. "I supposed that at my age, vanity must seem a bit pathetic. Sixty-five years is a long time to contemplate anything, I suppose, even oneself."

Her slight smile widened, warm with affection. "You look great."

"So," he said, rising and looking out the window at the city of Madrid spread out below, "the regression went well?"

"Lynch is the one," she stated. Rikkin raised an eyebrow. Sofia was nothing if not cautious, as befitted a scientist, but she was obviously completely confident in her assessment. "A direct descendant of Aguilar. Everything was clear in there. For the first time. We've done so many regressions, and they've all had varying degrees of success, but this one... quite remarkable."

She kept her eyes on the father on the screen rather than the father in the room with her, listening to his speech raptly.

"With your help," that Alan Rikkin was saying, his lined but still handsome face radiating earnestness, "Abstergo can go from market leaders to pioneers of what we all dream of—a more peaceful world."

The G7 audience erupted into thunderous applause. Sofia smiled.

"I see you stole my lines again," she quipped.

"I only steal from the best," Rikkin replied. From another man, it would have been a joke. Sofia knew her father was utterly serious. "And the Apple?"

"It's within our grasp." She was cool, but still confident as she turned to him, a hint of a victorious smile playing on her lips.

"What happened in there?" Rikkin asked, dropping any pretense of small talk. "You said it went well. Why did you pull him?"

"I had to," Sofia replied. "We have to keep him healthy. He was still recovering from the tetrodotoxin when McGowen tranquilized him, and we put him straight into the Animus. Hardly the best of ways to earn his confidence. But I think I can do it. And once we've got that, I know he'll lead us to it."

Rikkin, fastening his cufflinks for the evening ahead of him, would have none of it.

"Push him," he ordered.

She smiled at him, almost indulgently. "That's *not* how the Animus works."

Rikkin knew he intimidated people, and he used that knowledge to his advantage. Most Templars would have leaped to obey his demand. Sofia had simply smiled. She had never been intimidated by him, not once, in all her years on the planet. This both pleased him and exasperated him, and right now, he was experiencing the latter emotion.

Rikkin thought back to his earlier comment about looking old. As he fumbled with the cufflinks, the arthritis in his fingers further reminded him that, as Sofia had so honestly said, he *was* old. His breath escaped in an irritated sigh.

Sofia stepped beside him, as dark and silent as a shadow in her black dress. Her nimble fingers fastened the cufflink, and smoothed the cuff affectionately.

"Here you go."

Despite her scientific detachment, Sofia had a kindness to her that Rikkin had lost long ago, if indeed he had ever possessed it. With quiet sincerity, he said, "Thank you."

Their eyes met. She had her mother's eyes, not his; blue and wide as the sky. But she had inherited his stubbornness, his single-mindedness of purpose.

And it was that, along with her ferocious intelligence, which had brought them both to this moment, poised on the brink of greatness.

"1917: Rutherford split the atom," Rikkin said quietly. He held her gaze as her eyes searched his, wondering where he was going with this. "1953: Watson and Crick find the double helix. 2016," and he paused, savoring this, permitting himself to relish the sense of pride sweeping through him, "*my daughter* discovers the cure for violence."

Sofia looked down, uncomfortable with the comparisons. She shouldn't be. No Templar should ever be anything but proud of their talents, skills, intelligence—and accomplishments.

Gently, he took her chin between thumb and forefinger, raising her head so that she looked up at him.

"We chose your name well, your mother and I." *Sofia* was Greek for *wisdom*. "You've always been brighter than me." A soft, perhaps regretful chuckle left his lips as he graced her with one of his few genuine smiles.

He dropped his hand and took a breath, steeling himself for the evening ahead. "Now

I'm late. I have to head back to London tonight.
I shouldn't be long."

"London?" she asked, curious. "What for?"

Rikkin sighed. "I have to report to the
Elders."

CHAPTER 8

Rikkin was not used to being summoned. But even he answered to someone, and that someone was the group of Elders. And when they called—specifically, when their chairwoman called—he came like an obedient dog.

Now, he stood alone in the boardroom, waiting with his hands clasped behind his back, gazing intently at the painting on the far wall.

The room was beautiful and, like many Templar spaces, superbly blended the modern with the historic. Comfortable contemporary chairs, sufficient to seat a few dozen, were set off by large, elaborate candleholders and other medieval relics. On the wall to his left was a stunning collection of four dozen matching medieval swords arranged in a dynamic, sweeping silver circle.

At the center of the circle was a shield with the unmistakable red Templar squared cross against a white background. Spears and small, gleaming hand axes completed the display.

But it was the painting that held Rikkin's attention. Its hues, even after so many centuries, were still warm and rich, and the attention to detail was striking, given so many small figures.

He recalled the term for the action depicted in the painting: *auto-da-fé*. Translated literally from the Portuguese, it meant "act of faith." It referred to a very specific act of faith—that of burning heretics alive.

The master artist had presented a variety of onlookers, from royal to commoner, watching, presumably with great delight and perhaps religious ecstasy, as figures met their Maker on the orders of the Grand Inquisitor, whose diminutive form was seated between an equally tiny king and queen.

He heard the click of high heels on the marble floor, but continued to regard the painting. The voice behind him was elegant and precise, and he turned to face its owner.

"Francisco Rizi's work," said Ellen Kaye, the chairwoman of the Board of Directors—and the leader of the Council of Elders. She was a slender, poised older woman, almost as tall as he, chic and conservative in a tailored navy business suit with a cream-colored silk blouse.

"The painting's title is 'Auto-da-fé in the Plaza Mayor de Madrid,' depicting the event held there in 1680."

"I *thought* the queen was too old for Isabella," quipped Rikkin.

"1491 was a much more significant year for us," she said, ignoring his attempt at humor. "War, religious persecution—and the closest Father Torquemada or any of our Order came to finding the Apple." Rikkin stepped toward her, and she smiled faintly.

"How are you, my friend?" she asked, not without a hint of kindness.

He bent and kissed her outstretched hand. "Well, Your Excellency," he replied, gracing her with one of his own smiles. "But I rather suspect you didn't call me back from Madrid tonight simply to look at paintings, fine and inspiring though they might be."

He was right, of course. Kaye was known for not mincing words and cut straight to the point, speaking briskly, but with a hint of regret.

The words were devastating. "Next week, when the Elders meet, we shall vote to discontinue your Abstergo project."

Rikkin's smile vanished as coldness settled on his heart. This wasn't possible. Abstergo had been working on this for years, *decades*. As long as Sofia had been alive. Just in the last few years alone, they'd progressed by leaps and bounds, developing technology light-years beyond what anyone thought was possible, and systematically knocking down barriers to their ultimate goal.

"Thirty years is a long time to pursue a fruitless dream," Kaye continued implacably. "We feel that three billion annually could be better spent elsewhere."

She knew nothing. His voice was ice as he replied, "Three billion is nothing compared to—"

"We've won."

Rikkin blinked, unsure as to what she was saying. "I beg your pardon?"

"People no longer care about their civil liberties," she continued. "They care about their standard of life. The modern world has outgrown notions like 'freedom.' They are content to follow."

Rikkin's voice was a purr, but rich with

warning. "I wonder how many of our forefathers made the same mistake? Sitting complacently on their thrones, while a single voice of protest brought them down."

The chairwoman blinked. She was unaccustomed to being contradicted. Rikkin went on.

"The threat remains while free will exists. For centuries we've tried, with religion, with politics, and now consumerism, to eliminate dissent."

His thin lips curved in a cold smile as he said, almost lightly, "Isn't it time we gave science a try? My daughter is closer than we've ever been."

"How *is* your beautiful daughter?" Kaye asked.

As if she cared, he thought. *My daughter is more than beautiful. She's brilliant. And we are not making pleasant conversation over a cup of tea.*

"She has traced the protectors of the Apple," he replied, and took satisfaction in watching Kaye's eyes widen. There was no pretense of false courtesy in her reply this time. He had made her hungry.

"Where?"

"Andalusia," Rikkin replied, adding pointedly, "1491." He permitted himself to savor the moment.

"The descendants?"

He had her now. "All the bloodlines have died out," Rikkin replied, then added with a satisfaction he could not quite hide, "... bar one. We've traced his back five hundred years, to the Assassin Brotherhood."

Rikkin's mouth twitched in a suppressed smile of triumph.

* * *

Sofia gazed at the pages she had regarded a thousand times before: images from an ancient tome, which depicted the usage of the Apple. It shone brightly, seeming to hover in a circle of enraptured, primitive people, wearing little other than feathers, woven grass clothing, and expressions of utter joy as they held hands.

The facing page was slightly more analytic. The long-ago artist had tried to break down the construction of the Apple, but despite his diligence that had survived centuries, the blueprint raised more questions than it answered.

But now, it had a fresh relevance. It was, as Sofia had told her father, within their grasp.

A sudden movement caught her eye and she turned to look at a clear screen. Cal had bolted upright, shaking and startled, from his bed.

He'd been unconscious for almost twenty-four hours, and Sofia was relieved to see him wake up on his own. After her father's admonition last night to "push him," she was afraid she might have to put more medications in his system in order to awaken him.

He looked around, as if expecting someone to be in the room with him, and she placed down her pen. He had her full attention now.

Cal swung his legs over the side of the cot and rubbed the back of his neck. His fingers found the marks left by the epidural that had been plunged into his spinal cord yesterday. He probed them gently, pulling his hand back and regarding it as if surprised to not find it bloody.

Then he spotted the three guards, separated from him by thick, unbreakable glass, observing him. Cal gave them a long stare, then promptly ignored them, got to his feet tentatively, and walked to the door.

It was locked, of course, and after a few tries he turned his attention to exploring the small room, devoid of everything except the spartan cot, an armless, narrow padded bench, and the small table beside it, which did double duty as a light.

Sofia was not at all surprised when, almost immediately, Cal homed in on the small camera. From her perspective, he was looking right at her.

This is a man intimately familiar with prisons, Sofia thought, but his familiarity with his situation did not appear to breed resignation to it.

A sudden wave of anger at her father washed over her. *I wonder how bad this will be....*

Cal stared searchingly into the lens, wondering who was on the other side of it. Another guard? The angel of promises and pain herself? It didn't matter. He returned his attention to the guards, not at all intimidated. He had stared down their like before, more times than he could count.

There was a flicker in the glass; a reflection. Had another guard entered the room? No, not a guard, they did not move with such feline grace. He turned and his eyes widened.

The figure's face was hidden by a hood. The head lifted—and Cal gazed into a face that was both intimately familiar and unspeakably alien: his own.

A killer's blue eyes gazed at Cal, then narrowed. He stepped forward, slowly, then quickening his pace as he snapped his arms down, releasing the twin blades, and sprang.

The blade was pressed to his throat. Aguilar drew it back and the cold-hot, thrillingly painful slice opened Cal's throat. He doubled over, coughing up blood, his hand to his gashed—

—whole...?—

—throat.

Nothing. No blood. It wasn't real. Just his mind, playing tricks.

Sweat dewed Cal's body as he lowered his arms, trembling.

There was a soft beep, and the door opened. For a moment Cal thought he was still hallucinating. His mother had been fond of old movies from the 1930s and '40s, and the figure who now entered looked like she might have stepped out of one of those films.

Sofia Rikkin wore a crisp white cotton blouse, pants with knife-sharp pleats, and black shoes. The style was almost masculine, but no one would mistake her for anyone other than an effortlessly attractive woman.

Or an angel.

"The hallucinations are part of what we call the Bleeding Effect," she said as she entered, closing the door behind her. "Images of aggression, the violent memories that you relived yesterday, layer themselves over your present-day field of vision."

"*Just* from what I experienced yesterday?" he asked.

She regarded him levelly. "They're memories of aggression. Some were from yesterday. Not all."

Cal turned away from her as she spoke, leaning against the glass. The guards stared expressionlessly back at him, but he didn't really see them. Myriad emotions were roiling inside him at Sofia's words. He wasn't sure he could properly name any of them, but they were strong, and unpleasant, and one of them might have been shame.

She stepped beside him, her eyes searching his face. "If you'll allow me," she said, softly, "I can teach you how to control them."

An emotion surged to the forefront at the words: *Rage.*

Cal's lip curled in a snarl and his hand shot out. It closed around the soft, vulnerable flesh of her throat. He could have crushed her trachea. Part of him wanted to. But he didn't.

He simply held her prisoner, as she held him prisoner.

"Stand down," Sofia called immediately, and Cal wondered if Abstergo security was smart enough to realize she wasn't being harmed if she could inhale enough to shout. "I have this."

Her voice was as calm as ever, though the pulse fluttering against his hand, like a small, trapped bird, belied that calmness. Cal knew he was in control now, and he took advantage of it.

He pressed Sofia against the glass wall,

watching the guards in his peripheral vision, but much more interested in her reaction. She was a cool customer, that was—

—Aguilar grabbed him, dragged the blade across his throat—

Cal froze, squeezing his eyes shut in agony, but the pain was a headache, nothing more. Nothing near as painful and as horrifying and disorienting as the obscenely vivid hallucinations he had been undergoing.

He had not released Sofia. The pain battered him, like a tsunami pounding relentlessly against a defenseless shoreline. Through sheer will, Cal opened his eyes and took a steadying breath.

"What was it? In the machine?"

"It's genetic memory," she replied, carefully and calmly. "By using the Animus, we can relive the lives of those who made us who we are."

"What I saw in there... it felt *real*."

She held his gaze and answered, carefully, "It was... in a way."

White-hot fury surged through him. Cal slammed his free hand against the glass. It made a shivering, unhappy sound that echoed in the empty room.

"*Don't lie to me*," he snarled. "I feel... *different* now." Surely, now, Sofia would crack. Would show fear.

Instead, her eyes remained calm. Unbelievably, even her pulse had slowed slightly. She almost smiled, as if she knew something he didn't.

"Why the aggression?" she asked.

"I'm an aggressive person."

"Perhaps the better question would be, *whose* aggression."

He did not want to play her games. Not now. Not when the feeling of a knife slicing his throat was still so vivid.

"What kind of prison is this?" he demanded.

"It's not a prison, Cal. What happens in the Animus is complicated. You'll learn more if you cooperate." Her voice was reasonable, almost conversational.

Then: "Let me go."

It wasn't a plea, nor was it an order. It was presented as a reasonable option, implying that he, Callum Lynch, was a reasonable being.

Maybe he was. Maybe he wasn't.

They stood for a long moment, the tension between them rising, their faces almost as close as those of lovers. Cal wanted to show her he was in charge. He could snap her neck, right here, right now, and that would shut up her smug rationality, wouldn't it, shut it up forever.

But part of him didn't want to do that. She was smug because she was fully aware that she had just tempted him with the one thing he craved more than violence: some kind of understanding of what had happened to him. What had been done to him.

His mouth was a thin, angry line, his breath coming quick and short from his nostrils. Then his gaze fell to his hand, and, gently, almost like he was releasing that small, trapped bird, he opened his fingers.

He expected her hand to go to her throat. He expected her to move immediately out of arm's reach. She did neither of those things.

Instead, Sofia Rikkin smiled.

"Come with me," she invited.

CHAPTER 9

Cal hadn't darkened the door of a museum in three decades, and he had never even graduated from middle school. But the rooms through which Sofia now led him evoked both... times about a thousand.

Men and women dressed in white—Sofia's researchers, he assumed—moved about with the kind of hushed, focused air he remembered from rare visits to a library as a child. There was plenty of light, but Cal could tell it was a special *kind* of light, and even as it illuminated it gave the room a secluded, almost cloistered feel, accentuated by the carved stone archways through which they passed.

Weapons were in evidence here, but only

as antiquities to be carefully catalogued and analyzed. There were shards of pottery, inkwells and quills, pieces of statuary. In one area, what was clearly a painstaking restoration of an old painting was going on. Ancient tomes were sheltered in display cases, and pages upon pages of manuscripts were mounted on clear walls of plastic or glass.

As Cal drew closer, however, he saw that most of the pieces of paper weren't manuscripts, as he had first thought, but transcripts of a much more contemporary nature.

And some of them were chillingly familiar.

Cal's pulse quickened as he stared into a photograph of himself.

The boy in the picture was the age he had been when he had fled a bloodied tenement. His blue eyes traveled along what seemed to be a bizarre and disturbing scrapbook of his life writ large: old Polaroids from when he was a little boy, their once-natural hues now faded oranges and yellows. Other pictures of a more guarded young adult from his ill-fated foster home years. A staggering array of his various mugshots.

Newspaper clippings trumpeted his life in blaring, catchy headlines : "Fears Growing for Callum Lynch: Help Us Find Missing Boy." "Gang Raids Local Offices." "One Dead After

Night Club Fight." "'Lynch Will Die': Jury Finds Pimp Killer Guilty."

There were small glass vials with color-coded tops in acrylic containers. The charcoal sketches he had obsessively drawn during his most recent incarceration were here, too. There was a fake passport, his fingerprints—and his name, etched into the glass—and finally what appeared to be a family genealogy that seemed to go back centuries.

A genealogy that he knew nothing about.

Cal felt his gut grow cold. He felt... violated. Exposed. "What is this?" he snapped. "What are you, my stalker?"

"I know everything about you, Cal," Sofia replied. Her voice and manner was unsettlingly unruffled. "Your medical data, your psychological profile, the mutations in your MAOA gene, your serotonin levels. I know about the foster homes, the juvenile halls. The harm you did to others—and," she added, gently, "to yourself. You're living proof of the link between heredity and crime."

Cal was stunned and sickened, yet captivated. He moved down his family line, and the "scrapbook" was now no longer filled with news clippings and photographs, but yellowed old daguerreotypes and spider-scrawl letters.

Teeth.

Wrinkled drawings of hooded figures and gauntlets with blades strapped to them.

"How did you find me?"

"We found Aguilar," she said. The word—

—*the name*—

—was at once meaningless and full of portent. "When you were arrested," Sofia continued, "your DNA matched his."

"Who is Aguilar?" Cal asked, although he realized he knew.

"Your ancestor."

Sofia turned and walked casually to another collection of images, her hands in her trouser pockets, her body language displaying no more distress than if they were walking together in a park on a summer's day. She nodded at an old sketch on yellowed parchment.

Cal's hands clenched as he resisted being catapulted back into the hallucinations. He breathed steadily through his nose as he took it all in. White quills of bird feathers—raptors, Cal knew, without knowing how—were sewn into the front of the coat. Cloth was wrapped several times around the waist, and bound on top of it was what looked like a leather belt, which upon closer examination was a whip. Daggers hung at both sides, and hidden blades were housed beneath the tooled gauntlets on the arms.

The face was mostly hidden in shadows, but it was a face that Cal knew all too well.

For a wild second, Cal thought this was some sort of gaslighting attempt; that the people here were playing some sort of elaborate trick. But to what end?

Cal hadn't played a video game since he was a kid. But he was damn sure that if anyone really had the ability to make him feel as he had felt in the grip of the giant arm, they'd either keep it a closely guarded secret or be making a massive profit on it.

"Aguilar's family were Assassins," Sofia continued. "They were burned at the stake by the Templars Torquemada and the black knight you saw—Ojeda. Aguilar de Nerha took up the Assassins' cause."

Torquemada. It was funny, what stuck in one's head; in elementary school Cal had studied the Spanish Inquisition, and somehow he remembered the name.

He continued looking at the bizarre display of his bloodline's history. Now, the papers were sketches and art exclusively, or pages in Latin from some long-lost tome.

His gaze traveled downward, to a monitor

on the desk below the colorful prints. Here, the only colors were a black background and white lines—but the images so created were beyond his comprehension; hundreds of intricate lines forming the shapes of part of a machine.

One thing he did recognize, vividly; the arm, with its grasping two-fingered claw.

"What is it? This machine."

"We call it the Animus."

"I know about the Animus. I thought it was a chair."

"Not anymore. How do you know about it?"

"Never played the games, but I shoplifted enough of them for quick cash."

She looked faintly amused. "Really? Then you know it allows us to observe, and you to relive, the life of your ancestors through the projection of your genetic memories."

Rolling his eyes slightly, Cal went to another display. "Do you get out much?" he quipped.

"More than you."

Her tone was light, almost friendly. Banter. How strange, to be engaged in it with Sofia Rikkin—his angel, his jailor.

She continued in that vein. "Do you ever wonder how a bird knows when to migrate south in winter?"

"It's all I think about."

A hint of a real smile graced her lips, vanishing almost at once. Her voice, though, held a trace of amusement. "It's genetic memory. As you recover those memories, you inherit something of their lives. If you allow me to guide you through this, there is no telling what you might learn or see."

Cal felt himself close off as he recalled Aguilar's presence in his room. "I've seen enough. And I don't like the idea of you stealing my memories to make a game."

All trace of lightness fled from Sofia now too, and she looked at him intensely.

"I'm not stealing. I'm utilizing. The memories are not yours. They belong to your ancestors. And believe me, this is *not* a game."

Cal turned a corner and sobered further as he looked at another wall, one that had nothing to do with him. It was plastered with colored sheets of paper, each with carefully typed notes on them. Attached to the papers were small, wallet-sized photos of a few of the other... people he had met here. *Mug shots*, he thought.

He began to put names to faces. The black man urging him to jump, it seemed, was Moussa. He only vaguely remembered seeing an Asian woman, Lin, and a young, pale, earnest kid who was named Nathan. Another one, Emir, was a man about Cal's age.

Cal's voice was hard and flat. "And the others in here? Are they lab rats, too?"

"They're Assassins. Murderers, like their ancestors." Sofia paused, then added. "Like you, Cal. All born with a predisposition to violence. Your DNA, like theirs, allows us to journey through your subconscious. To the root of your very being. All those hidden impulses that have driven you your whole life."

The realization and all its implications was an ugly one. Cal walked away a few steps, keeping a tight rein on his emotions, then turned to face her.

"Murderer," he said. "So that's what you think of me."

"You killed a man." She said it without judgment of any sort. It was, to her, a simple fact.

"A pimp," Cal clarified.

The image of the scene rose up again in his mind: the sneering, ugly face of the man who sold women's bodies. The bruises on the prostitutes' faces, imperfectly concealed by heavy makeup. Their forced laughter. The stench of too much perfume and sweat and above all, fear.

And that moment when the pimp grabbed the throat of a girl who couldn't have been more than sixteen and slammed her face into the bar. The moment that could not be reclaimed when

Cal Lynch had decided that the human stain would never, *ever* hurt a terrified girl again.

And if Sofia knew his history as well as she had to, given what he'd just seen here, then she should damn well know that, too.

"I didn't like the way he treated women," was all he said, though.

Sofia stepped closer to him, her words expressing both curiosity and a challenge.

"Would you kill again?"

Cal did not answer. As he looked down, his gaze fell on a photograph. Unlike his, it was framed, with care and respect. He picked it up and examined it.

It was an older one, though it had been taken within the realm of memory. It looked a bit like the pictures of himself he had just seen, with the colors fading but the images still clear.

There were two people in the picture. One was an attractive, laughing woman with shoulder-length dark hair, wearing a crisp white blouse and jean overalls. Her arm was protectively around the second subject of the photo—a toddler with wide blue eyes seated atop an old-fashioned rope swing. There was something about the little girl's expression of focus as she gazed at something other than the photographer that he recognized.

"Nice," he said. Then, archly, "Happy families. Apple of your mother's eye. She must be very proud."

Sofia's expression had gone from lively and curious to soft and a little sad, even as a wistful smile curved the corners of her lips.

"I wouldn't know," she said. "She was killed by an Assassin. Like your mother." She let the words linger there, letting him absorb what she had just said.

"Sorry," he said. And to his surprise, he realized he meant it.

Cal let the silence stretch on for a long moment before he said, "My old man killed my mother." Which, doubtless, Sofia knew too.

"And how does that make you feel?" The girl mourning her mother had retreated into the shadow of the scientist.

"Like killing *him*," Cal said bluntly. He turned and continued his perusal of the room.

Sofia followed. "Either we let this affect us for the rest of our lives, or we do something about it. You turned to violence; I turned to science."

Cal's attention was drawn to a row of metallic spheres arranged on clear plastic stands. They were all of the same size, smaller than a baseball, a little larger than a tennis ball. Each was subtly different in its design, however, and he idly reached to pick one up. It was heavy.

"The Templars call it the Artifact; the Assassins, the Apple," Sofia said. Cal examined the orb, glancing at the various pieces of parchment that had sketches or commentary about the item as she spoke. "The Bible tells us it contains the seed of man's first disobedience."

Cal was fascinated by the decorated sphere in a way he couldn't understand, absently pulling up a chair and sitting as if he belonged in the room, rolling the thing around in his fingers. Sofia perched on the desk area in front of him, reaching around for a mouse and calling up something on the monitor.

As she spoke, she clicked the mouse, and myriad blueprints of the Apple appeared on the monitor. They appeared to be similar to those Cal had seen of the Animus, and he wondered if it was based on the same technology.

"But there are those of us who believe it has its basis in science. That within its genetic code, God—or some ancient civilization—has left us a roadmap to understand why people are violent."

They locked gazes for a moment, then Sofia's blue eyes traveled back to Cal's board.

"Aguilar was the last person known to have had it in his possession." And then Cal understood, even before her eyes traveled back to his.

"We need you to find out where he hid it."

He was oddly disappointed, though he knew he shouldn't be. Everyone had an angle, it seemed. Even angels. He kept his voice light as he said, "I thought I was here to be cured."

"Violence is a disease, like cancer. And like cancer, we hope to control it one day. We're searching for the root cause of what makes you sick. And we're seeking to control it. We're after the evolution of humankind." She swallowed. "So that what happened to your mother... and mine... will never happen again."

Quietly, Cal said, "Violence is what kept me alive."

She cocked her head and regarded him. Her black hair fell across her forehead. He wanted to reach and brush it back. "Well," she said, "technically... you're dead."

She had a point. Cal's brain hurt, and his body, which was definitely *not* dead, reasserted itself.

He tossed the gray orb back to Sofia, who caught it deftly.

"I'm hungry," he said.

CHAPTER 10

"What's in it for me?" Cal asked as they strode down the corridor. They passed orderlies in white, gray stone arches, and tree trunks that may or may not have been actual wood. He was growing used to the strange juxtapositions of the corporate with the creative, the historical with the antiseptic cleanliness of the present.

Still, he was growing weary of the cool blue, gray and white palette of the place. Something in him yearned for the blazing sun, explosive and urgent yellows, the taste of dust in his mouth. And he wasn't sure if this was a longing for the Baja California life he knew as a child, or if it was Aguilar's sun-baked Spain that was bleeding into his consciousness.

As they rounded a corridor, he caught a glimpse of a large screen. It was a talking head on some kind of news show, and there was something oddly familiar about the neatly styled gray hair, the sincere expression, and the piercing brown eyes. His eyes dropped to the name scrolling under the face: *Alan Rikkin, CEO, Abstergo Industries.*

Ah, he thought. *No wonder you have a seemingly unlimited budget, Dr. Sofia Rikkin.*

"There are legal ramifications, obviously," Sofia was saying, "but once my research is complete, there's no reason to keep you here."

Cal slowed, stopped. Sofia turned to face him.

"I get my life back?" he asked, uncertain that he had understood her correctly.

Sofia smiled at him, hands primly clasped behind her back, her eyes bright, as if she were giving him a present on Christmas morning.

"Better," she said. "A *new* one."

Given what he had seen here, Cal had no question that Abstergo was capable of it. A new life. A fresh start. With, perhaps, none of the hot, irresistible yearning for violence to plague it.

She gestured toward the door where they had stopped. "You're hungry," she said. She made no move to follow him. Keeping his eyes on her, he moved to the door, and then stepped inside.

What Cal assumed was the common room was similar to everything else he had seen thus far in the Abstergo facility. Orderlies wore white; the patients wore the same white T-shirts, gray pants, and gray V-necked top as Cal did. It was hard to believe that they were all murderers—Assassins, as their ancestors had been.

The walls were slate gray, and Cal immediately spotted the mirrored glass, behind which he knew security was observing everything. There were a couple of guards in the room as well, keeping to the sides, trying—and failing—to be unobtrusive. The room definitely had similarities to the prisons in which Cal had spent far too much time.

Still, it was a somewhat more pleasant sort of environment. There was exercise equipment, and two men were taking turns shooting hoops. Cal heard the distinctive *ka-pok*, *ka-pok* of ping-pong. Over it, he could hear birds chirping. A variety of foliage, from trees to shrubbery to fruits and vegetables, appeared to be thriving.

The thought of food made Cal's stomach rumble. But he couldn't settle down into this environment despite his very real hunger, and found himself facing the mirrored walls, trying to peer within.

As he was staring at the guards he couldn't see, someone approached him. It was the black man with the neat white beard Cal had "met" on his first day. The one who had encouraged him to jump.

Now, he was smiling. He stood exaggeratedly straight, one arm held stiffly behind him. He stepped back a pace or two, sweeping his other arm out grandly toward one of the group tables.

"How about here, sir?" he said, as if he were the maître d' of the place. Cal looked at the two tables as the man patted an empty spot on the bench. "It's an open menu, but we do recommend the chicken."

Keeping his eyes on the man, Cal slid onto the seat. Across from him was an older Asian man, his long gray hair falling in a tight braid halfway down his back. He paid Cal no attention.

A young orderly approached, her voice and manner pleasant, her hair in a tidy, professional bun.

"What can I get you, Mr. Lynch?" she said, smiling. "It's an open menu, but we do recommend the chicken."

The man's eyes danced, but his face remained solemn.

"I'll have steak," Cal said, never taking his eyes from his odd companion.

"Steak for the Pioneer!" the man exclaimed, as if instructing the orderly in her duty. "And how would sir like that cooked?"

Cal turned to the orderly. "Walk it through a warm kitchen."

The orderly left. The man, uninvited, immediately sat down beside Cal. He brought up three small cups from seemingly nowhere and placed them on the table, lip side down, in a tidy row.

"Who are you?" Cal asked. He remembered noticing his companion's picture in Sofia's research lab, but the name escaped him.

The man picked up the middle cup with deft fingers. "They call me Moussa," he said, using the cup to point toward the mirrored glass. He leaned in conspiratorially to Cal. "But my name is Baptiste."

His dark face took on a strange, serious expression. "I'm dead two hundred years, now," he said. Then he added, his voice lowering, "Voodoo poisoner."

He held Cal's gaze for a long moment. Cal tensed, ready to defend himself. Then Moussa's face dissolved into an impish grin. "I'm harmless," he laughed, giving Cal a wink.

No, you're not, Cal thought. *You're a killer, just like me.*

And you told me to jump.

Cal felt eyes on him, and his gaze wandered to meet that of a tall, gangly young man with tousled brown hair. The kid didn't flinch or look away, instead staring intently at Cal with a hard look on his face. *Nathan,* Cal remembered; he had also been in the garden when Cal had stumbled in, still fighting the drug in his system.

"Ah," Moussa said slyly, "they're watching you." He looked past Cal in the other direction. Cal turned to see that someone else was staring at them: the Asian woman, Lin, her long, sleek black hair tied back in a ponytail. She, too, stared at Cal with open suspicion for a long moment.

"Have you met him yet?"

Moussa's question brought Cal's attention back to him. Cal did not reply. Moussa repeated the question, his expression hardening, his words deliberate.

"Have you met him yet?"

There was nothing of a playful, "harmless" trickster about him now. When Cal still did not answer, Moussa wordlessly rose, plunking down his three small cups that, Cal now realized, were designed to perform the old "find the missing ball" trick.

"We are the last to protect the Apple, my friend," Moussa warned as he walked away. "All the rest... most of them are on their way to... infinity." And he made a waving motion with his hands, grinning one last time.

Another man, bearded and heavyset, walked up to him. Cal recognized him as Emir. He had his hands clasped behind his back, and his expression appeared to be genuinely pleasant. Smiling, he said, "'So the last shall be first, and the first last: for many be called, but few chosen.' This belongs to you."

And he held out an apple. It was smallish, a little green, a little red; clearly a product of the on-site garden rather than a big-box grocery store. Cal's mouth watered at the scent of the apple, and his mind flashed back to that golden moment, lying in his mother's arms as she quoted Robert Frost.

And another voice, also female, also kind: *The Templars call it the Artifact; the Assassins, the Apple.*

And then there was that bizarre comment of Moussa's about "protecting the Apple."

He took the apple. Emir's dark eyes searched his, looking for something, then he nodded and wandered off.

Cal watched him go, baffled, and shook his head.

First this place was a lab, then a torture chamber; now an insane asylum.

He sensed someone coming up on his other side. Fingers closed on the piece of fruit. Without removing his eyes from Emir, Cal's hand shot out and closed on the would-be thief's wrist. Casually, Cal turned to see Nathan, quivering with intensity.

"You're going to lead them right to it," Nathan said. His voice suggested not just outrage, but personal affront.

"No," Cal replied in an exaggeratedly calm voice, "I'm going to *eat* it."

An appetizing smell announced the orderly approaching with Cal's steak. She set it down in front of him, a look of concern on her face, but did not intervene in the standoff. Nathan released his grip on the apple and walked away, but not without an angry backward glance.

The orderly melted into the background. Cal stared for a moment, then shook his head.

"What the fuck is going on?" he muttered, laughing a little at the craziness.

He shrugged and cut into the meat. In the midst of all the madness, it was a comfort to see that at least the kitchen in this place understood how to prepare a steak. It was rare, cool in the center, and smelled like heaven. Red juice poured onto the place. Cal's mouth flooded with saliva as he popped the first bite into his mouth and chewed. The wonderful, slightly iron flavor of the juicy—

—bloody—

—a face, hidden in a hood, turning slowly toward him, grief and regret in his face even as the blade dripped—

Agony knifed through Cal's temple and he dropped the fork, pressing his left palm into his eye as if to physically force the pain back. He was trembling, his breath coming in quick gasps, but he didn't want anyone to notice.

Moussa and Nathan had made it plain that they considered him hostile. He'd spent enough time in prison to understand those dynamics. He couldn't afford to appear weak, not now, not in this pit of vipers, or they would destroy him.

Cal forced his breathing to slow, and brought the pain down from unendurable to merely excruciating. Better.

Slowly, he lowered his hand and looked around.

A figure glad in leather and thick cloth stood near the mirrored observation wall. His clothing appeared gray in the light, but Cal knew it was dark red. The man's hooded head was bowed and arms were out to his sides, a blade protruding from each wrist.

Slowly, he turned, fixing his piercing gaze on Cal.

No. It's the hallucinations—the, what did Sofia call them, the Bleeding Effect.

Cal gritted his teeth, willing the figure to disappear—

—and suddenly he was in his room, his tiny gray cell, and *they* were there. All of them. Cal knew their names: Aguilar.

Benedicto.

Maria, with her kohl-rimmed eyes.

"Our own lives are nothing," Maria whispered as she brushed around him, her face with its blue, beautiful tattoos only a few inches from Cal's.

"We defend mankind against the tyranny of the Templars," Aguilar said, his voice so familiar and yet so alien. Cal's own blue eyes blazed in Aguilar's bearded, sun-dark face.

"Do you swear?" demanded Benedicto, the Mentor.

Their blades were no longer hidden, and they circled him, whispering words he did not understand, watching his fear—

Cal blinked.

He was indeed in his room, with no memory of how he had gotten there. But the Assassins weren't here.

He was alone, except for the silent, watchful eyes that were always present behind the glass.

CHAPTER 11

The new kid—Mr. Lynch, the orderly had called him—was having a rough time of it, Moussa thought as he watched the convulsing form being dragged away. He had some empathy for the man, having had his own experiences with the horrorfest that was the Bleeding Effect.

He hadn't caught Lynch's first name, but someone else would know it. Each of them was like a part of a whole; one would hear something, another something else. That's what a Brotherhood was.

Moussa grinned as one of the guards approached, trying to act all casual. He'd been watching the interplay between the two inmates—they were supposed to think of themselves as "patients," but that was bullshit—and was suspicious of it.

"Want to sit down and play a game with me, big man?" Moussa asked genially, placing his cups on the table.

"You got nothing I want if I win," the guard pointed out, quite reasonably.

Moussa cackled. "You got that right!" he said, then added thoughtfully, "Or do I? I got me a pair of sharp eyes and sharp ears." He nodded his head at the door through which the hallucinating Lynch had just been dragged. "Could be useful things."

The guard eyed him, and then cautiously sat down at the table. Moussa lifted the cup on the right, showing him the small round ball hiding underneath it.

The guard grimaced and pointed at the others. "Let me see them." Moussa, grinning, obliged. "And the bottoms of all of them," the guard added.

"Your mother didn't raise a fool," Moussa said, though as far as he was concerned that remained to be seen. Others were taking an interest now. They always liked to watch Moussa perform.

That hadn't always been the case. When he had first been brought in, drunk as a lord, he'd been mostly a simple street thief in Atlanta: lifting wallets, snatching purses, engaging in the occasional bar fight, nothing more complicated than that.

Except for that time—or two—when he'd had to fight for his prizes.

Cops had found the bodies, but they'd never found him. He was too clever.

But in the five years since he had been here—was it five? It was hard to reckon time in the changeless blue glow of this place, and that damned machine played tricks on the mind— things had changed. Moussa's natural deftness had increased a thousandfold, and whereas he had once been content to let others play the games and manipulate and control, he was now the ringleader of this little circus.

"We don't know who he is, what he is, anything," Emir had said when Lynch had first come into the room, walking with that cautious stance that Moussa fully understood.

"We all started out as strangers," Moussa pointed out, adding, "Some of us started out as enemies."

Emir frowned. He could not deny the truth of Moussa's statement, but he had the best instincts of all of them. And it was clear that something about the newcomer troubled him deeply.

"Look how he moves, Moussa. How he holds himself. He is closer to his ancestry already than we were for a long time. But we don't know which ancestor it might be. That makes for a dangerous man."

But Moussa was curious. Plenty of others had come this way with just that expression and attitude. Including Moussa himself.

"Give him a little more time, Emir," he had said to his friend. "The man may prove to have some noble blood in him yet."

He had introduced himself to the Pioneer with a second name—Baptiste. Everyone here had second names. Or was it a first name? Because as he had told Lynch, Baptiste, who had indeed been a voodoo poisoner, had also been dead for two hundred years.

But the Abstergo Foundation had found Moussa, and through him, they had dug up Baptiste. And after all this time spent in the Animus, living through his ancestor's memories, the sly, intelligent killer of centuries past had come to reside comfortably alongside Moussa in that man's skin.

Baptiste had not been a nice person. Not at all. He had been trained as an Assassin, and had been a member of that Brotherhood for thirty years. But when his Mentor was killed,

Baptiste had abandoned the Brotherhood. Pretending to be his Mentor, Baptiste formed his own cult, and reveled in directing his followers to kill as suited him. Later, he would plan to join the Templars.

And so, quite reasonably, as he had reminded Emir, the inmates hadn't trusted Moussa. And at first he'd proved them right. He'd gone along with what the Templars had asked of him, just as his ancestor had, for some time. Until the day came that Moussa realized that today's Templars weren't about to keep their word any better than yesterday's Templars had done, and that they had been the only ones to benefit from the knowledge they had ripped from him.

Hell, the Templars hadn't even given him cake when he had asked for it on his birthday, which was... he didn't remember anymore. What kind of ungrateful shit was that? Too bad he couldn't get his hands on any poison; the plants that the Templars allowed the inmates to grow were all completely harmless.

Moussa manipulated the cups swiftly, his fingers feather-light as he touched them. The guard kept his eyes glued on the swiftly-moving objects, his mouth a thin, determined line of concentration. After a few more feints and shifting, Moussa stopped and looked at the guard expectantly.

The other man reached out and tapped the cup in the middle. Feigning sadness, Moussa lifted it to reveal that the cup concealed nothing, and then lifted the one on the right. The small ball sat beneath it.

"Aww, too bad. Best two out of three," he offered. The guard glowered, then nodded.

Again, the cups moved quickly.

Moussa had turned to the Assassins. It had taken time, but he had proved his trustworthiness to them. Now, he was the one *they* turned to. Each had his or her own skillset, their own knowledge and strengths. But it was Moussa, the trickster, the one who played the fool and the madman in order to glean information, who had the final say on things. They listened to him, trusted his judgment. He was always the one sent out to vet the newcomers. And there was something about this Pioneer that had seized his interest.

Lynch could be the one they had been hoping for... or the one they feared above others.

Their Protector... or their doom.

Moussa was feeling charitable, so he slowed his motions down just enough so that the guard, this time, was able to select the correct cup.

"Well, look at that," he exclaimed, "I got a shiny little thing hiding out underneath this. You got some sharp eyes, man. Bet nothing gets past you."

"I won. So what do you have for me?"

"Not one for chitchat, are you?" Moussa looked around, as if making sure they wouldn't be heard, then leaned in closer to the guard. "I know something about the new patient," he said, his lips almost brushing the guard's ears.

"Yeah?"

"He likes his steak rare," Moussa said, then pulled back, looking completely serious.

The guard flushed beet red, but Dr. Rikkin had forbidden any violence against her "patients" unless absolutely necessary. Still, Moussa was well aware that the guard would probably find some way to get back at him, but he didn't care.

Inside, Baptiste was laughing his head off.

* * *

Sofia's stomach knotted as she watched Cal gasp and cower, strike at empty air, and shout defiance. She had seen this before, many times. The first time she had witnessed it she had been distressed by it. Eventually, though, she had grown inured to it, though she took no delight in watching. It was a necessary part of her research, and she always had to keep the end goal in mind.

Sofia understood that this manifestation of the Bleeding Effect was terrifying and also physically painful for the patient. She also knew that it would pass with time, and that everything she knew about Cal's psychological state told her he was a strong candidate and would almost certainly suffer no lasting harm.

But something about Cal's suffering felt different to her. Sofia told herself it was only because he was so important to the Templar cause right at this moment.

"The Bleeding Effect is getting worse," she said to Alex, who was standing beside her watching the screen. "He's more affected by it than the others. Give him four hundred milligrams of Seroquel for the hallucinations."

Alex looked at her, a little surprised by her concern, but nodded and left, silent in his rubber-soled shoes.

She stood a moment longer, watching Cal and gnawing on a thumbnail. The Seroquel should do him some good. If not... she'd have to think of something else.

Sofia returned to her work, which had always been a source of comfort, pride, and distraction. And, she had to admit, a way to get her father's attention and approbation.

It was no real surprise to her that she had gravitated to science and technology rather than other interests. With the horrible shock of her mother's murder, her father had increased the amount of security in their two main houses in England and France, and brought in governesses and later formal teachers to instruct her. She didn't know how to interact with her fellow humans, and computer technology had been a key part of her lessons and her entertainment.

Despite the trauma of the nature of his mother's death, Cal at least had had her presence in his life till the age of seven.

Sofia had lost her mother when she was four.

She didn't remember much. A faint image here and there; the sound of a laugh, or a line from one of the books her mother often read aloud. The pet name of "Sofie." The scent of lilacs and the softness of a cheek. Butterfly kisses.

Sofia even had memories—happy memories—of her father from that time. He was kinder then, and laughed more. She remembered being swung up on his shoulders, going from the smallest to the tallest in the room, and looking up at the comforting shapes of both parents tucking her in bed.

But once the bright light that was Mama had winked out of her daughter's life, everything had changed. Sofia would wake at night screaming, terrified that the "Sassins" had come for her father, too, and she would be all alone in the world. She'd wanted her father to come to her room on those awful nights, to scoop her up and tell his Sofie that the Assassins would never come for either of them, that he would keep her safe.

But that had never happened.

Sofia—no longer Sofie—had been largely left to her own devices. Her father had a global corporation to run, after all, and had duties she had only begun to learn about as a teenager in his role as a Grand Master Templar. As the years passed and Sofia began to contribute more and more to advancing Abstergo's Animus technology, he had given her more important tasks and titles.

The Madrid center was hers. Except, like all things, it wasn't, really. "Not to ourselves, but to the future, give glory," was a commonly heard phrase among the Templars. It was a lovely thought, but more often than not, it was to the Elders and to Alan Rikkin that glory was given.

Sofia heard soft footfalls behind her and smelled her father's aftershave. She smiled to herself. *Speak of the devil*, she thought.

"He has to go back in the Animus," Rikkin said without preamble. Sofia looked up from her work. "*Now.*"

She looked at him incredulously. "Can't you see what's happening to him?" Sofia asked. "The Bleeding Effect is hitting him very hard. He needs more time before he goes in, for us to prepare—"

"We don't *have* time," Rikkin interrupted, cold and deliberate.

A chill went through Sofia. "Why?" she demanded. What was her father keeping from her?

He did not answer. It would not be the first time. Sofia understood the demands placed on him, though she did not know the particulars. There were certain things he was not permitted to say, questions he wasn't allowed to answer. Although, the older she grew, the more she wondered if it was less that his hands were tied than that he simply liked to keep secrets.

This time, though, she knew it wasn't the playing of a game that made him hold his tongue. Something had happened. Considering he had flown back to London last night to report to the Elders, she made the assumption that they had told him something that had forced this new urgency upon him.

The silence stretched uncomfortably between them. His brown eyes were fixed on the screen.

It was not a pleasant sight. Despite the medication, she had prescribed for him, Callum Lynch was now curled into a tight ball on the floor, rocking back and forth. Alan Rikkin was used to being in charge, to having all his orders obeyed immediately and without question. Father and daughter had butted heads before. He was not a scientist, he was a businessman. And he was more interested in results than in... well, in anything.

"Send him back in, Sofia. Not in a couple of days, not in a few hours. Now."

Sofia knew she could not risk growing too attached to her test subjects. But she was also their protector, and she made a decision.

"You know as well as I do that he'll die in there if he isn't ready."

"Then see to it that he *is*."

She closed the distance between herself and her father, turning her face up to him defiantly.

"I won't risk his life."

That got his attention. He looked at her for a moment his expression... sad. Then, reluctantly but firmly, he said words that chilled his daughter to the bone.

"Then I'll have to find someone else to do it."

Sofia stared at him as he walked out without another word or a backward glance, and groped for her chair, almost collapsing into it. She gripped the back of the chair till her knuckles turned white, forcing herself to breathe deeply.

When she was eight years old, she had found a stray dog. He had been a mutt, absolutely crawling with fleas, big and gangly and uncontrollable, but she had fallen in love with him on the spot. Her father had told her that under no circumstances would Oscar, as she had named him for no reason she could fathom then or now, be allowed to stay.

Sofia wasn't a girl of many tears, but she'd flung herself on the animal, sobbing her heart out. She'd felt the matted fur against his cheek, his body heat against her, his heart beating quickly. For the first time since her mother's death, Sofia experienced a connection to some other living creature, one that needed her, that she could take care of, as her mother had taken care of her.

Of course, she couldn't articulate such a complicated thought at that age. All she could do was cry, and cling to Oscar, and beg.

Sofia promised her father she'd take care of everything. She would feed, bathe, and train him. He would be a good dog, she had vowed. The *best* dog. Oscar would be grateful to have been rescued, and he would love her.

And if he would let her have Oscar, she, Sofia Rikkin, would be a good girl, the *best* girl. She wouldn't let her grades slip, she'd do everything her teachers asked of her. Eventually, her father had relented, but said he'd hold her to her promises.

Sofia kept her word. She bathed Oscar, and fed him, and worked diligently on housetraining him. She even taught him to sit and stay. Then one day, while she was taking him for a walk, he'd slipped his leash to go after a squirrel. He refused to come when she called and finally, she cornered him and made a grab for his collar.

He'd been overexcited and frightened, and, not unexpectedly for a stray animal, had bitten her. It hadn't been a bad bite, but it had broken the skin. Bleeding, Sofia had gotten the leash reattached and they had gone home, blood streaming down her arm.

Her father had gone through the roof.

Sofia had been bundled into the car and taken to the Rikkins' private physician, where she had received ten stitches. She still had the scar, and now, as she stared at the monitor, at Callum Lynch curled up weeping, shivering, and striking out savagely at enemies that existed only in his mind, she found herself tracing the almost-invisible white line on her wrist with a thumb.

She'd gotten stitches.

Oscar had gotten shot.

When she had found out and confronted her father, all he had said was, "I don't like seeing you get hurt."

Growing up, looking back on the incident, Sofia had rationalized that her father had indeed been upset at the thought of his only child being attacked by an animal—even one whose reaction to the situation had not been unexpected or even severe. She had told herself that, so soon after losing her mother, her father couldn't bear to think of anything bad happening to his daughter.

But now, she understood. Alan Rikkin hadn't been an overprotective father trying to protect a beloved child. He had been exercising his right to control the situation.

He had been telling her that he had the ability, at any time, for any reason, to eliminate anything—and anyone—that was precious to her, if he so chose.

Cal Lynch wasn't the first casualty of Alan Rikkin's need to control his daughter's life.

He was just the most recent.

CHAPTER 12

Cal had revived, and eaten; they brought another steak to his room, cut into pieces so that he wouldn't require a knife. He felt better after he'd had some food, and for a while he wondered if he'd beaten the hallucinations.

But he hadn't. Now Cal stared into the room at the end of his, where the guards kept constant vigil. This time, they weren't the ones regarding him.

This time, it was Aguilar.

Cal was tense and alert, sweat coming off him in rivulets, but the Assassin did not attack. He simply stared at Cal for a long moment, then stepped into his room.

Through the glass.

Cal stared for a moment into his own face, but one that was harder, adorned with both scars and tattoos. *This is a hallucination. It's not real. What happens in the Animus is not real, not for me. This is just the Bleeding Effect.*

He was surprised the image was so calm. Perhaps his mind was working through this and was going to have the Assassin speak to him. Instead, as he had done before, the Assassin lunged.

But this time, Cal was ready. He got his left arm up in time to knock aside Aguilar's attempted stiff-handed jab at his throat, and his right to strike hard at the Assassin's second attempt. Aguilar feinted, then whirled and kicked out, his foot barely missing Cal's stomach.

Cal was no stranger to brawling. He had gotten into more fistfights than there were stars in the sky since... since that day. But now, for the first time since the Bleeding Effect had descended upon him, twisting reality and grabbing him by the throat, Cal was in control of his actions. Before, the images of Assassins had simply terrorized him: whispering accusations, stabbing him, slitting his throat. His brain had been flooded with unreasoning fear. But this time, things were very different.

He knew how Aguilar had behaved previously, when he was trying to kill Cal. He had succeeded then. This wasn't an attack—at least, not like the others had been. Dimly, Cal realized that this was... sparring. Training.

Dodging a kick. Blocking a strike. Executing his own punches. He fell into the motions easily, comfortably. This kind of fight, he knew. In this kind of fight, he could hold his own.

Abruptly he whirled, kicked out—and nothing was there. Cal paused, barely winded, and looked around the room. Was Aguilar gone? Then he felt a prickle at the back of his neck and turned around.

He was no longer alone. Others were coming into the room now. They were his enemies, too, but unlike the angry Assassins who had descended upon him earlier, they wore crisp white uniforms instead of hoods. This was not a hallucination. They were coming to put him back into the Animus, but he would not go quietly.

Two orderlies approached him. Adrenaline shot through Cal. He couldn't go back there. Not again. Even the hallucinations were better than being grasped by the arm and being plunged back into a dead man's memories. Cal darted forward, seizing the first orderly, and slammed his face into the wall. He whirled, head-butting the second, then blocked a blow from the first one, seizing his arm and flipping him over to land on his back.

Three guards now raced forward, carrying batons instead of hidden blades. Cal took down the one on his left first. He shoved his arm into the guard's elbow and the black-clad man stumbled. Cal immediately went for the one on his right, landing a solid punch to her jaw and sending her reeling backward.

A fourth guard had entered the room, and he and the middle one managed to seize Cal's arms, attempting to immobilize him. He would have none of it, using their grip on him as leverage to lift his legs and land a brutal kick into the midsection of the newcomer.

But the guard he'd punched had recovered, and she smiled with grim pleasure as she struck him across the face with her stick. It almost, but not quite, knocked him out. His body succumbed even as his spirit raged, and he sagged in their grasp, his world blurry as they dragged him out of the room.

They paused at the door. His head throbbing, Cal blinked, steeling himself against the pain as he raised his head to look up into a large man in a guard uniform with heavy-lidded, expressionless eyes.

"You're up, slugger," the man said.

No. He couldn't do it. Abruptly Cal seized on his greatest fear, and weaponized it.

"I'm crazy," he said through the blood that was pouring out of his mouth.

They ignored him, and began dragging him down the corridor. As fear spurted through him at the thought of again entering the body and mind of Aguilar de Nerha, an image from that long-ago day flashed into his mind: the old, battered radio, playing the Patsy Cline song "Crazy".

Cal started to sing—or, more accurately, scream, the song.

He sang, wildly off-key, desperate to prolong the inevitable.

* * *

It was a simple game of poker, and it was anything but.

Nathan's turn to deal was up, and he passed out cards with seeming calm. Ordinarily the guards were kept out of sight, behind the two-way mirrored wall. A few had come out when Lynch had appeared earlier. Now, the place was crawling with them.

Emir glanced up, then back down at his cards. "They're putting him back in again," he said. No one said anything. They all knew.

Moussa picked up his cards without looking at them, his eyes on the orderlies. "They're rushing him. He ain't ready to go back in again, not with a breakdown like the one we saw. Pioneer couldn't even stay steady long enough to eat that nice juicy steak he ordered. That man doesn't even know who he is yet, much less which side he's on."

"Then," Nathan said, fanning his cards out, "we should stop him before he betrays us."

The others were calmer than he was. Nathan had been brought in spoiling for a fight, ready to take a swing at anyone for looking at him wrong. He had gradually learned to exert better self-control, but not completely. Moussa had chided Nathan for his words to Lynch earlier, but the boy wasn't sorry. Everything in Nathan screamed that the man Moussa was fond of calling the Pioneer was a threat. And sometimes it was better to be wrong and safe than right and dead.

Every night, Nathan awoke covered in sweat and absolutely terrified. Intellectually, he understood what was going on. Dr. Rikkin called it the Bleeding Effect, and suggested that, since Nathan was younger than most of the patients at the center, the effects might manifest more intensely with him.

"A man who is fifty has lived with himself for more than twice as long as you have," she had told him in her calm, gentle voice. "He has more memories that are his own. Therefore, he has more to draw upon to remind himself of his own identity when the lines begin to blur."

And she'd smiled, that sweet smile that always made Nathan wonder if maybe he was wrong, maybe she wasn't entirely on the Templar side of things. And even if she was, maybe the Templars weren't so bad.

Of course, that wasn't really him. That was bloody Duncan Walpole, traitor, sticking his nose in where it didn't belong.

Second cousin to Robert Walpole, Britain's first prime minister; Duncan Walpole, born 1679, died 1715. It sickened Nathan to think that any part of that man lived on in him. Duncan Walpole was a turncoat, just like Baptiste had been. But at least the voodoo poisoner had a right to his anger. He had been born a slave, and later had felt betrayed by the Brotherhood.

By contrast, Duncan had lived an easy life. He had followed the path of a naval officer, but was an arrogant, self-centered prick who balked at taking orders. Unhappy with the navy, he had been seduced by the ideals of the Assassins. It had appealed to his better angels.

But even in a Brotherhood where "everything is permitted," the spoiled Walpole eventually grew discontent. He again challenged the older members of the Brotherhood, and nursed grievances, most of which were imaginary.

Given an assignment in the West Indies, Duncan learned everything he could about the local Assassin guild while he was there. Then, once he had obtained enough information to be valuable to them, Walpole contacted the Templars, who knew exactly how to flatter him... and pay him.

Nathan had been in and out of school because he was always picking fights. An almost stereotypical East Ender, he'd fallen in with a gang and dealt drugs for a while. The gang leaders sent him to peddle drugs near the local schools because he looked so sweet and harmless. Harmless until he lost his temper; he'd beaten one member nearly to a pulp with his bare hands.

"You'd know about such things, wouldn't you, Nathan?" Emir said now. Once, it would have been an insult. Once, Nathan would have taken it as a challenge. Now, he knew it was an acknowledgement of what—or who—Nathan had to live with every single day.

And night.

Nathan forced himself not to shiver.

He didn't want to be like Duncan. He wanted to be better. He wanted to be more like Moussa, or, when he was feeling particularly hopeful, like Lin or Emir. The two of them—as far as he knew—had no skeletons in their closets.

Knowing how despicable his ancestor had been was why Nathan was always so suspicious of any newcomer. *Guilty until proven innocent*, he'd been known to say, *and let's face it, we're all guilty*.

Nathan trusted Moussa's judgment. More than any of them, even the level-headed Emir, he seemed in harmony with his two sets of memories. He acted like a buffoon for the benefit of the guards, but in reality, he was the sane one.

"I do know about such things," Nathan replied calmly. His gaze flickered to one of the guards. *They're watching us like hawks.* "Moussa's right. They shouldn't be putting him back in the Animus yet. If they're pushing him that hard, that's because he knows something very important. And he might decide to pick the wrong side."

They couldn't afford to give this newcomer the benefit of a doubt—not if, as Moussa suspected, he was going to be either the one to get them out of here, or the one to get them all killed.

Moussa met his gaze; two Assassins who had turned Templar, and who understood one another well. Moussa looked back down at his cards and grunted.

"Well, will you look at that," he said, and placed down four cards. There were two black aces and two black eights. "Dead man's hand."

Four cards. Four guardians of the Apple.

"What about the fifth card?" asked Nathan.

"Fifth card was a bullet to the brain," Moussa said.

They were all in agreement.

* * *

Cal's broken howling of song lyrics reached Sofia's ears before the man himself did, and she had to force herself not to wince in empathy. It was too soon—far too soon—to put him back in.

She had heard that tone of despair and terror in the voices of previous subjects. Sometimes, the essence of who that person truly was vanished shortly after Sofia heard that tone... and that person never returned.

Dammit.

"Set the date for the sixth," Sofia told Alex.

Cal's voice, high-pitched and desperate, continued to shriek ghoulishly appropriate lyrics.

Sofia's hands clenched. "If his condition deteriorates..." She took a deep breath. "... pull him out."

Alex turned to her, his high brow furrowing. "But your father—" he began. Sofia cut him off.

"I don't *care* what my father said," she murmured, acutely aware that the man under discussion was watching everything from his office window. She strode out onto the floor, and looked as the arm, gripping Cal firmly about his waist, raised him over her head.

Cal all but sobbed now, his face a rictus of a smile, as he wondered along with Patsy Cline what he had done.

He looked terrible. He was bloody from being "subdued" in his room. His eyes were wild, he was sweating, and his chest heaved as he hyperventilated. Sofia's own chest ached in sympathy. Damn her father, anyway; this should not be happening.

Once, as a little girl, she had sat for hours outside her childhood home, patient as the hills, sunflower seeds cupped in her tiny hand, waiting for squirrels or chipmunks to accept her offering. Her body grew stiff from sitting, and one of her feet fell asleep. It didn't matter.

It was all worth it when one small, bright-eyed creature poked its nose out from around a tree. With jerky movements, ready to flee, the chipmunk made an indirect approach. It had just placed its tiny, clawed forepaws on her thumb, staring up at her with big eyes, its heart pounding so fast she could see the motion through the fur on its white chest, when her father had emerged, shouting at the chipmunk to go away. It had vanished in a brown blur. The next day, and the next, despite her father's orders, she had sat outside. Waiting.

It had never returned.

Cal bore more resemblance to a wolf than a chipmunk, but he, too, was wary. And he, too, had started to trust her, she believed. But instead of simply chasing him away, her father had issued instructions that Cal be beaten into submission, hauled forth, and shoved into a machine he barely understood and was obviously terrified of.

It was cruel, it was *wrong*, and in a bitter irony she knew it was going to, in the end, set them back, perhaps irrecoverably, while her father was so keen on getting results instantly.

Sofia had one shot at protecting Cal from

damage, right here, right now, and she had to make it count.

"Cal," she said, her voice strong and commanding. "Listen to me."

He only sang... shouted... louder, trying to drown her out. Trying to put up some kind— any kind—of barrier to protect who he was before experiencing what he was going to be forced to endure. The irony, the danger, was that the only way for his mind to be safe was if he completely embraced what was going to happen. If he did not try to hold it at arm's length, or drown it out by screaming louder than the memory.

"*Listen to me!*" she shouted. "You have to concentrate! You have to focus on the memories." Was she getting through? Sofia couldn't tell. She pressed on. "You have to stay with Aguilar."

The name caught his attention, and Cal looked down, blinking, trying to focus, still madly singing. Except it wasn't madness—it was a fierce bid to keep a grip on sanity.

Sofia had studied this man intently. She did, as she had told him openly, know everything about him. And the man suspended above her, panting and struggling not to shatter, reminded her of the little boy in the old Polaroids so strongly it hurt.

What was the line from Shakespeare? she thought distractedly. "*I must be cruel, only to be kind.*"

She had to drum it into him. He would listen, do as she said—or he would become like so many others before him, a body with a shattered brain, caught eternally between the past and the present.

Sofia would not let that happen.

Not to Cal.

She repeated the command. "Cal... *you have to stay with Aguilar.*"

There was nothing in this world that he wanted less, she could tell. But she could also tell that he heard her.

And then—he was in.

CHAPTER 13

The belowground holding area was hot and stifling. Dust wafted in air that reeked of sweat, blood, urine, and feces. Aguilar, Maria, and Benedicto were not alone in their captivity; over a dozen other prisoners joined them. There had been more, a few hours ago. Guards had come for them, a few at a time, marching them out and then locking the metal gate behind them. No one, of course, ever returned.

Aguilar knew what the Assassins' crime had been. He neither knew nor cared what the other poor wretches had done to earn a fate such as that which awaited them. Some wept quietly, others sobbed, rackingly and loudly, begging for mercy. Still others sat with blank expressions, as if completely unaware of their present circumstances.

All were in various states of agony and exhaustion, and were securely chained with their backs to the cold stone walls, their arms cuffed at the waist and linked to rings a few feet over their heads. Movement was limited, but possible, and while the pose was extremely uncomfortable, it was not in itself an extra torment.

The three Assassins had been the last ones brought in a few days ago. They were the only ones left of their Brotherhood; all the others had been killed in the attempted rescue of Prince Ahmed.

Maria and Aguilar had been shackled beside one another. Their proximity offered them no comfort. Aguilar was furious with himself. He and Maria had come so close to escaping with the boy. But Ojeda had hauled him up by his own grappling rope, and Aguilar had been forced to watch the boy be handed right back to his captors.

What was a thousand times worse was discovering that Maria had not been able to elude the Templars. He was resigned to his own fate, as he had been ever since his family had perished at the hands of the massive, implacable

Ojeda, and he had joined the Brotherhood to avenge them.

If only Maria had escaped.

They had fallen silent hours ago, and now she stared ahead, her eyes focusing on nothing. Then, she spoke.

"Soon they will march on Granada."

"Sultan Muhammad is weak," Aguilar replied. His mouth was as dry as the sun-baked earth and his voice was a raspy croak. The ever-compassionate Templars had reasoned that their prisoners would be dead soon, and what did a corpse need with water?

"He'll surrender the Apple and betray the Creed for the prince's life. He loves his son."

She had turned to look at him while he spoke, her chains clanking soft. Now, she gazed him with that blazing intensity that was as much a part of her as her hands or her voice.

"Love makes us weak," she said, her voice shaking ever so slightly.

Aguilar couldn't tear his gaze from her. He had not been able to, really, since the first time they had met. He shifted position so that his whole body turned to hers, and ignored the pain his battered frame expressed at the moment. There was so much he wanted to say that had remained unsaid. But in the end, the words were not needed. She knew—and so did he.

Instead, he found different words coming to his lips. There was only one thing to say, at this moment. Maria knew it, too. The Templars had taken everything from them. There was only one thing left that they couldn't take, no matter what they did to their bodies.

She spoke at the same time, together with him in this as they had been in so many things before the sun had dawned on their final day. In unison, they repeated the vows each had made, separately, upon their initiation.

"I would gladly sacrifice myself and everyone I care for, so that the Creed lived on."

Her eyes were wide, unblinking, and he could see the pulse in her throat even in the dim light that filtered through holes above. Aguilar's own heart leaped even now to see the passion in her eyes; she lived every moment, every breath, with that passion, and now savored it more than ever.

Aguilar leaned forward, straining against the chains to reach her one last time. She did the same, but the Templars, it seemed, had been unkind unintentionally, for once. The chains were but an inch too short. Maria and Aguilar would not even be allowed a final kiss, before they tasted that of the heretic's fire.

They heard the metal door open, the tramp of boots. The red-cloaks were unlocking the prisoners' chains. It would not be long, now.

Bound at throat, wrists, and feet, they were hauled up. Aguilar bit back against the hiss of pain as his body was forced into movement after being obliged to be still for so long. Side by side, as they ever had been, Aguilar and Maria faced the door.

"When I die today," she said, her voice taut but strong, "do not waste your tears."

He wouldn't. Simple tears would never do this remarkable woman even a shadow of justice. The only drops that he could shed that would properly mourn her would be those of his own blood.

They were marched upward along a slanting corridor, up to the sunlight and the heat and the dust, straight into a carnival of insanity.

Aguilar's head was laid bare for the sun's harsh rays to beat upon, as was Maria's, revealing rows of braids. All three of the Assassins' hoods had been pulled down, robbing them of any mystery or hint of anonymity. The only hoods worn were those of the executioners, who stepped to either side of them—two muscular men, whose faces were hidden by black cloth.

Cal blinked. He could see both the crowd clustered around him, and the lab assistants at their stations. And, of course, the angel's face, a pale oval of both aloofness and concern. Superimposed on both these images was a memory, short and sharp, of sitting on the floor in his cell, sketching, sketching like a man possessed; the crude charcoal drawing of a large, broad-chested man with a black hood—

"Stay with it, Cal," came the angel's voice, and Cal fell back into the place of pain and heat.

* * *

Ahead of the group of prisoners strode a cluster of churchmen, clad in white vestments, their miters perched atop their heads as they bore their croziers in front of them. They waved blessings at the throngs, whose cheers were muffled at first, growing increasingly louder until the Assassins were buffeted by the noise. Drums thundered in their ears, adding to the cacophony and the sense of disorientation.

Blinking in the bright light, Aguilar beheld bizarre costumes, people who had painted their faces strange colors, and row after row of spectators shouting hate-filled epithets at them. He wasn't sure of the purpose of it. Maybe those who capered about, dressed as demons, were performing a sort of passion play, or were trying to ward off evil spirits summoned by the death of so many sinners. Or perhaps it was to frighten the sinners themselves, to give them a foretaste of what surely must await them in hell.

Indeed, the red-cloaks were placed in the unusual role of being the Assassins' protectors, as a wild crowd struggled to reach the prisoners, wanting to tear them to pieces with their own hands.

Aguilar only pitied them. *If you only knew,* he thought, *that you are cheering for the deaths of those who would defend you.* They, too, were prisoners of the Templars, but they wore their invisible chains unknowingly.

Walking in front of Maria and Aguilar, Benedicto twisted around to look at them. His face was calm; peaceful.

"We die today," he assured them, "but the Creed lives."

Aguilar envied him his tranquility—and his certainty.

The three of them continued to be shoved forward, stumbling up steps to an enormous, open platform to be confronted with the true reality of their approaching, agonizing deaths. Stakes were affixed to the platform, and at their bases were piled huge bundles of twigs. Elsewhere were large barrels of oil, beside which one of the costumed tormenters stood at attention.

The arena had been constructed for a solitary purpose—the torture and execution of heretics—and was much larger than Aguilar had expected it to be. Hundreds, perhaps thousands, of spectators crowded and overflowed three levels of seats on all four sides.

Yet despite the other "heretics" that had kept them company in the prison belowground, only the three Assassins had been brought up. Clearly their deaths were meant to be the highlight of the event.

Gazing down from a high scaffold above them were the Inquisitors, crosses around their necks. With a pang of guilt, Aguilar noticed that, standing to one side, was the young Prince Ahmed the Assassins had tried so hard to rescue.

In the center, on what could only be called thrones, sat three imposing figures, all with stern, judgmental expressions. Aguilar recognized them all—King Ferdinand and his wife Isabella, the former Queen of Castile, and

Tomás de Torquemada... the Grand Inquisitor. For all the power he wielded, and all the terror he inspired, he was a small man, almost dwarfed by the regal king and queen as he sat in a chair between them.

If Ojeda had been the man who had captured Aguilar's parents and brought them to a place such as this, then it was Torquemada who had issued the orders for—and presided over—their deaths. Pure, undiluted hatred rose in Aguilar at the sight of the man.

Aguilar had made it his business to learn everything he could about the Dominican friar. Torquemada had advanced swiftly through the ranks at a young age, becoming a prior at the monastery of Santa Cruz in Segovia. It was there he met the woman who now sat on her throne, staring with loathing she did not attempt to disguise at the Assassins now ascending to the platform. Torquemada had been advising Queen Isabella most of her young life, becoming her confessor. He had even convinced her to marry King Ferdinand in order to consolidate a power base that Torquemada—and the Templars—could draw upon and manipulate for their own purposes.

His adoring chronicler, Sebastián de Olmedo, enthused that Torquemada was "the hammer of heretics, the light of Spain, the savior of his country," and "the honor of his order." Aguilar wondered which "order" de Olmedo meant—the Dominican, or the Templar.

Now the Grand Inquisitor rose, his tonsured pate gleaming in the sun, his tiny eyes and harsh mouth radiating his disdain. He looked over the three Assassins as his queen did: with contempt, not seeing human beings, only enemies. Not enemies of God, as the Templars so wanted the populace to believe, but enemies of the Templars and their quest for absolute domination of the human race.

He stepped forward, standing remarkably straight for a man of seventy years, and lifted his hands for quiet. His voice had grown no weaker with age, it seemed; it was strong and thrummed with certainty.

"'Do not think that I have come to bring peace upon the earth: I have not come to bring peace, but a sword,'" Torquemada quoted from the Bible. "'I will make mine arrows drunk with blood, and my sword shall devour flesh.' 'They shall die grievous deaths: they shall not be lamented.'"

As he spoke, the three Assassins were taken to the stakes and roughly shackled to them. Benedicto, as the Mentor, stood unaccompanied at his stake. Aguilar and Maria were led to a single one, the chains that bound their hands looped up and held in place by a spike at the top, their throats still encircled by links of iron.

One of the costumed demons scooped up a bucketful of oil, grinning in anticipation, and emptied it at Aguilar and Maria's feet.

"'They shall be consumed by the sword, and by famine; and their carcasses shall be meat for the fowls of heaven, and for the beasts of the earth,'" continued Torquemada. He was relishing every moment of this. Another grotesquely costumed man, looking like an enormous red bird with hands for claws, emptied a bucket of oil on Benedicto's pile.

Torquemada lowered his hands. "For decades," he continued "you have lived in a land torn apart by religious discord. By heretic vermin who think freedom of belief is more important than the peace of a nation. But soon, thanks to God and the Inquisition, we will purge this disease. And God will smile on you again, for only in obedience can there be peace!"

The crowd went wild, cheering and flailing in their excitement. *How comforting it must be, to think it is this simple to end discord,* Aguilar thought.

His gaze traveled from the deluded crowd and Torquemada's posturing to land on Ojeda. The other man stared at him, expressionless and cold.

Do you recognize me, you son of a dog? Aguilar thought. *Do you remember what you did? Are you pleased to be here so that you can complete your twisted task?*

Ojeda's ugly face contorted even further into a deep scowl. He swung himself off his horse and accompanied one of the bare-chested, black-hooded executioners as he went up to the platform toward Aguilar and Maria.

Torquemada smiled benevolently, sharing the crowd's joy. "The sinners before you sought to defend the heretic prince of Granada—the last heathen stronghold in our holy war. And so today, before our king and queen, Ferdinand and Isabella," and he turned and bowed, just deep enough to be respectful without being obsequious, "I, Torquemada, swear that we shall wash ourselves clean in the holy fire of God!"

The executioner had reached Aguilar and Maria's pyre. He bent to shove a spike through a link their lower chains, securing them to the platform. Aguilar was having none of it. His Mentor and even his Maria might be resigned to death today, but he would resist it to the last moment, and he kicked savagely at the executioner.

The man reeled back, but recovered quickly. He was angry now, and drew a dagger, intending to impale the Assassin's foot to the platform instead. But Aguilar was too nimble, jerking his feet out of the way at the last minute, and the dagger embedded itself solidly in the footrest, resisting the executioner's frustrated attempts to pull it loose.

Ojeda tried nothing so elaborate, instead stepping in and almost casually landing a solid blow to Aguilar's stomach. Aguilar doubled over, prevented from curling into a fetal position only by his restrained, still-raised arms. He was glad now that the Templars had given them nothing, not even water. He did not want to give his enemies and the ecstatic crowd the pleasure of seeing him vomit.

"You will watch your Mentor burn," Ojeda promised, looking from Aguilar to Maria and then back. "And then you will die the slowest." He smiled cruelly, and added, "Just as your parents did."

Aguilar tensed. So. The black knight had recognized him after all.

"They suffered, and they screamed," Ojeda continued. "I watched them turn to ash then, and I will watch you do the same now. Your filthy lineage dies with you."

As Ojeda picked up a torch and strode to Benedicto's stake, waiting while a bucket full of oil drenched the Mentor's pyre, Torquemada cried, "Behold God's will! I am Alpha and Omega, the beginning and the end! I will give unto him that is thirsty a fountain of the water of life!"

Unable to hide a smirk of satisfaction, Torquemada, his eyes on the Mentor of the Assassins, made the sign of the cross.

***

Standing, barely breathing, Sofia's entire being was focused on the holographic images of Ojeda, Maria, and Torquemada reenacting a scene from over five centuries ago. Incredible, what the Assassins were capable of enduring. Admirable, the lightning speed with which they could assess a situation and figure a way out of it....

***

With the attention now on Benedicto and Ojeda, Aguilar acted, kicking with all his strength at the hilt of the dagger impaled through the chains at his feet. Trapped between his ankle manacle and the sole of Aguilar's boot, the hilt came off. The blade, and the metal core around which the hilt had been crafted, remained embedded in the wooden footrest.

Maria was chained with her back to him, but she gasped and he knew that she had seen—and she knew what it meant. So many times they had worked together so smoothly, as a single entity, knowing what the other was thinking. Now he could feel her tension, her readiness. He was so grateful to have her. They were the perfect team, in all things.

Again and again, Aguilar brought his ankle shackle down, using the slender core of the dagger to push at the shackle's pin. With each blow, he shoved the pin up just a little further.

Come on. Come on....

The crowd was almost frenzied now, whipped to a fervor by the Inquisitor's words and Ojeda's actions. Some of the strangely costumed onlookers were dancing among the crowd, and the roar was almost deafening.

Ojeda peered up at Benedicto, who lifted his head defiantly. Assassin and Templar regarded one another with utter loathing.

"Not to ourselves, but to the future, give glory," he told the Assassin Mentor.

Benedicto closed his eyes tightly, steeling himself for what was to come.

Ojeda touched the flaming torch to the oil-saturated wood. And orange flame sheeted up around the Assassin Mentor.

CHAPTER 14

Aguilar had wrested free and spun himself around, but he froze, transfixed with horror and unable to tear his sickened gaze away from the spectacle. He saw not only his Mentor, but his parents, standing at their own stakes just like this, "blessed" by a man who served no God, but only himself.

Padre... Madre....

Benedicto screamed in agony, his body engulfed by hungry orange-yellow flames, and the stench of burning flesh—

* * *

Cal gagged, sickened by a smell that was not present, his mind galloping back again to the art he had plastered on the walls of his cell: The image of a dark shape, unrecognizable, surrounded by a nimbus of fire that consumed and enfolded him. His mother, staring, her life blood drip-dripping on the linoleum.

He shut his eyes, turning away from all of it, seeking reprieve—

"Cal! Don't! You must stay with Aguilar!"

The voice of the angel, sweet, and cruel, and commanding. He was Cal, and he was Aguilar, and someone he loved was dying the worst death conceivable.

But someone else was still alive—

"Maria," Cal shouted, and hurtled back into the memory.

* * *

Aguilar shook off the paralyzing moment of fear, where past and present converged in a grotesque conflagration. His parents and Benedicto would want him and Maria to live, to complete their mission, and his Mentor would be honored to know that his death had given them the chance to do so.

Aguilar hoped that, somehow, Benedicto knew.

There was nothing he could do for his Mentor now. Like a fish leaping from the water,

Aguilar hurled himself forward and around so he faced the stake, then placed his feet against it, climbing it and somersaulting so that the chains fastened to his wrists unlooped and he had room to maneuver. He and Maria were still linked together by the chains around their neck, and his movement away from the stake yanked her closer to it, choking her.

Aguilar seized a sword from one of the guards, pulling it from its hilt and bringing it sweeping across its owner's throat. He continued the sweep all the way around, slamming the sword into the chains that bound Maria's feet.

Though still linked at their throats, they fought together, in harmony; he with the sword, she, hands still chained to the stake, with booted feet and powerful legs.

* * *

Sofia stared, watching Cal with wide eyes. He was no longer simply being *moved by the Animus; he himself was moving, the blows that turned holographic Templars into ghostly black nothingness coming smoothly, easily. Naturally. He was an active participant in the regression now, not a helpless puppet manipulated by a machine.*

She had been concerned earlier, as she watched Cal twice appear about to slip out of the simulation—

something that could easily mean the death of Sofia's attempt to locate the Apple—and the death of Cal Lynch. She wasn't sure what had upset him so greatly. She could only see his actions and their effects; she could not read his mind. Only he had known what he saw.

But it seemed that he had crossed some sort of threshold that would forever be hidden from her, and she was so very grateful.

"He's synchronizing," she whispered, and her lips curved in a tremulous smile.

This was going to work....

* * *

One of the guards recovered enough to seize a torch and hurl it onto Maria's pyre. He paid for the move with his life, as Aguilar hurled his sword across the distance straight into the guard's chest.

The wood had not yet been saturated with oil, so flames did not leap wildly, but the dry tinder caught nonetheless. Maria spun on the stake, keeping her body as far away from the fire below her as possible.

The bloodthirsty cries from the crowd had turned into shrieks of panic. Torquemada, his beautiful ceremony thrown into chaos, was shouting orders to his followers. The flames were starting to climb now, and with a fierce growl Aguilar ran toward Maria's stake at top speed, slamming his shoulder into it with all his strength. The wood groaned in protest as the stake cracked free and toppled. Maria twisted, hitting the platform hard.

Aguilar reached down to her. Maria's eyes flew wide at something behind him, and she pulled him down instead. He rolled to see one of the executioners raising his axe, and realized Maria had saved his life. Grabbing her leg, Aguilar pulled her backward. The executioner could not halt the blow already in motion, and so the axe, meant to sever Maria's neck, severed her chains instead.

Liberated, she flipped forward and landed on her feet. Aguilar charged the executioner, who was strong but slow. As always, Maria knew what he was thinking. Together, they wrapped the chain that connected their necks, pulling it tight around the man's thick one to throttle him. A quick tug and it was over, and the executioner sagged and slumped toward the planks.

Aguilar seized the dead man's axe and hurled it toward one of the barrels, then he and Maria raced toward a set of stairs leading up into the stands. Oil began to spill across the stage, flowing seemingly like a living thing into Benedicto's pyre.

The stage exploded with a deafening boom, birthing an inferno.

As the pair of Assassins leaped up the stairs, Templars were burning to death in their stead, screaming in torment. It would seem that Grand Inquisitor Torquemada had been over-eager for his fiery entertainment, as there was scaffolding that had not yet been cleared away. Aguilar made straight for it, with Maria right at his heels. They launched themselves at it, climbing furiously.

When they reached the top, Aguilar and Maria paused for a moment, catching their breaths and assessing the situation. Below them, the white smudge of Torquemada's face, contorted in anger, stared up at them. He was shouting and gesticulating, and Aguilar saw that his enemy had somehow eluded the flames: Ojeda, cape flapping behind him, had mounted his black warhorse and was giving chase.

Wordlessly, the pair flipped up their hoods, reclaiming their identities as Assassins with the gesture, then headed for the roofs of Seville .

Black, oily smoke mixed with the near-om-nipresent dust as they ran. They were not unchallenged; Torquemada, or perhaps King

Ferdinand, had anticipated that there might be an escape attempt, and archers had been positioned on the rooftops. Now they flung aside their crossbows and drew their swords, charging the two. But skilled though the soldiers might have been with their weapons, they lacked the agility and grace of the Assassins, who found fighting and running on rooftops as easy as breathing.

Mindful of what had worked so well before, Aguilar wrapped his wrist chains around an enemy's sword, twisting and snapping one of the links. The guards were easily knocked off balance, toppling down into the maddened crowd below who were seeking an escape from the flames.

Others arrived to take their places, though, and it was immediately apparent that these were not ordinary guards. Torquemada had sent Templars after them; too many for two Assassins to defeat. Still attached by their neck chain, Maria and Aguilar raced to the edge of the roof and leaped off, sailing over a gap to land on a sloping, brick-tiled roof.

They slid down on their backs, looking ahead to a narrow buttress, and launched themselves toward it. Aguilar and Maria then began to leap from ledge to overhang to roof, always making sure they were never too far away from one another, trying desperately to shake off the dogged Templars at their heels.

Aguilar heard one of them cry out as, in a futile attempt to follow the Assassins as they jumped nimbly from one small foothold to the other, the Templar lost his footing and tumbled to the streets far below. A quick glance down revealed to Aguilar that the broken body of the Templar had fallen not amongst terrified crowd members, but amongst his own brethren. They were running through the streets, their faces peering upward, some on foot and some on horseback. Aguilar heard a humming sound as a crossbow bolt whizzed past, too close for comfort.

Maria and Aguilar had reached the end of this stretch of rooftop, and leaped in tandem to a narrow balustrade. Aguilar, slightly ahead, landed solidly, but Maria's foot slipped. She fell, grasping onto the chain that still bound them together. Aguilar's hand shot out, seizing the chain as well, and hauled her back. Old stone crumbled beneath them, and they immediately leaped again.

This time, they surprised a group of bare-chested, dust-covered stonemasons, who stared at them blankly in shock. They offered no resistance or complaint as Maria's hand darted out and closed on a chisel. She squatted, letting the chain stretch out flat on the roof's surface, and looked up at Aguilar expectantly.

He was already grabbing a hammer out of one of the mason's unresisting hands. With a single powerful blow, the chain snapped, and they were off and running again, the masons staring after them. Aguilar allowed himself a hint of amusement at the thought of what these men would be telling their families at the next mealtime.

Aguilar had lost track of the layout of the city at this point. But as long as they were on a roof, they had the advantage. Assassins were trained to maneuver in such places in a way the Templars were not.

But the Templars *did* have numbers, and it now seemed they were swarming in every direction, like insects emerging from their nest to descend upon their enemies.

Aguilar and Maria jumped through crenellations onto a flat roof. A church, Aguilar realized absently. They had barely landed when a Templar appeared, racing after them. He launched himself at Maria, slamming into her, and the two tumbled down into a courtyard below.

She recovered quickly, but so did her foe. Maria easily dodged his sword strike, darting forward to seize his overextended arm and turn it—and the sword it grasped—to strike the staff of a second Templar coming up behind her. A quick jab to the abdomen laid the second Templar out on the stone, and Maria made short work of the first.

A level above her, Aguilar lithely sprang from bridge to parapet to roof, supple as a cat. Half a dozen Templars descended upon him, but he was ready.

A few short minutes ago, he had been staring at certain death. The memories of his family had threatened to overwhelm him, but he had pushed them back and not surrendered to grief or fear. Benedicto's execution by fire had been horrifying to witness, but it had bought Aguilar the precious time he needed to free himself and Maria.

He had been thirsty, hungry, exhausted. Had even tasted the first prickling of despair. But now, he was not about to let a mere handful of Templars become an obstacle.

Aguilar's blood sang and he felt alive, so *alive*, and when they descended upon him, it was child's play to strike one down with a whirling, leaping kick, seize his staff, and turn with a fierce, demonic grin of pure relish to fight off the other five. This was his heritage. His parents lived through him, now, and he would not dishonor that gift.

Maria appeared beside him as the lone remaining Templar gasped out his last breath. Their eyes met, and she jerked her head toward the next roof. No sooner had they made the jump than Aguilar caught a flurry of movement over his head.

Running along the ledge above them was a line of Templars, firing down at them.

CHAPTER 15

It was time to go down instead of up. This time, when they reached the edge of the roof, Maria dropped to the sloping stone arch of a balcony's roof and swung herself inside.

Aguilar followed. They crashed through the wooden slatted door and tore through a small, long room. The church attendees screamed and dove for cover. Without even slowing, Maria and Aguilar leaped out the next window they saw and clung like burrs to ledges about six inches wide. The overeager Templar who followed them missed the handhold and plunged downward, screaming.

Up they went, leaping from a ledge on one building's side to a higher ledge on the one about six feet away, zig-zagging steadily upward, to emerge on the front of the great cathedral. They were afforded a splendid view of the city, and a more sobering one of the now-dozens of Templars, on other roofs and at street level, who had come to join in the hunt.

One of them, Aguilar saw, was Ojeda. Their eyes met and the Templar shouted incoherently, kicking his great warhorse violently and plunging toward the church.

Aguilar heard footsteps behind him. Planting his feet on the narrow ledge, high above the city streets, he turned and bodily seized the charging Templar, using the man's own onrushing motion to hurl him down to the stone street. He hauled Maria up beside him and they turned, racing across the flat, wide-open top of the church.

Templars were crawling up the sides now. Maria, running full tilt, slammed the top of her boot underneath one's jaw, lifting him up and breaking his hold on the side of the roof.

They had to throw the Templars off somehow. Pausing to catch his breath, Aguilar looked down at the lines of rope that stretched between this building and the one nearest it. They had been erected so that colorful banners could be hung from them, but they appeared to have been tied off solidly.

There was only one way to find out.

He steadied himself and jumped, right foot landing on one rope and then his left on the next. Maria followed him, and the two raced across the taut ropes effortlessly, as if they were leaping from stone to stone across a river.

A furious bellow came from behind and above them. Somehow, Ojeda had managed to bring his horse through the church and out onto its flat roof.

An instant later, Aguilar's next step landed on air. The Templar had sliced the rope free. Aguilar reached out, grasping it as it passed. Maria fell with him, clinging to his leg as they swung crazily, without direction, slamming into the shutters of a closed window and smashing the delicate wood to pieces as they tumbled inside.

Scrambling to their feet, Maria and Aguilar pelted down a corridor. Up ahead, running figures came to meet them. They veered abruptly, dashing down another hallway to the left, into a storeroom of privately-owned weapons—and a pair of guards coming from a door on the far end of the room. Maria balled up her fist and punched one square on the jaw. He stumbled backwards, shaking his head and blinking.

Aguilar quickly dispatched the other in a similar fashion. Each Assassin seized a bow and an arrow. Back to back, as they had fought so many times before, they faced in opposite directions—and each fired an arrow directly into the chest of a Templar. Maria sprinted for the door Aguilar had been facing, while he turned around once more and sent another arrow singing into a foe.

The door opened onto a walkway that ran along the entire side of the building. A red-cloak with a sword swung at Maria, but with her usual grace she ducked, grabbed his sword arm, pressed it against the railing, and pinned it there savagely and efficiently with an arrow that she shoved the entire way through the man's arm.

Emerging from the door, Aguilar fired an arrow at the Templar racing futilely to help his companion. More and more of them were coming onto the walkway, seemingly crawling out of the woodwork.

Aguilar released shot after shot, turning one way and then the other, while Maria dispatched the ones who came too close for him to shoot.

At one point, she turned to him, her eyes bloodshot from the smoke and strain and exertion, but still smoldering with the raw excitement she always experienced when the two of them fought side by side. He knew his own eyes were bright with intensity as their gazes met for the briefest of instants before he turned, slamming a red-cloak with his elbow in the very same movement that he used to draw back the bow and let another arrow fly straight and true.

They raced down the walkway, leaping over bodies, and took a hard right into another room. It was not empty, but this time it was not crowded with Templars—only a nobleman and his family, who had clearly been sitting down to the midday meal when the sounds of fighting on their balcony had disturbed them.

Stay your blade from the flesh of the innocent. The first tenet of the Creed.

These people would come to no harm through him or Maria. Aguilar could only hope, as he looked at a mother holding her child tightly, her eyes enormous with fear, that the Templars who would pursue them would leave the family be as well.

Even as he had the thought and was almost through the room, the shuttered windows crashed open. An enormous, solid figure burst through. Impossibly, it was Ojeda. The bigger man hurled himself upon Aguilar, shoving the

Assassin into the table.

Maria snatched up a knife used to carve the roasted fowl and hurled it at a second Templar moving in on Aguilar, sword at the ready. The knife caught him in the throat. Ojeda whirled to stare at her, but she had already fled, and Aguilar darted through the door.

They joined up a moment later, both racing as fast as they could down the long balcony beneath hanging laundry, drying herbs, and other symbols of ordinary life.

The Assassins knew they couldn't simply outrun Ojeda. They were pushing their limits, first fighting to rescue Ahmed, then languishing in prison without food or water, and then fighting their way to freedom. Ojeda had had opportunities to rest and eat. He was a large man, but he was startlingly fast. He would simply run them down. Even as Aguilar had the thought, he risked a glance back to see that Ojeda was within a few strides of seizing Maria.

They were coming up on a tower that appeared to be part of Seville's massive cathedral. It had scaffolding around it, and both knew that this was their only chance. Without slowing, they leaped, slamming into the platform that was little more than crude slats of wood. Ojeda was right behind them, his bulk crashing through the outlying slats of wood to land heavily on the platform below them.

Maria gazed at him for an instant, then began to climb after Aguilar. There was nowhere for them to go but up. Ojeda recovered after a moment and continued to pursue them as they surged ever upward, craning their necks to find the next hand- or foothold.

Aguilar's heart slammed against his ribcage. His muscles burned with each movement. He refused to acknowledge their threats of cramping. He had been born into an Assassin family; bound by blood and choice to the Brotherhood. His body was fit, strong, and lithe—and under control of his will and his discipline. It would obey.

But the Templars had spotted them. They, too, had been climbing, pacing them on nearby buildings and jumping onto the scaffolding. To anyone watching, it would appear as though the Templars had surrounded and trapped their prey.

Even as the two Assassins reached the top of the massive tower, the town spread out below them looking like a jumble of children's toys, a crossbow bolt sang across Aguilar's path, barely two inches in front of his face.

Maria sped to the edge of the scaffolding and

did not slow, launching herself off, spreading her arms wide and embracing the empty air. Aguilar glanced back over his shoulder at Ojeda.

* * *

Cal's face furrowed, the tension in his body changing subtly. Sofia's breath caught as his eyes refocused, and realized that, in this moment, Cal had surged forward, displacing Aguilar.

No... please, not now, Cal...

"Jump!" she shouted. "Jump!"

* * *

Aguilar had done this many times before. It had been a key part of his training. Confidently he ran off the scaffolding's platform, gracefully raising his arms as if in a dance, as much at peace in this freefall as he ever was. Below was a market; he would land safely, as he always did. The white squares of the vendor's canopies raced toward him as—

* * *

Cal's arms pinwheeled, his body wrenching itself back from the rapidly approaching stone floor, from the perception of impending death. The arm holding him halted, and he hung limply in its grasp.

"Complete desynch," barked one of Sofia's technicians, and her heart leaped in horror.

"Get him down!" she cried, racing toward him, begging the universe, *No, no, don't let this happen*—

Cal's unconscious body suddenly twitched, then erupted into full-on spasms, flailing frantically as the Animus arm lowered him to the ground. Sofia crouched beside him, trying stupidly to still his frantic movements with her own small hands.

"Where are the medics? *I need help!*" she cried.

Three of them were on the floor now, two holding down a leg each, one keeping Cal's head immobilized. Cal's body fought them fiercely, trying to buck and thrash. His eyes had rolled back into his head so that only the whites were visible.

Ordinarily, Sofia, the researcher and scientist, would step back and let them attend to the patient. But this time she stayed where she was, reaching out to grasp Cal's hand, holding it tightly in one of hers while the other ran soothingly along his chest and shoulder.

Simple human contact. Potent. Powerful.

"It's okay," she whispered, blinking back tears that suddenly, unexpectedly stung her eyes. His face was flushed a dangerous purple hue, and there was foam dripping out of his mouth.

"It's okay, Cal, stay with me—"

She looked up, and she, Sofia Rikkin, who never lost her self-control, screamed at the fourth medic running toward her, "*Hurry up!*"

She couldn't lose him. She couldn't. She pressed Cal's hand to her heart as the medic lowered a clear mask over his mouth and nose. His eyes opened, and they were wide with terror as he bared his teeth in a grimace beneath the plastic of the mask.

Sofia squeezed his hand, trying to exude calm when inside she felt anything but.

"Look at me," she urged him, and the rolling blue eyes fastened on her. Something wet plopped down on his white shirt, making a darker spot. She hadn't realized she was crying.

"It's okay," she whispered, and as his spasming slowed, she smiled, shivering herself as relief crashed through her.

CHAPTER 16

Rikkin was in his office, lost in thought and savoring a snifter of Hennessy Paradis Imperial, when his daughter stalked in. He had expected to see her sooner, but McGowen reported that Sofia had instructed Alex to inform both the head of security and her father that she was "unavailable until further notice."

Rikkin had accepted that, but with poor grace. It was reasonable for Sofia to want to take the time to find out what the hell had gone wrong, and to see to Lynch's safety. Now she was here, and he wanted answers.

His daughter's anger was contained, but he had learned how to recognize it. It flashed now in her eyes, revealed itself in her body language in the tight press of her lips and the way she folded her arms when she stopped in front of him.

But he was angry, too. He'd watched her with Lynch, holding his hand, talking to him like he was a child. Or perhaps, something else. He'd never seen behavior like that before from his daughter, and he should not be seeing it now, when so much—when everything—was at stake.

His face was as hard as hers as he demanded, "What happened?"

"He desynched," she answered in a clipped voice.

Irritation flared. "I *know* that, why?"

"He wasn't ready." She did not say *I told you so*. She knew she didn't have to. He waited. "We lost him. We lost control of the Animus. We don't know where he went, what he did... nothing."

Sofia placed her hands on his desk and leaned forward. Her eyes were sapphire fire. "What if we lose him again?"

Rikkin did not reply. If they lost him again... they would lose everything.

* * *

Cal was being crucified and drowned at the same time. He was in a cage, feet together, arms spread, engulfed by water. Terror spurted through him. His lungs cried out for air. Above him, only dimly glimpsed, was a ripple of gray in the aqua-blue, lit only by flashing ribbons of light. Gray, and white, and a face.

Aguilar.

Cal screamed, expelling air, inhaling water—

He blinked, his chest heaving. He was not immersed in the water, not now; he floated atop it as an orderly patiently waited for his breathing to slow, for him to take another deep breath, before steadily submerging him again.

He recalled now, bits and pieces at least, about what had happened. The horror of seeing—smelling—someone being burned alive. The sharpness and clarity of everything, and the speed with which Aguilar's mind raced. The rightness of the violence against the Templars, who had performed such atrocities. The bone-deep connection of passion and trust between Aguilar and Maria.

And the city laid out, far below, with Templars on every side and—

Cal had awoken to a mask over his mouth and nose, providing oxygen as he lay in the salty, body-temperature water. They had said something about *electricity* and *galvanic stimulation* and something else, enough for him to understand that this was a treatment, not a torture. Cal wanted to have some measure of control and insisted they remove the mask, which meant that every half-minute or minute or so, they'd pull him up.

Dim blue light emanated from below him. The room was walled in black metal, with a band of low-level light running horizontally along it. The water steamed gently. If he had been there of his own free will and not strapped down in a damned cruciform cage, it might have been pleasant.

He had no idea how long this had been going on, but realized that his ability to think was returning—and the hallucinations had ceased. So at least in this, the orderlies were telling the truth.

They did not ask how he was feeling; he did not volunteer the information.

On the fiftieth or maybe about the thousandth time that they pulled him up, a figure stood over him. But this time, it was not Aguilar. It was Sofia, and he understood that she was real. And he wasn't sure if that was good or bad.

* * *

Sofia was still fuming as she entered the recovery room. While she was appreciative of the funds the Templars sent her way for her research—and she could not have come this far without them—she had always done her utmost to stay out of the politics surrounding both the Templar Order and Abstergo Industries. Up until now, she'd largely managed it; a feat almost as remarkable as the one she hoped to achieve through Cal's help.

She checked his stats before coming fully into the room, and was relieved to see he was recovering well. Sofia still wasn't sure about how she felt regarding her actions when he had desynched. The avalanche of emotion was foreign to her.

"I can't feel my legs," Cal said as Sofia stepped to the edge of the pool and regarded him. He was admirably calm, making such a statement.

Now, she replied in kind. "The paralysis is temporary."

Cal seemed to accept that. "What's the bad news?" he asked.

"You desynchronized. It caused a neurological split, but we got you through it." She paused. "*This* time."

Cal looked at her, the reflections of the water causing light to dance and break over his body. His eyes were the color of the pool, and they showed fear and pain.

"I'm going to die in there, aren't I?"

Sofia didn't answer at once. She sat down beside him, crossing her legs and leaning forward.

"No," she answered. "Not if you go in there of your own free will." She gave him a gentle smile. He turned his head away from her, staring up as the light moved back and forth across his face.

"We can put an end to pain, Cal," she continued, speaking from her heart. "For everyone."

"I can't do this," he said. It was not a cry of protest or despair. It was a simple, blunt statement, and Sofia found it hurt her.

"Yes, you can," she replied. He looked at her now, wanting to trust her, but too wary to do so. That, too, brought unexpected hurt. She thought again of her childhood vigil; of wild creatures, and taming, and lost chances.

Sofia took a breath and considered her next step. Her father wouldn't like it. It could backfire spectacularly. But something told her that it was the right thing to do.

If he was to trust her, she had to trust him. Trust him to understand what he was being asked to do.

"I want to show you something."

* * *

Within twenty minutes, the orderlies had removed Cal from the recovery pool, bathed him, dressed him, and placed him in a wheelchair. He met her at the door of his room, his frustration and resentment at his current helplessness coming off him in waves. Sofia attempted to push the chair, but Cal would have none of it, instead gripping the wheels himself and staring up at her defiantly.

"Where to?" he asked.

"The Animus Room." His face hardened, and she added, "You're not going back in."

"You're right. I'm not," Cal replied. He let her lead; his previous trips down the corridors to the room had not been conducive to making note of the turns.

She had dismissed her team, so they had the room to themselves. Natural sunlight filtered in from above, but most of the rest of the area was bathed in the cool blue of the after-hours lighting.

Once they reached the Animus Room, Cal permitted Sofia to roll the wheelchair next to a cabinet before she unlocked it with a set of keys and removed a single item. She looked at it for a moment. Her back was to Cal; he did not see it. This was her last chance to change her mind.

Once she gave it to him, what she would set in motion could not be halted.

She took a deep breath and stepped in front of Cal, offering the necklace, its pendant gently swinging from its silver chain, to him.

He looked at her first with mild interest, but as his eyes fell on the necklace, she saw recognition flow over his face like water.

* * *

An eight-sided star with a diamond shape in the center. Etched on it in black was a symbol that looked almost like the letter A, if that letter's lines had been made from stylized, slightly curved blades.

Cal had seen this pendant every day for the first seven years of his life. The last time he had laid eyes upon it, the silver lines on the pendant had been etched with dripping blood, and the chain had been tangled around a dead hand.

The memory thrust itself into his vision: the hyper-clarity of each fat drop glistening on the tip of his mother's fingers before falling slowly with a soft *plop* to the linoleum. The tinny sound of Patsy Cline, a bizarre soundtrack for a horror show.

The warm hues of the room, of his mother's strawberry-gold hair.

The emptiness in her dead eyes.

Anger and sorrow, more dangerous and powerful than the rage, washed over him. But it was *his* rage, *his* sorrow, and he would not share it with the woman who stood before him now.

Slowly, he lifted a hand and took the necklace.

"Where did you get this?" he said, his voice a rough whisper.

"My father recovered it from the scene of your mother's murder. He brought it here for safekeeping."

A muscle twitched near his eye. His mind went back to the fleet of black SUVs that had roared up in front of his childhood home. The pale, angular-featured man with the black sunglasses and dark clothes in the passenger side of one car. So... it had been Alan Rikkin, the man the child Cal had seen speaking on the television, after all.

The man who had fathered the angelic-looking woman who, impossibly, was currently regarding him with compassion in her large eyes.

"Safekeeping," Cal repeated, disbelieving. "You stole it."

"It's your mother's necklace," Sofia replied.

"I wanted you to have it."

She truly had meant this as a kind gesture. She couldn't understand what it was doing to him. Briefly, Cal's thoughts flitted to the old photo, of another smiling, murdered mother, this one with the little girl who would grow up to stand in front of him, handing him his own murdered mother's necklace.

Cal focused on her words. Her father had been present; he had recovered it. "Why was he there?"

"To save her."

Sofia was still compassionate, but she answered in a straightforward manner. It helped him stay calm. Cal knew she knew that. Even so, he could feel the façade cracking; could see his vision blurring with tears.

"From who?"

"Her own people."

"What's it got to do with you?"

Something flashed in the blue depths of her eyes. "Assassins and Templars have been at war for centuries. I aim to change that."

It was almost funny. "That's right," Cal replied, exaggeratedly. "I *forgot*. We're all here to combat *aggression*."

Their gazes were still locked, and the urge to spout gallows humor faded beneath true anger. He kept it in check, under control, as he replied, "I don't think I like your methods. I don't think I like Templars that much, either."

That seemed to sting, somehow. Sofia replied, "I'm a scientist."

"I'm here to be cured of violence." Cal shook his head, adding, almost sadly, "Who's going to cure you?"

"I'm trying to create a society without crime. We can remove violence from the human genome, but we need the Apple to do it. Our choices seem our own, but they are governed by what has come before us."

"You see what you want to see. Prisons are full of people like me, and it's people like you who run them."

She looked at him, uncomprehending.

Cal was done. She couldn't see it. Dr. Sofia Rikkin, scientist, had tried to be open and aboveboard with him—as much as someone in her position could be. But like many clever people, she had grown quite adept at lying to herself—or, at the very least, she had cultivated willful blindness. Sofia truly believed in what she was trying to do, and her eyes pleaded with him to believe it, too.

He was no longer angry. He just felt sorry for her.

Cal reached down to the wheels of his chair and began to propel himself back the way they had come, leaving her with a final, scathing comment.

"I think you're missing something."

CHAPTER 17

Sofia had not lied to Cal about his legs. Two hours later, he was on his feet again, the wheelchair discarded beside the bed. There was a vague tingling sensation still, but the orderlies had assured him that it would soon pass completely. Cal actually welcomed it after feeling absolutely nothing in his lower extremities for so long.

He ran his thumb over the ridges and points of his mother's necklace, then lifted his head and stared, as he had done so often, at the thick glass covering one wall of his spartan room. But there was a major difference this time.

This time, no guards stared back.

The observation area was completely empty.

The only thing looking back at him was his own reflection. But even as Cal stared into his own eyes, they hardened, slightly. A hood took shape around his face.

Aguilar de Nerha stared back at him, and Callum Lynch smiled.

The Assassin stood beside him now, not ambushing him from behind, nor stabbing down with razor-sharp blades emerging from gauntlets with a practiced gesture. He stepped forward with a shout, moving his arms in a motion as if breaking an opponent's strike. Cal moved alongside him, emulating him. Learning.

Training.

***

Alan Rikkin was not happy with how his daughter was choosing to do things. She was revealing too much. Trying to get Lynch to trust the Templars; to like them, to want to go back into the Animus to help them in their quest.

This, of course, was idiocy. Sofia was brilliant, no question, and she might understand much more than he did about the Animus and its effect on the human mind. But Rikkin knew people, and he knew Assassins in particular. Some Assassins, of course, had turned their coats to ally with the Templars. But most of the wretched breed were too stubborn or "honorable" to be swayed. He had seen what Sofia had seen in the regressions, and he knew that Aguilar de Nerha, unlike Baptiste or Duncan Walpole, would never desert the Brotherhood. And Rikkin was certain that in this case, the breeding ran true.

Callum Lynch might be taken with his daughter's beauty and calm manner. He might even think he wanted to be cured of violence.

But Rikkin knew better.

He stood now in his office alongside McGowen, who had just told him to activate the camera in Lynch's room. Together, the two men watched, silently, as Callum Lynch, descendant of an Assassin, practiced martial arts intended solely to kill Templars.

"We're feeding the beast," McGowen said quietly. "We're making him stronger."

This was intolerable. It was past time Rikkin did something about it.

* * *

Behind him, Cal heard the door opening. He didn't bother to turn, thinking it was just another orderly. He was in no hurry to be dragged back to the Animus.

"I'm Dr. Rikkin," came a cool, precise British voice, adding, "Alan."

Mildly surprised, Cal turned. Before him stood a tall, slender older man. He wore a black turtleneck, a gray wool sweater, and slacks. His face was aquiline and elegant, the graying hair sporting what was clearly an expensive, but conservative, cut. Every line of the man bespoke money and power. He had dressed casually, but looked like he belonged in a boardroom in a power suit.

Cal could see now that this was, indeed, the man he had seen on that day so long ago. And the knowledge stirred a myriad of emotions.

"I look after things here at Abstergo," Dr. Rikkin—*Alan*— continued.

"Like to keep things in the family, huh?"

Rikkin gave him a smile. It was practiced, and charming, and completely false, though Cal was willing to bet that it had fooled more than a few people.

"Yes," Sofia's father said, with a faint chuckle. "I'm sorry if we've caused you any discomfort. Is there anything I can do?"

"Fresh towels would be nice."

Again, the warm smile that lacked any genuine emotion. "I'm certain that can be arranged."

"While we're at it, how about you let me out of here?"

The smile was devoid of pleasantness now as Rikkin ambled, hands in pockets, to the long, backless bench where he sat, spreading his hands out on either side.

"That's something I can't manage," he said, with false regret. Then the fake smile shifted, becoming wry and cunning—and much more real. He was dropping the act.

Good. No more bullshit.

"I'm here to make a deal," Rikkin continued. "We need the Apple of Eden, and we need you to get it for us."

Cal had spent enough time around predators to know when he was in their presence, and Alan Rikkin struck him as one of the most dangerous he'd ever met. Cal would not trust the man, but....

"I'm listening," he answered, carefully.

The dark eyes searched his, flickering over his frame. Analyzing and evaluating. Rikkin seemed to reach a decision, getting to his feet. He gestured at the still-open door.

"Why don't we stretch our legs?" he said. "Work that last bit of tingling out."

* * *

"Any more hallucinations?" Dr. Rikkin asked Moussa, peering into his eyes with a scope.

"Only everything around me," he quipped. She offered a smile of her own at that, then clicked off the scope and reached for a clipboard and began to jot down notes.

"Your bloodwork is excellent, all tests are positive, and your eyes look fine."

"You sending me back to the machine?" Moussa asked. He kept his voice easy, his body posture relaxed, but he figured Dr. Rikkin had his number.

No one was ever eager to revisit "the machine."

Sofia had had Moussa brought in for another series of tests. He was fit and healthy. She'd informed him that orderly reports stated that he mixed well with the others, ate well, and worked out vigorously. But even though he'd called on all of Baptiste's charisma, Moussa was well aware that Dr. Rikkin didn't trust any of the patients.

His eyes flickered to one of the walls. It was covered with images—old Polaroids, newspaper clippings, a timeline. *Well,* Baptiste inside him amended with a shrug, *maybe the doc does trust* one.

"No, you don't have to go back," Dr. Rikkin said briskly in answer to Moussa's question, her dark head bent over the report as she finished jotting down her notes. "You've already shown us what we needed to see."

Moussa had no desire to return to the Animus. But he was suddenly aware that he had no idea what would happen to him—or, indeed, any of them—when they were no longer "needed." And he had a terrible suspicion.

"Then can we be free now?" he asked, sincerely; none of Baptiste's playfulness now.

Dr. Rikkin obviously wasn't expecting the query, and looked up at him, struggling to keep her emotions from showing on her face. She might not be as cruel as McGowen, and she certainly was a lot easier on the eyes, but she was one of *them*. She was the master of the Animus, and decided their fates. Moussa thought he saw his answer in the simple fact that she refused to answer the question.

Shit, he thought, his stomach sinking.

Her eyes flickered away from him, and a frown creased her pale forehead. She walked over to the monitor and leaned her hands on the desk, peering at it intently.

Moussa followed her gaze. He saw the other Dr. Rikkin walking down a corridor. Her father appeared to be engaged in in pleasant conversation with Lynch.

Moussa's gaze went back to Sofia's face.

Whatever was going on, it was upsetting her. He didn't know if that was good or bad.

He resumed looking around at the display cases. Baptiste was on high alert, and wheels were turning in Moussa's head as he analyzed the cases' contents. Old swords, manuscripts, pieces of art. Daggers. Jewelry.

And one thing Baptiste—and Moussa—recognized: blown glass containers, small enough to fit in a man's hand, covered with decorative filigree.

His eyes still on the small items, Moussa asked, "What do you hope to gain from the newcomer?"

Sofia had clearly almost forgotten about his presence. Absently, her attention on the scene unfolding in front of her, she replied, "Something that will benefit us all. You too, Moussa."

* * *

"You've been desynching in the Animus," Rikkin said to Cal as they went past a few expressionless guards. They gave Cal not so much as a glance. It was an odd feeling. "We need you to not do that."

He had paused at the door to a room Cal had never entered and tapped in a code.

"We call this the Infinity Room," Rikkin said. The door swung open and Rikkin stood to the side, allowing Cal admittance.

The Infinity Room was full... but no one was home.

It was crowded with patients, all wearing the same gray uniform and white shirt Cal had seen in the common room. But these people weren't shooting hoops or eating chicken. They walked aimlessly, stood in place, or sat quietly. Staring... at absolutely nothing, their faces as blank as a sheet of paper. Some were old, some were young; all were broken.

The room had many chairs and beds. Some of the patients here seemed unable to move from the beds without assistance. The oddest thing about it was the ceiling. The silhouettes of birds, black against a white background, was projected against its flat surface. Cal's first thought was that the rhythmic, gentle motion unfolding above their heads was soothing to the patients. But then he wondered if anyone here could even actually see the display.

Cal recalled Moussa's bizarre comment before he had left Cal alone in the common room: *All the rest... most of them are on their way to... infinity.*

Cal looked at Rikkin, but the other man's

face was unreadable. He looked again at the occupants, and then, carefully, moving slowly, he stepped inside. Those who shuffled through the room moved to avoid him, but otherwise it was as if he wasn't even there.

This was, without question, the most horrifying thing he had yet seen in this place. Violence, as Sofia would be quick to point out, was something he understood. It was urgent, immediate. It was alive.

This...

"What have you done to them?"

"They call it 'splitting'," Rikkin explained. Cal wanted to look away from the empty shells, but didn't seem to be able to tear his gaze from them. "It's what happens if you don't enter a regression of your own volition."

You desynchronized. It caused a neurological split, but we got you through it.

This time.

The words had been chilling enough when Sofia had spoken them earlier. Now, Cal's bowels clenched as he understood the fate that he had eluded.

This time.

With seeming casualness, Rikkin removed something from his pocket and regarded it thoughtfully. Cal struggled not to react, but sweat broke out beneath his arms and his palms as he regarded the metallic contraption.

"Do you recognize this?" Rikkin asked rhetorically. "It's an Assassin's blade."

Oh, yes. He recognized it.

In the cool, soothing blue light that appeared to be ubiquitous throughout the rehabilitation center, the blade appeared sterile. The almost mystical aura it had radiated in Cal's memories—both those that were his own from that awful day and those that belonged to Aguilar de Nerha, who had a completely different relationship with the weapon—was utterly dispelled here. There was no intricately crafted gauntlet concealing it, and the inner workings of its spring-driven mechanism, which appeared almost childishly simple, were laid bare for anyone to see.

Cal remembered how easily, quickly, cleanly he had been able to activate or retract the storied weapon of the Assassins. How it had felt, to plunge it into a bare throat and experience the patter of hot blood spouting from the carotid artery on his hand as he pulled it back.

How it had looked on an ordinary late afternoon three decades past, with blood running off its tip to drip onto linoleum.

Rikkin pressed something on the device.

The sharp *shing* of the blade's activation, and the startling speed with which the lethal metal sprang forward, snapped Cal back to the present.

"This is the actual one your father used to take your mother's life," Rikkin continued in a conversational tone. He was examining the blade—admiring its construction, weighing it in his hand, as if fascinated by the thing.

Absently, almost as an afterthought, he added, "He's here, you know."

Rikkin lifted his eyes from the weapon. They were cold as a snake's. Cal understood immediately that Rikkin did not simply mean that his father was here, at the facility.

He meant that Joseph Lynch was in the Infinity Room.

So this is the deal, Cal thought. He said nothing, but looked out again at the room full of things that were once people. But this time, he was looking for one of them in particular.

His searching eyes suddenly stopped their quest. A muscle in his jaw tightened and he swallowed hard.

"A mother's death, Cal," Rikkin said quietly. For the first time since Cal had met him, the man sounded genuinely regretful. "It's not something a boy should ever be made to see."

Cal turned back to Rikkin. The older man stepped forward, extending the blade hilt-first to him. Cal stared at it. He could knock it to the ground and spring on Rikkin. He could step back—walk away.

Drip.

Drip.

Red on the linoleum.

A giant man, a hooded man, staring out the window.

Slowly, Cal extended his hand to take the blade. Deftly, Rikkin turned, moving the weapon out of Cal's reach and placing it with great precision on a gleaming metal table with curved edges. He stepped back, and looked at Cal, a hint of a smile quirking his thin lips.

Then he turned and sauntered out of the room.

Cal continued to stare at the blade, barely registering Rikkin's departure. His arm trembled, ever so slightly, as he reached out and gripped the base of the knife. He had expected it to be cold, but it was warm from Rikkin's touch.

And it was warm and growing warmer as Callum Lynch turned around and began to slowly make his way through a sea of shuffling zombies.

CHAPTER 18

"This is wrong," Sofia said the moment Rikkin walked into his office.

He was mildly annoyed to find her here, waiting for him, but unsurprised that she had caught him out. His daughter was indeed a clever girl, and she knew him well. Though perhaps not quite as well as she thought.

She was standing in front of the monitor, watching the mindless shells amble about the Infinity Room. Her arms were folded tightly over her chest in a hunched, anxious pose, and her large, expressive eyes were full of accusation.

Rikkin didn't even break stride as he brushed past her, heading for the bar and pouring himself a snifter of Hennessy Paradis Imperial.

"You left me no choice," he told his daughter. "He has to go in of his own free will. You said that. I had to negotiate."

"You mean *manipulate*."

Rikkin paused for just an instant. The words were accurate, but they stung, and that surprised him. Lifting the liquor to his nose, he inhaled the spicy, orange blossom and jasmine scent.

"I assured the Elders we would have the Apple for London," he said, too irritated to enjoy the cognac as it properly deserved and instead taking a gulp, feeling the warmth trickle down his throat.

"That's in two days!" She had turned to stare at him, her eyes even wider than he would have thought possible. Well, perhaps now she would understand his recent desire to push the murderous bastard.

"Sofia," he said, "he doesn't want to know his past, or his father. He wants to destroy them... both."

Sofia looked like a startled doe, Rikkin thought. One hand was wrapped tightly around her midsection, the other clenched into a fist. She was trembling; something he had not seen her do in years.

He felt a long-dormant desire to comfort

her stirring, but he couldn't surrender to it. Sofia had to learn that cruelty was a tool, and a damned useful one at that, and that these Assassins she treated were not pets.

But her words made him realize that she wasn't shaking with fear or hurt.

His daughter was furious.

"We're not in the business of creating monsters," Sofia said. She got the words out with an effort; an effort not to refrain from breaking down, but from physically lashing out at him.

He looked at her, kindly, but experiencing the barest hint of contempt for her compassion.

"We've neither created them nor destroyed them," he explained, rationally. "We've merely abandoned them to their own inexorable fate."

* * *

The orderlies saw Cal with the knife. They made no move to intervene. Rikkin had doubtless had a quiet word or two with them.

The man he approached was both larger and smaller than he remembered. Cal was almost of a height with Joseph Lynch, now. Such a thing had seemed impossible when he was a little boy of seven. Then, his father had loomed as a giant to him, in all aspects. In the intervening years, Joseph had put on bulk; not muscle, but soft, sad flesh that gathered around his midsection and tugged his now-beardless face downward toward his thick throat. The red-blonde hair Cal remembered adorning his father's head was now mixed with gray.

Cal moved silently to stand beside his father. Joseph turned toward him. Defeat was etched in every line of his face and stooped body as he said, in an Irish brogue that had not lessened in the thirty years since Cal had heard it shouting at him to *Run! Go, go now!*, "You are your mother's son."

The words were not at all what Cal had been expecting, and it threw him.

"What does that mean?" he asked in a rough whisper.

"The blood that flows through you is not your own." Almost the same words he had last said to Cal. *Your blood is not your own, Cal.*

While crimson drops splattered on the floor.

"It belongs to the Creed," Joseph was saying. "Your mother knew that. She died, so the Creed may live."

Cal moved in an instant from standing perfectly still to placing the blade against his father's throat.

"Remind me how, exactly," he ground out.

His right hand clutched the blade. His

mother's necklace was wrapped around the fingers of his left.

The room was empty, now. Sometime over the last few moments, the orderlies had ushered out all those who had suffered in the Animus.

Cal and his father were alone.

Soon, it would just be Cal.

Joseph did not look afraid. He looked... resigned to his fate, almost as if he welcomed it. As if he had been waiting for this moment, and was relieved that at last, after so much torment at the hands of the Templars and their cruel machine, it had come.

"What you saw, I did," Joseph said quietly.

"You murdered her," Cal rasped.

Still calm, still quiet, Joseph answered, "I took her life, rather than have it stolen by that machine." His voice cracked slightly on the last word; the only sign he had yet given that any of this had affected him.

"A man grows with the greatness of his task. I ought to have killed you." His eyes, milky blue behind cataracts, stared into his son's. "I couldn't."

"Well, here." Cal flipped the blade in his hand, offering it hilt-first to his father. "Do what you couldn't do thirty years ago."

Joseph shook his head. "It's in your hands now, Cal. This is what they want."

"It's what *I* want."

But Cal knew he lied. He no longer knew what he wanted. The man before him was not the loving father, nor the heartless murderer. He was a pawn in the hands of the Templars, who had broken him so badly that he was now in the Infinity Room.

Cal was frantic for Joseph to make a decision, *any* decision, so that he himself could react.

"Spill my blood," Joseph said, the weight of the world in his words, "but do not go back into the Animus."

"Why?"

Joseph's eyes burned into Cal's, as if they had, at last, slowly flickered to life. Joseph did not care about his death—or life. But what he said next, he obviously cared about with all that was left to him.

"The Templars want us all dead. The Apple. It contains the genetic code for free will. They will use it to destroy us."

Cal stared, unable to process all that he was learning. Was this nothing but madness born of too many hours of resisting the Animus? Or was it true?

Could this really be what the graceful, calm, beautiful angel Sofia was after?

A tear trickled down Cal's cheek. "I'm going

to find it," he stated. "And watch them destroy you... *and* your Creed."

Strangely, something seemed to soften in Joseph at Cal's words.

"You cannot kill the Creed," he said, as if he were speaking to a child claiming to kill a mountain. "It's in your blood." And then he spoke the last words that Cal had ever expected to hear from him: words from a poem Cal had last heard uttered by a young, sympathetic priest. Words about picking apples.

Cal's eyes filled with scalding tears and he blinked them back fiercely. A lump suddenly swelled in his throat, threatening to choke off his words. He forced them through. It seemed important, now, that he say them to this man.

A faint, but genuine, smile touched Joseph's lips as his son recited the next line of the poem. "You do remember," he said, obviously moved.

A long pause. "It's all I have of her."

"The Apple is everything. Your mother died to protect it."

Cal's gaze fell to his left hand, clutching the back of his father's shirt; the necklace wrapped around his fingers.

"She had no choice," Cal said, understanding at last and wanting his father to know it.

Sofia and Alan Rikkin had told Cal what would happen if he refused to enter the Animus of his own free will. He could see the evidence that they spoke the truth all around him, shuffling purposelessly or staring blankly into space. His father had been here for thirty years, and it was clear Joseph Lynch had refused to go into the Animus without a fight.

Yet somehow, though he was broken beyond repair, he'd still clung to his mind. His memories—*his*, not those of some long-dead ancestor. He'd clung to them like he was clinging to the blade of a knife, slicing himself more the harder he gripped.

Cal knew what the Animus could do to one's mind. He had come close to breaking himself, and he had only been here a few days. His father's strength was humbling.

Cal relaxed his grip on his father's shirt, and lowered his hand.

Cal unwound the silver, small-linked chain, observing that it had left small red marks on fingers from where he had bound it so tightly. He placed it around his father's bull-thick neck, fastening it with fingers that trembled and still held the blade with which one man had murdered the other's mother.

Cal rested his hands lightly on his father's

shoulders for a moment, looking into his milky eyes.

"I do."

Father and son, bound by blood and love for a woman whose smile had filled both their hearts, regarded each other for a moment. Then Cal turned away, placed the knife down on one of the beds, and walked calmly toward the door.

He knew what he had to do.

* * *

A guard met him at the door. Cal informed him where he wanted to go, and the guard nodded. Cal was lost in thoughts of the past, present, and future—some not his own—and tried to focus on what was about to happen.

The guard stepped into a small, circular room with several doors. Cal had been here before; it was a hub room. One of the doors led to his destination. But the instant the guard stepped inside, there was a flurry of movement and he dropped like a stone.

A thin sliver of metal or wood protruded from his neck.

Some inner instinct alerted Cal. Before he even realized what he was doing, his hands had shot up to his throat, his fingers slipping between his flesh and the thin wire that was being twisted tight around his neck.

Had he moved a fraction of a second later, he would have been dead by now.

As he and his unknown assailant struggled, Cal saw that the would-be killer wasn't alone. He recognized Lin and several of the others from the common room, where they had stared appraisingly at him. Now they stood, watching their fellow Assassin struggling to kill Cal.

He caught a glimpse of white, and realized that the woman he had mistaken for an orderly was in fact one of the patients. They had planned this out carefully. And Cal realized it might yet work—the wire wasn't slicing this neck, but it pulled his own hands tightly to his throat, forcing him to participate in his own strangulation, and he would pass out soon if he didn't escape.

Cal slipped his right hand out from under the wire and elbowed his assailant hard. He struck the soft flesh of the abdomen and was rewarded with a sharp grunt.

He switched hands quickly, and caught the attacker in the face with his left elbow. The grip slackened enough for Cal to wheel around, seize Nathan, and barrel toward the sealed doors with him.

Nathan stubbornly kept his grip on the wire, tightening it even as Cal pressed his palm against Nathan's cheek and forced him back. Once the boy's arm was at full extension, Cal slammed down on the inner bend of the elbow.

The hold was broken, but Nathan refused to give up. He pummeled fiercely, squirming in an attempt to get out of Cal's implacable grip, but Cal would not release him. He slipped a powerful arm around Nathan's throat, choking him as the boy had tried to choke him.

The doors burst open, the guards having overridden the hijacked controls. The head of security, McGowen, rushed toward Cal with his baton raised and aimed at Nathan.

Cal kept one arm around Nathan's throat, while the other one came up and grabbed the baton before it could strike the boy's skull. He released Nathan once he halted the baton's brutal motion, and locked eyes with McGowen.

More guards pelted inside the room, heading for the Assassins, even the ones who had simply stood there watching. Two of them wrestled Nathan into submission. As they hauled him off, still struggling, he shouted to Cal, "You're going to kill the Creed!"

Cal watched him go. He reached up to his neck, grabbed the makeshift garrote, and dropped it to the ground. McGowen was still staring at him, with his heavy-lidded, seemingly unblinking eyes.

Catching his breath, Cal jerked his head in the direction of the door he had been approaching before the attack.

"Take me to the Animus," he said.

CHAPTER 19

The guards had been alerted to Cal's imminent arrival, and Sofia had her team standing by. Both she and her father had watched the tense confrontation between Cal and his own.

Sofia had been surprised at how pleased she had been to witness Cal turn away from what surely had to be the greatest temptation of his life: a single, swift act of violence that would have been exactly the revenge he had probably always wanted.

She dared to hope she had gotten through to Cal; that despite the pain and cruelty that had been shown to him, both outside these walls and within them, he had listened to her. Cal had seemed to want to be cured; the fact he had walked away from his father instead of taking the older man's life was evidence that on some level, he truly could learn to set aside the violence that was not just part of his life's experience, but his very genetic code.

And if he could learn, so could other Assassins. Once they had the Apple, the combination of genetic manipulation and properly directed therapy could render a world that was, truly, without violence. Her project, her faith, all she had done for most of her adult life—all would be vindicated.

Even so, the faint cobwebs of doubt still clung to her as she watched Cal stride into the room. With a quick tug, he pulled off his shirt and discarded it, as if in an effort to remove as much of his identity as a patient as possible.

Was it that he was tired of being regarded as less than human? Or was he sick of anything involving the Templars' control over him?

His eyes met hers and, to her surprise, her heart jumped slightly. The Callum Lynch she saw before her now could not possibly have appeared more different from the scattered, raging, frightened man who had first entered the Animus such a short time ago.

He was moving like an Assassin now, she

realized; smoothly, gracefully... proudly. Certain of what he was doing, confident in his ability to do it. It was profoundly attractive... and alarming.

Doubt crept into her again, and found herself withdrawing even as she wanted to connect more with him. To thank him for what he was doing.

Cal strode toward the overhanging arm like a boxer meeting an adversary in the ring, or a samurai bowing to his foe.

"Put me in," he said, not an offer, but almost an order.

"Prepare the Animus for voluntary regression," Sofia told Alex, not taking her wary but still hopeful gaze from Cal. She watched as McGowen himself held out the gauntlets and Cal slid his arms into them; easily, familiarly, never taking his eyes from McGowen.

"Do you know how the Assassins came to be named?" McGowen was saying.

Sofia was surprised; the head of security was as taciturn as they came.

Cal remained silent.

McGowen continued. "From an Arabic word, 'hashashin.' They were society's outcasts—those who stole, who murdered in cold blood. People ridiculed them as rebels, thieves, drug addicts. But they were wise."

Behind Cal, Alex was fastening the arm to the belt around Cal's waist.

"They used this reputation to hide a dedication to principles beyond those of even their strongest enemies. And for that, I admire them. But...." McGowen paused. "You're not one of those men."

Sofia tensed, waiting. McGowen's half-closed eyes were glued to Cal's face. Then the question came.

"Are you?"

Cal held the other man's stare as he reached behind him and grabbed the epidural unit out of Alex's hands. Startled, Alex glanced over at Sofia, who shook her head for him not to intervene.

"Let's find out," Cal replied.

And then, with only the barest flinch, Cal plunged the epidural unit into the base of his own skull.

You screamed the first time, Cal. And I know how badly it hurts.

There was a whining, mechanical hum as the arm lifted Cal into the air. This time, Cal's body was relaxed, at ease with all that was happening. When the arm reached the proper height, it dropped slightly, settling into position.

Cal snapped each wrist with a familiar flick, activating his hidden blades. With the light playing over his bare chest and catching the determined, almost grim set of his face, at this moment he looked more like Aguilar than Callum Lynch.

What if he is?

"Commencing regression," Alex announced, back at his station.

Sofia stepped out onto the floor in her usual supervisory position, her eyes raised to Cal's. As he looked at her, his face softened slightly.

Sofia's history had not predisposed her to trust easily, or even show warmth. But she wanted to say something to Cal, to thank him for his cooperation, to reassure him that yes, this *was* the right choice, for him, for humanity... for Templars... and Assassins.

Words crowded her mouth, and Sofia couldn't speak for a moment. Finally, haltingly, her voice thick and trembling, she managed, "This is my life's work."

Cal gazed at her, kindly, but unsmiling.

"This is my *life*," he said.

She continued to gaze at him raptly, fearful and joyous and tense with anticipation, and then he was in.

***

Granada was aflame.

Dozens of fires sent thick black smoke up into the air to mingle with yellow dust. Set by the Templars, the myriad infernos had done their vicious work, flushing out any enemies and destroying their hiding places along with anything that was precious to them—including family members, if that was what it took to obtain victory.

The great walled city had finally been forced to open its gates, offering surrender after a price dearly paid. The Templars were no longer slaughtering the Moors, but a river of red now flowed along the streets nonetheless; a river of red cloaks and uniforms, marching toward the great Alhambra, ready to claim their final reward.

In the center of the river of soldiers rode Father Tomás de Torquemada. He sat straight in the saddle, unable to hide a pleased smirk. Riding beside him as always, towering over him, was the Templar's loyal Ojeda.

Maria and Aguilar, perched atop the highest tower of the great Moorish palace, watched the enemy's steady approach in silence. They knew that somewhere in that sea of Templars, likely chained, certainly watched, was Prince Ahmed. And they knew that the dark bargain, bought with pain and treachery and with lives that numbered in the hundreds, perhaps the thousands, would soon be completed.

Then Maria stirred, reaching her hands up behind her neck. "For the Creed," she said.

He turned to her and saw that she held out a necklace. It had come to her from her parents, he knew.

Now, she was giving it to him.

Slowly, reluctantly, Aguilar held out his hand and let it settle into his palm, staring at it as she continued to speak, observing the eight-sided star with a diamond shape in the center. Etched on it in black was the symbol of the Creed—the letter A, curved at the ends to look like blades.

"Our own lives mean nothing. What matters is what we leave behind."

He did not like that she was giving it to him. He wanted to refuse it, to give it back to her and tell her that neither of them was going to leave anything behind today but Templar corpses. She had predicted her death at the auto-da-fé earlier, had she not? They had both survived.

But such a reassurance would be a lie. He knew no such thing. They were Assassins. No day, no hour, no breath was taken for granted. One or both of them could die at any time— including today.

And she wanted him to have it.

Aguilar tightened his fingers over it. To him, it was as precious as the object they sought together.

The last two remaining Assassins settled into position and waited. Patience and stillness, their Mentor Benedicto had once told them, were brothers to action and swiftness. An Assassin needed to master them all.

Aguilar did not know how long it took for the snaking stream of Templars to reach the Patio de los Leones, but at last, the hated figures of Torquemada and Ojeda stepped inside the courtyard. The contrast between the peaceful interior, with its graceful statuary, gently bubbling fountain, and beautiful flowering plants, and the bloodied, soot-dusted soldiers of the Templars could not have been more striking, or more offensive.

The Grand Inquisitor had his hand on Ahmed's narrow shoulder in an avuncular fashion, but the hollow expression of a child long past fear on the young prince's face told the true story.

Torquemada's fingers dug into Ahmed's flesh like claws, and at once the boy halted beside him.

His father, Sultan Muhammad XII, stood

beside the centerpiece of the courtyard, a beautiful fountain of white marble encircled by twelve roaring lions. Water flowed in two directions, enabling the lush gardens to flourish. The fragrance of roses filled the air, almost, but not quite, driving out the burning smell.

Muhammad was regarded as a strong and benevolent leader who cared deeply for his people. His eyes were deep and dark. His thick black hair was concealed by his turban, and his chin was adorned with a well-groomed black beard. The sultan wore a dagger at his waist; more ceremonial than functional, for Aguilar knew that here, at this moment, Muhammad would make no move to unsheathe it.

His kind face was etched with pain and love as he regarded his child, and he made no effort to conceal his emotion. Around the square stood the sultan's court, standing in the shaded colonnade area, watching intently.

They and their people had fought bravely, and with honor, but all knew the battle was over now.

All save one final act.

"Sultan," said Torquemada, his voice smooth and pleasant. "I come in peace."

"The slaughter of innocents is no basis for peace," the sultan replied.

The hawkish answer seemed to bother Torquemada not at all. The benevolent expression never wavered.

"Granada is ours," he said, matter-of-factly. "But give me what I seek," and he stroked Ahmed's matted, dirty hair gently, "and I shall let your boy live."

Muhammad could not tear his eyes from those of his son. Aguilar and Maria watched tensely, their bodies flattened atop the roof.

"The Spanish army claims the Alhambra for the king and queen. They may have it. My ambitions are greater."

Torquemada's thick lips curved in a smile. "Surrender the Apple. Your Assassin protectors are gone. They cannot save you. The Creed is finished."

For a long moment, Aguilar thought Muhammad would refuse the command. He had been a loyal friend to the Assassins, and they to him.

But he had not sworn, as Maria and Aguilar had, to place nothing and no one before the Creed.

Aguilar's mind flashed back to the prison, where he and Maria had gazed into one another's eyes and said together, *I would gladly sacrifice myself and everyone I care for, so that the Creed lived on.*

The boy's eyes were large and wide and frightened, and the sultan had a great heart.

In the end, as both Assassins had expected, he could not sacrifice his beloved child for another's ideal. Lowering his head, the sultan sighed deeply, then turned and walked into the palace, moving as if he had abruptly aged twenty years.

Aguilar and Maria moved, too, traveling swiftly across the roof to one of the skylights and peering down to watch. Maria, Aguilar knew, was more than ready to fight. But the moment was not yet.

The sultan led them through several arches, to an inner room with an ornate pattern of carvings on the wall. Dozens of flickering candles in delicately wrought glass containers provided some light, while the sun illuminated patches of the floor.

Muhammad halted in front of the carved wall and pressed his palm against a section of it. A small drawer slid open, revealing a small chest of decorated white stone, or perhaps ivory. Aguilar wondered how many other drawers were perfectly concealed in the large carving, and what each of the others contained. But for now, only one mattered.

Muhammad's booted feet made the only sound, other than the omnipresent trickling of water.

He halted within six feet of the much shorter Templar, who was perspiring either from the heat, swathed as he was in heavy layers of ritual garments, or anticipation.

"My son," the sultan demanded.

Torquemada gestured to Ojeda, who stood a few steps behind him. The black knight, who had had both hands clamped down on Ahmed's shoulders, now released him. The boy immediately darted past the priest to his father, who caught him and pulled him safely behind him. The sultan never broke eye contact with Torquemada.

Muhammad held the chest out in front of him, forcing Torquemada to come to him. After a moment's hesitation, the priest did so. His smug self-confidence ebbed with every step, and his hands trembled as they eased open the chest.

From their vantage points, the two Assassins could not see what was inside, but they could see the effect it was having on the Grand Inquisitor.

Seeming to barely breathe, his eyes wide, his mouth open slightly, Torquemada reached inside the exquisitely carved box, and drew out the Apple of Eden.

It was beautiful, and red, a perfect sphere that glinted like a giant gem, and Torquemada held it up to the shaft of light streaming from the open section of the roof.

"Here lies the seed of man's first disobedience," the Grand Inquisitor proclaimed, joy and wonder filling his voice. "Of free will itself."

* * *

The Apple of Eden, *Sofia thought, almost dizzy from the importance of what she was bearing witness to. Her life, her whole life, ever since she had been able to comprehend the concepts of DNA and the potential to manipulate the gene that controlled violence, had been spent in search of this.*

It was for this moment that she had forced her heart to harden to what she had to do. This precious relic was the key to healing humanity.

It was the Artifact to the Templars, as she had told Cal, and the Apple to the Assassins.

But for Sofia Rikkin, scientist, it was the Holy Grail.

* * *

It was time.

Let the Templars be overwhelmed by the Apple, eyes wide, mouths open in awe as they beheld it. It would make the Assassins' job easier.

Aguilar nodded to Maria, who eagerly moved into position at the side of the roof, her body perfectly still and taut as she waited with wild, excited eyes. Aguilar stayed where he was, looking down on the scene unfolding inside. The Templars would be allowed to gloat a bit longer.

Torquemada was still staring at the sphere with a mixture of wonder and proprietary enjoyment.

"Thanks to the Apple of Eden, the known world shall be ushered into a new age, one of peace, in which all the warring populations of mankind shall bow in perfect obedience to our one Templar rule."

As their leader spoke, Ojeda and the other Templars knelt in reverence, to him and to the object that he held aloft before them. It was strange to see the massive knight's broad, scarred face filled with a sense of awe and wonder. Ojeda was looking upon something greater than himself, greater than the Templar Order, and the knowledge seemed to humble, even soften him.

It was then, smiling a little, that Aguilar dropped two small items down onto the tableau. They were round, like the Apple; decorative, as it was.

But these two objects had a far different purpose.

As soon as the twin orbs struck the stone floor, they exploded into dense clouds of thick, gray smoke.

And the Assassins exploded into action.

In perfect synchronicity, though they were facing away from one another, they raised their arms, drew themselves up, and leaped—Maria down into the courtyard crowded with Templar guards and soldiers, Aguilar into the palace vault room currently wreathed in billowing gray clouds.

He landed directly in front of a blinded Templar, dispatching him quickly and efficiently with a single blade thrust through leather armor and into the heart. Another stumbled in his direction.

Aguilar whirled and slashed his throat, moving easily and surely. Assassins spent time training while wreathed in the smoke from their small bombs. Unlike the Templars, neither Aguilar nor Maria would be distracted as their eyes stung, and he knew from long practice how to set enemies against one another in the protective smoke.

One was frantically turning this way and that. Aguilar easily stepped up behind him and snapped his neck. He heard the sound of Maria slamming the door's bolt home, and the thud and cries of the Templars she had locked out as they threw themselves impotently against the heavy metal gate.

The only Templars now left for the pair of Assassins to worry about were the ones trapped inside with them, and their numbers were dwindling by the second.

The room was filled with the sounds of blows, grunts, the thuds and splashes as Templar bodies fell. Then there was an abrupt silence. Aguilar froze, listening. He knew what the sudden quiet likely meant—that, between himself and Maria, the Templar threat had been eliminated.

Or it could mean that some of them, cleverer than their fellows, were staying quiet, rooted to the spot, trying to control even their breathing in hopes that the Assassins would not find them. Aguilar saw a shape; the sultan, pressed against a wall, holding his son tightly.

The Assassin moved on to the other shapes, and caught a flash of white in the smoky dimness.

Torquemada.

The Grand Inquisitor was looking around wildly, thoroughly disoriented. And he still clutched the Apple.

Slowly, Aguilar approached Torquemada, activating his blade. Then he lunged forward. One hand shot out and snatched the Apple from the Templar's grasp. Aguilar's other hand descended to give the killing blow.

At that instant, Aguilar saw movement in the shifting shadows. Another Templar yet lived. The shape was large—too large to be anyone other than the despised Ojeda.

And in front of him, the black knight held Maria, his dagger at her throat.

CHAPTER 20

With nearly inhuman reflexes, Aguilar managed to halt the blade's trajectory, its sharp tip making only a slight indentation in Torquemada's neck.

The smoke was starting to clear sufficiently for Aguilar to see Maria's wide eyes and flaring nostrils. Ojeda's beefy left arm pinned her firmly to his body. She was not a tiny woman, but suddenly, Maria looked so small, standing against Ojeda's massive frame. So fragile. But she was always so fierce, so lithe....

"The Apple," Ojeda demanded in a cold voice. "Give it to him. Now."

Aguilar found himself paralyzed. One quick move would secure the Apple for the Brotherhood. Would save humanity from the grasp of the Templars. Would preserve free will. To kill Torquemada, to deny the Templars the Apple, was the outcome to which Benedicto and had pledged their lives.

They had died for this. And if Aguilar honored those deaths, Maria would join the slain.

She saw his hesitation. "For the Creed," she said, in her low voice. Reminding him of their oath. Of their duty.

But it would seem the Templars had an oath of their own as, daringly, Torquemada spoke.

"Not to ourselves, but to the future, give glory," said the Templar.

Aguilar wasn't listening. His whole world had narrowed to Maria's eyes—wide, shimmering with tears that might or might not have been from the smoke.

Maria.

Not so long ago, they had stood about to enter the arena of the auto-da-fé. She had turned to him and had told him to not waste tears for her. In that prison, she had spoken the words of their vow, to serve the Creed before themselves or even one another.

That Maria was prepared to die, Aguilar knew.

But now, he also knew, as he gazed into her eyes, that she did not *want* to die.

He had killed for the Creed. He was willing to give his own life for it, if need be. But he stared into the eyes of this woman, lithe and loving and passionate and proud, she who had been *everything* to him, Aguilar de Nerha realized that he could not sacrifice her.

Not for Benedicto's memory. Not for the Brotherhood. Not for the Apple.

He retracted the blade.

A softness, a sweetness flooded Maria's face for just an instant as she saw what he had done; as she truly comprehended the vast depth of his love for her. Maria gave Aguilar a tremulous smile, and he saw in her gaze that his love was returned.

Then she shot up her hand, clamped it around Ojeda's massive paw, and jammed his blade into her own throat.

Dying for the Creed, with love in her heart.

* * *

Dying for the Creed, exactly as his mother had done. With no hate in her heart for the death.

The Apple was everything.

Callum Lynch screamed the single, ineffective word:

NO!

* * *

Time slowed down to a sickly, sluggish crawl.

Maria fell, languidly, like a leaf drifting down to the earth. Her eyes were open.

Aguilar's throat felt raw. Had he screamed? He did not remember.

It was the rage that saved him.

White-hot, scalding, pure, and irresistible, it descended upon him like a benediction of poetic violence.

Torquemada had lurched away from Aguilar, but not swiftly enough. One of Aguilar's blades caught him, ripping through the thick layers of his vestments to find the flesh beneath and laying open a raw, wide wound. The friar stumbled and fell with a cry.

Aguilar paid him no heed, not now. Everything in him was afire with rage as Ojeda—Ojeda, Torquemada's dog, who had methodically taken from Aguilar everyone he had ever loved—charged him. The Assassin struck out, but Ojeda dodged with that swiftness that always seemed to take Aguilar by surprise. He struck Aguilar full in the face and for a moment, he stumbled.

The Assassin ducked as Ojeda swung his sword in an arc that was intended to remove

Aguilar's head from his shoulders, and the sword shattered plaster and paint as it struck one of the pillars.

Aguilar dove behind another pillar, surging up at Ojeda from below with his blades.

* * *

Sofia watched, her eyes round with astonishment, as the battle between these two men unfolded. It was nothing new to her to watch a subject grow into their role as Assassin; learn how to move, when reliving an ancestor's past.

But this was different somehow. The way Cal fought now was not the same as he had before. Then, it had lacked something she was seeing now: Ease. Grace. Full presence. It was no longer Aguilar de Nerha fighting, with Callum Lynch along for the ride.

This time, Cal was in there, too.

It was Aguilar's memory; Aguilar, who had fought with preternatural speed, power, and agility. But Cal was now inhabiting these memories on a level no subject had previously achieved.

It was breathtaking to watch, and terrifying, and even as Sofia wondered if she should halt the simulation, pull back, give Cal a chance to gain perspective on the situation, she was almost afraid to. As if, should she do so, she would somehow change the outcome.

She couldn't, of course. Time flowed in only one direction. This was a memory, nothing more. Or so she told herself.

She was watching a warrior being born.

It was the most beautiful, horrifying, wondrous thing she had ever beheld. And even as she watched, she felt something inside her stir, as well, as if something that had lain dormant for most of her life was slowly, inexorably, being called from its slumber.

And that was the most frightening thing of all.

* * *

As Ojeda bore down on him with the sword, Aguilar countered. His body seemed to be moving of its own accord, anticipating each lunge or feint and getting an arm up to knock Ojeda's arm aside.

He activated his blades and slashed at the Templar's arm. The only reaction was a grunt, but Aguilar knew the blade had met flesh.

Ojeda dropped his sword arm slightly, wincing in pain, but when Aguilar surged forward to press the attack, Ojeda met his rush with a fierce and powerful kick. Aguilar was caught off-balance and stumbled backward, slipping in the blood that had flown from opened Templar jugulars, and striking the mosaic-covered wall.

Grinning, Ojeda pressed his advantage, bringing his sword down. Aguilar surrendered to the momentum of his fall, coming up at the last moment to seize Ojeda's over-extended arm and stab toward his throat with his left blade.

Crying out, Ojeda jerked back, and the Assassin's blade laid open only his cheek. Aguilar slammed his elbow into the Templar's face. The bigger man went crashing to one knee, but instead of trying to rise he lowered his head and, bull-like, slammed it into Aguilar's mid-section.

The Assassin fell, hard, but got up almost immediately. He grabbed the nearest weapon to hand—a slender iron candlestick that was taller than he was. It was heavy, but his pain and fury gave him strength he had not known he possessed.

He whirled on Ojeda, using the candlestick as both a staff and a spear as he first struck the Templar, knocking the sword from his grip, then hurling the huge iron thing at him.

But he had miscalculated. As he used his body to fling the sharp-pointed makeshift weapon at Ojeda, he left himself open. Ojeda curled his fingers into a fist and landed a powerful blow squarely on Aguilar's jaw.

Stars spun in front of his eyes. He toppled backward, landing in a shallow pool. And in that moment where he was not moving, the pain from every one of his injuries seemed to strike him at one time. He gritted his teeth, and through sheer will, rolled over and got to one knee.

He flicked his right wrist. The blade sprang to obedient attention, jutting forward to fill the space where his ring finger had once been.

Ojeda strode up to him and before Aguilar could rise, the Templar's booted foot slammed into his face.

Aguilar fell back again, and this time, he could not seem to summon the strength to rise. He lay there, sucking in air, hearing Ojeda moving about.

He's found the Apple, Aguilar realized sickly. *They've won.*

His head lolled to one side, and he found himself staring into Maria's eyes. Tears welled up in his own.

Maria....

It was over. He had tried, but he had failed. Failed his family, his brethren, his beloved. All of them. Death would be welcome now. Perhaps, as some of the faiths preached, he would be together with her in some happy afterlife.

He reached out a hand, bruised and bloody, to touch her cheek.

It was warm. And as he watched, her lips parted.

She was alive! But even as stunned joy surged through him, he realized that although she yet drew breath, her life was almost gone.

Maria...!

Somewhere, as if from far away, he heard the sound of footfalls approaching, of leather creaking.

Her eyes boring into his, Maria's lips moved. He could barely catch the whisper, but her right hand jerked, ever so slightly.

"Go."

It took everything in him to tear his eyes from hers, but he could not refuse her urging. He looked up to see Ojeda standing over him: bruised and bloody, as he was. Injured. Weary.

But a snarl of victory contorted his ugly, bearded face, revealing clenched yellowed teeth, and his bloodshot, unmatched eyes gleamed.

Aguilar's hand left Maria's face, dropped onto her arm. Her wrist. He remembered her unique blades. One, with its twin prongs.

And the other—

Just as Ojeda was about to bring the sword down, impaling Aguilar straight through the heart, Aguilar's hand clutched Maria's gauntlet, lifted her arm, and pressed the release.

Maria's blade shot free, speeding upward like a bolt from a crossbow to all but bury itself in Ojeda's chest.

He dropped the sword with a dull clang and staggered back, peering down in disbelief at the two inches of blade protruding from his body. Savage glee filled Aguilar.

Later, he would have no recollection of getting to his feet. The next thing he would remember would be his own blade, eight inches long, embedding itself in Ojeda's chest alongside Maria's.

Ojeda swayed, but then seemed to rally. He bellowed and charged at Aguilar, swinging wildly. The Assassin sliced once left, once right—and then brought both blades sweeping across Ojeda's midsection.

The knight's black leather armor was now ribbons... as was the flesh beneath it, pouring forth scarlet liquid like a fountain.

His face was contorted, teeth bared with hate, but instead of triumph, Ojeda's eyes were wide with fear. He struck at Aguilar, and there was still force behind the blows as they landed on the Assassin's shoulders.

But no amount of stubbornness could prolong the inevitable, and both Assassin and Templar knew it.

Aguilar brought his blades up and then swept them down with all his strength, all but severing both of Ojeda's arms. The huge man dropped to his knees, gasping for breath, lifting his eyes to Aguilar's.

He had thought that at this, his moment of revenge, he would feel joyful. Triumphant. Vindicated. At peace. But Aguilar felt none of those things.

Ojeda deserved to die, many times over. He had issued orders that an entire town be put to the torch. He had subdued and brought Aguilar's parents to the stake, and had gloried in watching their agony as they—and Benedicto, too— had been burned while still alive to feel the pain.

Ojeda had *not* killed Maria. She had robbed him of that triumph, at least. And now, Aguilar was about to take the life of one whom many whispered could not die.

But Aguilar did not feel joy. He was surprised to find that he felt pity. For as he stared upward, looking death in the face, the black knight Ojeda was not angry, or raging, or contemptuous.

In those odd-colored eyes, now, at the last moment, Aguilar saw nothing but simple human fear.

He lifted his blades, and brought them down, burying them deep into the Templar's neck.

Still, the mountain would not crumble. Ojeda swayed again, but stayed on his knees. With an odd gentleness, Aguilar brought his bloody fingers to his enemy's face and gently closed his eyes.

There was a long, low sigh, and then, slowly, Ojeda fell to the floor.

Silence in the vast room, except for the trickle of water, and Aguilar's own labored breathing heavy in his ears. Then a quiet sob drew Aguilar's attention, and he slowly turned his burning gaze to the frightened face of young Ahmed, and then upward, to his father—Muhammad.

Muhammad, whose weakness, whose love for his child, had brought all this upon them.

Had cost Maria her life.

"Forgive me," said the great sultan, his arms about his son.

I could kill him right now, Aguilar thought.

He knew that Muhammad would not resist. The sultan had betrayed the Brotherhood, and so many of those Aguilar had loved had died for that act of paternal devotion.

But Aguilar knew he would not kill the sultan. The first tenet of the Creed was "Stay your blade from the flesh of the innocent." Muhammad had been guilty only of loving his child, and the boy certainly was an innocent in all of this.

And had not he, Aguilar de Nerha, been willing to surrender the Apple to Torquemada for Maria's life? He could not condemn another for the same crime he himself had committed.

He would stay his blade.

Slowly, feeling every blow, every cut, every broken bone, Aguilar turned to Maria, hoping against hope that he could hold her one more time. But as he looked into her eyes, he saw that his beloved had gone ahead without him on the last, greatest journey of all.

He knelt beside Ojeda, and felt for the Apple. It was there... solid, round, filling his palm. Even now, he would gladly hand it over to Torquemada, if it would only bring his Maria back, even if she despised him for eternity for the betrayal.

Torquemada....

Aguilar looked up to see the Grand Inquisitor standing about twenty feet away, his hand pressed to his bleeding side. Their eyes met for a fraction of an instant, then the wounded priest stumbled as fast as he could toward the huge, bolted door. Aguilar would not be able to stop him in time.

Torquemada fell against the door, fumbling for the bolt, and then shoved it back, gasping with pain at the exertion. The great iron doors swung open, and Torquemada scuttled out of the way as men poured into the room.

But Aguilar had already lifted a heavy metal grate and slipped down, into the drains below the palace.

CHAPTER 21

Aguilar landed gracelessly and hard, hissing in pain and pressing a hand to his side as he got to his feet and ran down the tunnel. Torquemada, though, had alerted his soldiers, and the way up ahead suddenly grew bright with pools of lights from above as Templars dropped down ahead of—and behind—Aguilar in an attempt to block his path.

The Assassin had moved beyond alarm or even strategy. Without slowing, he snapped his wrists and activated his blades, running headlong into the first surprised soldier and dispatching him with an almost mechanical rhythm.

When the second one dropped down, Aguilar simply raced, not toward him, but toward the wall, running up it and launching himself into a roll on the packed earth, completely bypassing the Templar, who swung his sword ineffectually.

Aguilar was on his feet and racing down the tunnel again before the Templar had even fully turned.

He knew that the secret was to not stop. At all. His task was to simply outrun the pain.

Two more Templars appeared in his path. One of them carried a torch to light the way. Now he shoved it toward Aguilar's face, thinking to burn him or blind him. The Assassin ducked, and came up swinging to knock the torch out of his enemy's hands, catching it deftly.

He thrust the fiery thing into the face of the Templar's companion, who screamed, and sliced the throat of the one who'd originally been the torchbearer. He heard noise behind him, and tossed the still-burning torch at them before again hurtling down the tunnel.

Light was up ahead—not a single pool that indicated a cover had been lifted off the floor above, but a flood of it. Aguilar realized that he was almost out.

Up ahead was a drawbridge. As Aguilar surged past the pulleys that controlled it, he slashed the ropes with his blade. The bridge started to lower. Aguilar ran up the wooden drawbridge as if it were a ramp and leaped off it onto the narrow stone bridge that led to the mountains and his freedom, striking the stone with his shoulder and rolling, absorbing the impact.

He shot to his feet—and froze, blinking in the bright sunlight.

They were waiting for him.

He heard those who had been in pursuit slow behind him, their breathing heavy, their feet scuffling on the stone. Up ahead on the bridge stood at least two dozen more, all armed with shields and spears. On the ramparts, crossbowmen had taken position.

And standing in the center, smirking down at his enemy, was Tomás de Torquemada.

The Grand Inquisitor's robes were saturated with blood, but the joy of his victory at last was clearly chasing away the pain for the moment.

Aguilar looked about, catching his breath, trying to find some escape route. There was none. Templars stood ready to obey their leader behind, before, and above him. Three hundred feet below, the uncaring Genil river raged, disinterested in the fate of any humans above it. Aguilar was well and truly caught, and Torquemada knew it.

"It's over, Assassin," he cried, shouting to be heard above the rush of the river. He extended his hand—inviting Aguilar not to simply hand him the Apple, which he was too far away to do, but to join him. All could be forgiven, once the Templars had won this ultimate prize. Aguilar could live out his days in a prison cell with food, fresh water and wine, and any comforts he desired.

Torquemada smiled, gently. Reassuringly, as a trusted father of the cloth should do.

Aguilar smiled back.

And then he leaped.

"Assassin!"

Torquemada's furious, despairing cry followed Aguilar as he plunged downward to the tumbling green-blue water, his ankles together, his arms spread. Templar crossbow bolts followed him down as well, singing past his ears like angry wasps.

One struck home. Aguilar grunted, his form thrown off as he lurched from the pain. The surface of the water was racing to meet him. He threw a dagger to break the surface tension, then turned his body in midair so he would strike feet first, and—Cal landed perfectly, like an acrobat.

Like an Assassin.

The Animus arm itself, however, seemed unprepared for the dramatic contortions performed by the subject in its two-fingered grasp. It twisted on itself and with a disturbing whirring, grinding noise, something snapped. It disconnected its grip from Cal's waist, undulated for a moment, then hung limply like a dead thing.

"Arm disabled," exclaimed Alex, alarmed. "Actuator rupturing!"

Cal was down on his right knee, his right hand on the floor beside his foot, his left hand raised. He was as still as if he had been carved in stone, or had been caught and held, frozen, in this moment.

Sofia seemed oblivious to the dire news about the Animus arm, instead stepping forward slowly, almost enraptured.

"A Leap of Faith," she whispered, gazing down at the still form.

* * *

Moussa was in his room, waiting for the guard to come and escort him to the common room. The guard was late doing so, which told him that the attack on Lynch had not been successful. While they had all been in agreement at the poker table, Moussa had chosen to not be involved... yet. If all of them were involved in the single attack and it went south, they would lose any opportunity for a second chance.

Obviously, he'd been right. And now that the initial attack had failed... something—maybe Baptiste—was telling him that eliminating this intense, blond man who preferred steak to chicken might not actually be the right thing, and he always paid attention to his instincts. He would be with his companions again shortly, and he would discuss what they had seen.

For no reason whatsoever, a chill ran along his spine. Gooseflesh erupted. In Moussa's mind, Baptiste opened one eye. When Moussa was a boy, his grandfather, dark eyes both twinkling and serious, had told him that whenever he got goosebumps, it meant someone was walking on his grave.

"Somebody's walking on somebody's grave," Moussa murmured, and instantly went on high alert.

* * *

Lin had spent some time in solitary for her participation in the attack on Lynch, but the guards told her they were releasing her for an hour, under observation, in the common room, if she continued to behave herself.

"My ribbons," she had said forlornly. "May I dance with my ribbons still?"

The Abstergo Foundation, she and the others had learned early on, was big on "constructive activities" and "artistic expression." That meant when Lin had displayed a fondness for dancing with ribbons, they had been inclined to permit her to continue. Just as they encouraged Emir to tend his garden.

Yes, she was told, she was free to dance with her ribbons, and Lin smiled, and looked content and vacuous.

She was the first they had released, though Emir and Moussa soon joined her. They did not ask about Nathan; Duncan Walpole's descendant had come close to killing Lynch. Common room time would of course be withheld.

But they had a plan for that.

Shao Jun was always just a whisper away in Lin's mind, but Lin always felt the strongest connection to her ancestor when she danced. Dr. Rikkin had told her that unfortunately she had to insert the agonizing epidural so that the arm could move her to match her ancestor's movement.

"It's called neuro-muscular facilitation—muscle memory," she had explained to Lin. And Lin had found it to be a useful thing.

Shao Jun had been born into slavery, and was raised to become a concubine of the Zhengde Emperor. She had become his favorite when she was in her early teens, but only for her dancing, her acrobatics... and her ability to spy on his enemies. Upon the emperor's death, Shao Jun's spying talents enabled her to discover the existence of the Assassins... and the Templar leadership in China, a group of ambitious eunuchs called the Eight Tigers.

Now Lin's fingers grasped the thick red ribbons she had been forced to fasten to cardboard paper towel tubes; they were the only objects deemed "safe." It didn't matter. She had no jian, and no means to recreate Jun's unique weapon, the hidden footblade. And of course, after the earlier incident, they would not permit her to access anything that could be crafted into throwing darts.

But she had her body. And that would be enough.

She walked out to an open area in the common room, and began to dance. Strong, fit, and lithe to begin with, she had learned the movements of the Ribbon Dance, birthed in the Tang dynasty, from Jun, who was a master at it.

As she posed and swirled, bending and kicking, the red ribbons flowing like animated streams of blood in breathtaking circles and undulations about her frame, Lin was accomplishing two things. One: connecting with her ancestor. And two... providing a distraction.

Unlike Baptiste and Walpole, Jun had no stain upon her name. She had lived a long, full life, achieving the role of Mentor among the Assassins. She had never turned to the Templars, for money, or greed, or fear.

Jun—and Lin—hated Templars. But all was well.

Soon, the Assassins would go tiger hunting.

* * *

"What's happening?" Sofia demanded. She couldn't take her eyes from Cal. A parade of horrible scenarios was crowding into her imagination, and she forced them away. Fear wouldn't serve her. Facts would.

"He's gone dark." Samia's voice was higher than normal. She, too, was struggling against unhelpful fear.

"Why have we lost him?" She paused, then asked, "Is Aguilar dead?"

The Animus had shown her the famous Assassin Leap of Faith before. Their genetics were extraordinary, and Sofia knew that. But she also knew that the bridge off which

Aguilar had leaped was taller by about fifty feet than San Francisco's Golden Gate Bridge. And Aguilar had been so *badly* injured, for so long....

What would being in Aguilar's memories at the time of his death have done to Cal? Had they come all this way for nothing? Had Aguilar, in the end, failed?

Had she, Sofia, failed—both the Templar Order and Callum Lynch?

She could not decide which fate would be worse.

"No," Alex said after checking Cal's brain wave pattern. "He's alive. Synchronization resuming."

Sofia had not taken her eyes off Cal, who was still kneeling on the floor, and at the news she felt both relieved and confused. This shouldn't be happening.

Her father's voice floated down from his office, saying the words that couldn't be true... but were.

"He's controlling it."

Sofia's eyes widened. This wasn't possible. No one had ever been able to wrest control of a simulation from her. But now, at last, Cal moved, slowly lifting his head to stare directly ahead.

And Sofia knew her father was right.

"Status?" she inquired, keeping her voice calm and steady.

"Back in," Alex assured her, pleased and relieved. Cal rose and stood in a relaxed but ready posture. The simulation began to take shape around him; she could now make out the silhouettes of ships and sails.

"Where are we?"

"It looks like a military port," Alex answered. Ghost vessels took shape around Cal's unnaturally rigid, still body; visible, but translucent and only faintly colored. "The architecture's Andalusian."

A suspicion began to form in Sofia's mind; taking shape, imperfectly and unclearly, like the port city the Animus was constructing around them. She tamped it down. She was a scientist, and she would wait for more facts. But the theory hovered, tantalizing... perfect.

"Elevation?" Sofia asked, her eyes flickering from the phantom vessels to Cal.

"Eleven meters," Alex answered. "Gulf of Cádiz. Palos de la Frontera." Her suspicion deepened. "The boats?"

"They don't look like warships," Alex mused. He scanned the holograms and added, "They're seventy feet by twenty. Lateen sails... ah, they're caravels. Used for exploration."

Cal was no longer present. He was seeing through Aguilar's eyes, looking up, and Sofia caught the spectral image of a holographic bird soaring overhead.

CHAPTER 22

Aguilar sat in the hold of the ship, gazing up through a slatted wooden frame at the eagle overhead, and envied it fiercely.

He was exhausted, filthy, and wounded in body and spirit. He had been traveling for five days, fighting off infection, taking odd routes, walking and stealing horses to throw any Templars off the scent. But he was alive, for the moment at least, and he was here.

Food had been spread out before him, but he touched nothing, and when the captain of the ship entered, Aguilar did not rise.

"Assassins died for this," he said bluntly. The captain did not move, simply stood quietly at the end of the table, as if Aguilar were the master of the vessel, not he. "Protect it with your life."

"I am a friend of the Creed," the bearded, slender captain assured him.

***

Sofia's eyes narrowed. She had grown up all over Europe, and she knew her own accent reflected her upbringing. Able to speak three languages fluently, she had an ear for accents, and she knew at once that this unknown captain was not a native Spanish-speaker.

***

Slowly, Aguilar extended his hand. In it, he bore the Apple of Eden. The captain reached to accept it from him, but before he could do so, Aguilar added, "Take it to your grave."

The captain paled beneath his tan, but met the Assassin's eyes.

"I swear," he said. His fingers curled around it securely.

"Following the light of the sun, I shall leave this old world behind."

***

Sofia stood, rooted to the spot, as Alex provided the translation. "'I shall leave this old world behind,'" she repeated. The words confirmed what she had almost dared not believe.

"It's Christopher Columbus," she breathed, and then Aguilar's words to the captain took on a sudden, powerful new meaning. "Where is he buried?"

Alex understood the import of her question. He was the most unruffled person she had ever known, seemingly born with the quintessential British stiff upper lip. But she noticed sweat gathering on his hairline as he quickly searched the Animus database.

"His remains were returned to Spain," Alex said. "His tomb is in Seville Cathedral."

Sofia stared at the images on the screen.

"We found it," she breathed.

*　*　*

It was time.

Moussa absently bounced the orange ball on the floor, then made a perfect shot. Scooping up the basketball, he bounced it a few more times, then rolled it from one hand to the other and behind his back as he assessed the situation.

Over in the greenhouse area, Emir was busy repotting rosemary, and gave Moussa a casual glance over his shoulder. *Rosemary; that's for remembrance.* Some snatch of a poem or something, long gone, but it made Moussa smile.

Several others were sitting at the tables,

eating placidly. Behind Moussa, Lin was doing Jun's ribbon dance. Since the confrontation, there were more guards on the floor than usual. The dance was beautiful, and provided an excellent distraction.

While two guards watched Lin, Moussa called out cheerfully to two others.

"Hey! All-stars! Care for a little two on one?"

In days past, before the arrival of the Pioneer, the guards had been more complacent. One or two of them had usually obliged him. But today, Moussa could smell the tension on the air. He could feel it, singing along his veins. Something very big was going down. So today, the guards simply stared at him. One of them narrowed his eyes in suspicion.

Moussa had mastered sleight of hand long ago. Or had that been Baptiste? He had forgotten, and in the end, it didn't matter. Certainly not now.

He tossed the ball down behind him and his hands came up, fists clenched but palms down.

"Pick one," Moussa invited. The guards were used to his games, but this time, they didn't play. "Any one," he encouraged.

When they did not, Moussa shrugged, lifted his hands, and hurled the pair of smoke bombs he had stolen from Sofia Rikkin's office to the floor. Their exquisitely wrought filigree glass exteriors shattered, and a wall of smoke surged upward.

Lin instantly executed a graceful, flying leap into the churning gray cloud. Her foot connected with a guard's abdomen and he doubled over, vomiting. Moussa snatched the baton that fell from the guard's fingers and cracked him over the head with it. As the guard fell to the floor, Moussa whirled, taking out the second guard the same way.

* * *

It was Emir's turn, now. His plants abandoned, he had positioned himself by the main entrance into the common room.

Alarms blared stridently, and ugly red flashes disrupted the cool blue of the lighting and the soft dove-gray of Moussa's smoke bombs.

The door burst open. Four more guards, batons at the ready, raced in to assist their fellows in quelling this latest uprising. Emir waited until the last possible second, then darted forward, seized the last guard by the back of his neck as if he were nothing more than an errant puppy, and slammed him face-first into the wall. The guard slid down to the floor, leaving a trail of red smeared on the concrete.

His escape unnoticed thanks to the concealing, eye-stinging billow of smoke, Emir turned to the corridor toward the surveillance room, breaking into a run.

Unlike Moussa and Nathan, Emir's Assassin ancestor had been someone he had been proud to be descended from. Far from being a traitor to the Brotherhood, Yusuf Tazim, born in 1467, had been a friend to one of the greatest Assassins of all time—Ezio Auditore da Firenze, even giving that famous man one of his trademark weapons—an exceedingly useful device called a hookblade.

Emir had grown up without family around him. His earliest memories were of foster homes, shunted from one to the other while uncaring so-called parents pocketed money intended for his upkeep. Yusuf, too, had grown up without knowing his father and had a similar unsavory early life. But at seventeen, he had attracted the attention of Ishak Pasha, the leader of the Ottoman Brotherhood of Assassins.

It was a family. And as Yusuf grew, he became almost a parent to the younger members he taught. Warm, with an excellent sense of humor, Yusuf was everything Emir wanted to have in his life; wanted to *do* with his life. The Templars had put him in the Animus for their own ends, but Emir wondered if they understood that, strangely, they had also given him a gift by introducing him to this noble man.

Yusuf had died at the then-respectable age of forty-five, exactly as he would have wished: defending an innocent against the hated Templars.

Emir was only in his mid-thirties. He had no idea if he would live to be a hundred, or if he would die sometime within the next few minutes. He did know that that if, as he now suspected, this Pioneer was the one they had been waiting for, should he die defending Cal Lynch, Emir would deem that death as satisfying as the one Yusuf had been granted.

As they had anticipated, Moussa and Lin's distraction had worked. The surveillance room's door was unlocked. Most of the guards had been dispatched, and only three remained in the surveillance room. McGowen was nowhere to be seen, which was an unlooked-for gift. That one would have been a challenge to take down.

Fools, Emir thought.

The three guards who were left behind were all focused on their monitors watching the common room, the Animus Room, and the corridors down which their fellows were racing. They did not even notice Emir walking right in.

One of them finally spotted him and charged, lifting her baton. Emir seized her arm and twisted, hard. He felt something snap. She grunted and paled, but her other hand rose and came close to colliding with his jaw before he knocked it out of the way and punched her instead. Her nose crunched beneath his fist, and a stiff-handed blow to the throat removed her as a threat. She collapsed to the floor.

The second came at him. Emir sent him reeling back with a powerful kick to his chest, snatching up his baton and using it to first knock its owner out and then to crush the trachea of the final remaining guard.

It had taken him less than thirty seconds to incapacitate the guards and gain control of the heart of security at the Abstergo Foundation.

Emir shook his head in contempt and set to his task. The ones who had claimed Yusuf's life had at least been competent.

He bent over one of the screens, tapping it to get a map of the compound, clicked on the common room, and then began opening the cell doors one by one.

Starting with Nathan's.

* * *

Moussa and Lin were holding their own, even though at least a dozen, perhaps two dozen—it was a bit hard to tell with the smoke, Moussa mused—armed guards had charged in once the smoke bombs had done their job.

Lin in particular fought the hated Templars like a caged tiger set loose. She leaped, spun, and kicked like the entire thing was a choreographed dance performance; a ballet of blood. Her small frame made the bulkier, armed guards underestimate her, which she used to her advantage.

Moussa, meanwhile, snatched up weapons that the unconscious or dead guards no longer needed, and shared the crossbows and batons. He kept one eye on the main door, and when he saw it start to descend he shouted out to his companions. They immediately turned and raced through it as it lowered.

Moussa waited till the last minute, to make sure as many as possible had gone first, and then he dove for the narrowing space between the floor and the bottom of the heavy metal door, sliding under it just in time.

Lin helped him to his feet, both of them relishing the sound of the trapped guards futilely pounding on the wrong side of the door.

"Looks like the inmates are running the asylum," he said, and grinned.

CHAPTER 23

Sofia was vaguely aware that something was going on outside the confines of the Animus Room. Perhaps a second attack from the patients; she'd been told that there had been an earlier attempt on Cal today. It had been readily handled. If this was another one, it was none of her concern; she would leave that to McGowen.

Her focus, her attention, her entire being, right at this moment, was focused on Callum Lynch.

The previous scene had dissolved, the holographic images of ships and sails and Christopher Columbus simply fading into nothingness. That much was normal. But Cal stood, still synchronized in the Animus itself although the maneuvering arm was disabled, the insectoid epidural unit still jammed into his brain stem.

And he was not alone.

Aguilar de Nerha stood with him, beside him and slightly in front of him. They stared into one another's eyes, and Sofia realized that they were actually seeing each other.

How is this possible?

Slowly, Aguilar nodded and stepped back. Cal looked around the room. Companions, Assassins all, were taking shape.

One was a soldier in a U.S. uniform, circa 1943. Another wore the olive uniform of a WWI doughboy, although a hood covered his head, not the distinctive round helmet. A third was clad in the navy coat of a Union officer.

Back they went, spanning first decades, then centuries. A French revolutionist, then one from America's revolution. Sofia's stunned eyes took in clothing from the English Civil War, everything from formal Elizabethan ruffs and the sweep of a Cavalier cape to peasant's tunics and roughly made leather armor.

"Is it a memory?" Sofia's voice was an awed whisper, barely audible, but Alex heard her.

He stared at Cal's brain patterns, then said, "No." He offered nothing further.

Assassins were springing from Cal's DNA, his mind, or his conscience—she was utterly unable to tell which.

"He's projecting images of the Brotherhood," she said, stunned.

How is this possible? What's Cal doing?

He was crashing through all the limits they had thought bound the Animus, as if what should have been inviolable laws of science were nothing more than guidelines.

Sofia had been standing beside Alex, looking over his shoulder, but as more and more of the holographic Assassins joined their brother, she, too, felt drawn to step out onto the floor and stand beside them.

They were so clear, so real. As real as her imaginary friends had been to her when she was a child, lost and alone, unspeakably lonely. She moved among them, looking into their faces. With what Cal was showing her now, what couldn't they accomplish going forward! The thought was intoxicating.

Another figure stepped into the circle of Assassins, one who would be dead if the figures were not holographic: Her father.

He was gazing at the holographic figures as well, analyzing, assessing. His brown eyes met hers, and all her joy and wonder turned to ash at his expression.

He would not be congratulating her on her achievement of a goal the Templars had spent over thirty years pursuing. He would not tell her how proud he was, would not raise a glass of his expensive cognac in a toast to her. Perhaps such acknowledgments would come later, though she doubted it. For now, in her father's mind, what was unfolding in front of them was not so much a breakthrough as a problem.

"Transport?" he said, not to her, but to McGowen, who stood behind him.

"Standing by," McGowen replied, his voice, as ever, flat and cold.

Sofia's eyes widened at the words. She became more aware of her surroundings, of the blaring klaxons announcing a security breach, but she couldn't believe that it was this serious. There was one guard per patient, and that included the guards in the so-called Infinity Room, whose charges were utterly and completely harmless. Surely her father wasn't suggesting leaving, not now, not when Cal was—

"He's given us what we want," Rikkin said. "Protect the Animus, and purge the facility."

"*No!*"

The word exploded from Sofia before she even realized she had spoken. She stood staring at him, shaking with fury, her hands clenched tightly into fists.

She knew what that meant. It meant that her father and everyone he deemed important would, in a doubtlessly calm and orderly fashion, get into waiting helicopters and depart, leaving the guards behind to kill *every single one of the inmates.*

Including Callum Lynch.

It was meant to be a last resort—something to enact if there were to be a disaster, and immediate departure was the only chance of survival. That wasn't the case here, and Rikkin knew it.

Her father didn't like what he saw when he looked at Cal, and at the myriad Assassins Lynch had conjured up. He didn't like it at all. As far as Alan Rikkin was concerned, Cal had given them what they wanted—the location of the Apple. And now, he was disposable... even a possible danger.

The decades-long experiment—which she, Sofia Rikkin, had taken to its ultimate successful conclusion—was being closed down.

Cal had served his purpose. The inmates had served their purpose. The facility itself, other than the Animus, had served its purpose.

And Sofia couldn't help but wonder if she,

too, had served hers in her father's eye.

His gaze slid to hers, hard, annoyed.

McGowen said, as if Sofia had said nothing at all, "I need to get you out of here first."

"No!" Sofia shouted again. She took a step toward him, her face flushed with anger. Rikkin strode toward her—no, not toward her. He strode *past* her, not even bothering to turn his head as he called back, "We have to leave, Sofia!"

It wasn't a protest. Or an argument. Alan Rikkin was *chastising* her.

Mortification washed over her hotly, followed by fury. Even now, when she challenged him over the deliberate murder of fifty people, some of whom weren't even sufficiently in touch with reality to comprehend that they were being threatened, he dismissed Sofia as if she were four years old and clinging to the leg of his trousers, crying over a dropped ice-cream cone.

He clearly expected her to follow, like a dog to heel.

She didn't.

* * *

Joseph Lynch stood in the Infinity Room. Lights were flashing, and the scream of the alarms pierced his ears. But he was the only one of the twenty or so people in the room who noticed.

For the better part of the last three decades, he had been the only one who noticed anything. There was nothing the Templars could tempt—or threaten—him with to get him to cooperate. He had killed his beloved to keep her out of their grasping hands, and his son had seemingly vanished from the face of the earth.

Joseph had taken care to befriend no one, so the Templars could not use one of his fellow inmates as leverage. He had never gone into the Animus of his own free will, and soon enough, he had paid the price.

But he was a stubborn man, as his wife had loved to remind him with a smile in her voice. He clung to her memory, including that of how she had left this world, as if he were gripping a knife by the blade. It hurt, terribly, and it was *because* it hurt that he held onto it so tightly.

Now he did not need to hold on to anything any longer. His son had come. Beyond any prayer or wish or hope or dream, Cal had found his father, and understood him. His boy was strong—that was *her* in him, Joseph thought, and smiled a little as the world around him, this impossibly ordered world, began to crumble into chaos. He did not need to worry for Cal any longer. The boy—no, he was man grown, and this man had chosen his own path.

Joseph still held tightly to his blade; the one he had buried in his love's throat, the one that Cal had pressed to his, the one that Cal had returned to him. Events had come full circle now.

Joseph heard them coming for him. He didn't need to see the foot-long steel knife in the guard's hands to know what would happen when they arrived. He could hear it in the quick sound of the man's determined stride.

When his would-be killer was a step behind him, Joseph turned, calmly, casually, and drove his Assassin's blade into the man's gut.

A final gift from his boy. Joseph Lynch could at last, as his wife had done, die for the Creed.

Three of them charged him, now. It was almost laughable, how easy it was to kill the first one—and the second. But, as was perhaps inevitable, the third guard slipped behind him and thrust deep with the razor-sharp blade.

The pain was a gift. It made Joseph feel alive, for the first time in so very, very long. The guard pulled out the blade, and hot red blood flowed down Joseph's side.

My blood is not my own, he thought. And as Joseph Lynch, Assassin, felt the last great coldness descend, and as his eyesight bled to black, he smiled.

He was free.

* * *

Sofia Rikkin, scientist, Templar, stood rooted to the spot as the tableau of Assassins seem to waken. One by one, they lifted their heads, gazing out from under their hoods at Cal. *Seeing* him, as Aguilar had.

Cal looked at them in turn, connecting with each one. Were these his ancestors? Were they standing here in silent condemnation—or in blessing?

Only Cal knew, and one way or another, her time with him was running out. And that knowledge pained her.

One of the recently manifested images was smaller, slighter than some of the others. As Sofia watched, the figure lifted its head and regarded Cal as the others had done.

Cal's mother, slender, elfin of feature, her hair a warm honey-red gold, regarded her son with a tremulous smile.

The years seemed to fall off of Cal's face as, for the first time since Sofia had known him— and, in a way, she had known him for most of his life—he looked unguarded. He moved, slowly, like a man in a dream, till he and the holographic image of his mother stood so close he could almost reach out and touch her.

Sofia had never envied anyone as much as she envied Callum Lynch at this moment—this moment that did not in any way belong to her. This moment was too intimate. It was for these two; these two, and the other Assassins, including the ones whose descendants even now were fighting in the rooms and the corridors.

A Templar was not welcome.

At that moment, another Assassin lifted its head. But this one, while part of the circle, was not focused on Cal. It was turned toward her—a slender figure, in a simple brown, linen hood.

Blue eyes, rimmed with kohl, met Sofia's evenly. A face Sofia knew, decorated with small, ornate tattoos, gazed at her.

For a moment, Sofia couldn't breathe.

The face beneath the plain brown hood was her own.

She stood rooted to the floor, buffeted by waves of emotion: horror, joy, fear, wonder. She started to step closer, but her arm was seized by McGowen, who yanked her roughly away from the circle of Assassins.

"No!" Sofia screamed, struggling with all her strength against him. But McGowen was used to manhandling men as strong as Cal, and she was dragged away from the greatest mystery of her life, from the answers to questions she didn't even know she had; hauled off, kicking and flailing, to the waiting helicopter, despair closing in on her like a smothering hand.

Over the sounds of her own struggle, she heard the noise of fighting coming closer.

The Assassins were coming for Cal—their brother.

And she was glad.

CHAPTER 24

Lin and Moussa raced down the corridors, armed guards in hot pursuit. Without the smoke bombs to disorient the enemy, they were completely exposed and weaponless. At least there were plenty of distractions as they raced full-tilt toward the Animus Room.

As planned, Emir had done what he could to trap as many guards in certain places, while releasing the other inmates. All of them were, to one degree or another, allies—brethren—but only their small group of Moussa, Emir, Lin, and Nathan had stayed both sane and deeply in touch with their ancestor's memories.

Only they... and Callum Lynch.

Moussa had longer legs and pulled ahead, racing toward the Animus door. He heard movement behind him, and a quick glance showed him that a guard with a crossbow had darted out from one of the doors and was taking aim.

She was quickly and efficiently brought down by Lin, who seized both crossbow and the guard's baton. Lin whirled, bringing the baton around in a brutal arc that smashed the guard's ribs.

Moussa jabbed at the intercom next to the door and yelled, "We're here, Emir!"

"Opening now," came Emir's voice through the intercom, and the silver doors parted. Moussa didn't dash through immediately, waiting for Lin, who was busy shooting crossbow bolts at charging guards.

There was a commotion on one of the walkways over Lin's head and a flurry of movement. Moussa grinned fiercely as Nathan leaped down lightly, and the three of them rushed into the Animus Room as Emir slammed the door closed behind them.

* * *

Cal was fully aware that he was still in the Animus. He understood that none of this was real, perhaps even less real than Aguilar's memories had been. He could see them, could hear them, but he couldn't smell his mother's lavender perfume, and, although he had been able to touch—even kill—the holographic images previously, he was afraid to reach for his mother, lest she dissolve like a fragile and perfect dream.

Her words, like her face, were beautiful. "You're not alone, Cal," she assured him. "You never were."

And oh, it was *her* voice. He could hear it now in his head, as he had heard it so many times, reciting the Robert Frost poem, deliberately, sweetly and subtly planting the importance of tending apples into the receptive brain of a well-loved, contented child.

Her image continued speaking, and he drank in every word. "The past is behind us... but the choices we make live with us forever."

She paused, her eyes searching his face. Then she did begin to quote. But it was not the childhood poem.

"Where other men blindly follow the truth, remember..."

"... nothing is true." His voice was rough and thick with emotion. He hadn't thought he would remember the words Aguilar de Nerha had spoken.

Perhaps he simply had never forgotten them.

"Where other men are limited by morality or law, remember..."

"... everything is permitted."

Her face was bright with pride, even as it was softened by sorrow. "We work in the dark to serve the Light."

Cal took a breath.

"We are... *Assassins*."

She turned slightly as an additional figure stepped forward into the circle.

Cal felt another stab of pain and joy commingled as the new figure lifted its head. He knew the face beneath that cowl.

It was his father.

Not as Cal had last seen him, aged and stooped and soft and so, so close to broken, with milky eyes and a face twisted by years of internal torment.

The man who stood before Cal was the Joseph Cal had remembered, would always want to remember, before the Templars had come, and his world had become a living hell.

More than anything, Cal wanted to hold onto this moment. It had been the basis of both his sweetest dreams and most horrifying nightmares. He didn't understand exactly what he was doing, and therefore could not prolong it.

So it was that, one by one, in the same haunting silence with which they had arrived, the Assassins turned and walked away, disappearing whence they had come.

His parents were the last to leave.

His mother gave him a final, loving look, then she and his father turned away from him. Cal watched their retreating, hooded shapes for as long as he could, but then his eyes blurred too much for him to see them clearly, and then they were gone.

But, as his mother had assured him, he was not alone.

New brothers and sisters had come to him while she had been speaking to him; fighting for their lives to reach this room, this moment. He looked at them as he reached back a hand and plucked off the epidural unit, which had proven to be both torment and unexpected, joyful gift. Unfastening the belt, with its hated Abstergo logo, by himself for the first time gave him a sense of severance.

"What now, Pioneer?" challenged Moussa; Moussa, who had once dared him to jump; who, Cal now realized, had been analyzing him the moment he had stumbled, half-blind and terrified, into the rooftop gardens.

Moussa, who was Baptiste. As he was, in a way, Aguilar.

Lin stood beside him, silent, expectant. Even Nathan stood with Cal now, after what he had witnessed.

"We fight," Cal said.

* * *

They were pounding at the walls now; not with their batons, not anymore. The guards were wielding heavy, sharp blades, weapons that looked as though they could double as batons and swords.

Emir had suspected it would come to this. The Templars might be thugs, without the grace and finesse of Assassin training, but both Rikkins were fiercely intelligent. They would know there was something different about the Pioneer. They would no longer send their people to torment or bully or beat; they had now sent them to kill.

There were so many, all hammering on the glass, trying to reach one lone inmate. Ten—a dozen—fifteen—Emir swelled with pride, and the part of him that still felt as Yusuf did was content.

Emir had done what he needed to. He had kept his word. He had held the Templars off long enough for his fellow Assassins to break into the Animus Room and find the Pioneer.

He had unleashed every other prisoner, so they would have a chance to fight for their lives, as Assassins should, and not die slaughtered in a cage like beasts.

The glass finally shattered and they poured in, a wave of black and the glitter of their bright metal weapons, and still Emir fought them. In the end, it took four of them to hold him still enough for one of them to stab him.

This is better, he thought fleetingly.

And Yusuf Tazim agreed.

* * *

There were weapons all around them. Weapons that had belonged to Assassins down through the centuries—antiques, relics, carefully removed from the immediacy and urgency of the present and kept in locked glass cabinets.

"Where's Emir?" Cal asked as they went to the cabinets and began to select their choice of weapons.

"Took control of the surveillance room," Nathan said. "Let me out. Let us all out."

And, Cal realized, had locked the door to the Animus Room to buy them some time.

He didn't ask when or how Emir intended on joining them. Cal knew, as he suspected the others knew as well, that Emir's choice to barricade himself in the surveillance room would almost certainly be a one-way trip.

Some of the weapons were deeply familiar to the four Assassins, though their physical hands had perhaps never held them. Cal strode up to a bow. A shiver ran down his spine as he recalled grasping it, nocking an arrow, and letting fly. He smashed the glass with his blade and reached to pick it up, shaking off the broken shards. As he turned to find a quiver of arrows, he saw the others doing the same.

Moussa had found a most unusual gauntlet, one that had sharpened claws on the tips that moved like an extension of his fingers. Cal couldn't be sure in the dim, pulsing light, but he thought he saw that the metal of the claws was dulled by some sort of black substance.

... My name is Baptiste... Voodoo poisoner.

Nathan went straight for a sword, a beautiful thing, with a basket hilt of ornately swirling metalwork. He lifted it, smiling slightly, and cut the air with it a time or two. His whole body changed, going from gangly and frenetic to poised and aristocratic. On his other arm, he wore a hidden blade.

And Lin... Cal didn't even know what it was she grasped. Something made of leather, with a hidden blade that sprang forth as smoothly as the day it was crafted, despite the passage of hundreds of years. It was only when she slipped it on her left foot and did a practice flying kick that he realized her hidden blade was on her shoe—and how lethal it could be.

Cal remembered Maria and her two unique blades, and felt the stab of another man's great loss as keenly as if it were his own.

He and the others readied themselves for battle. Cal nocked his bow and pulled the long, slender arrow back smoothly, the sharpness of its tip undulled by time. Moussa had his claw hand flexed and languid for now, and at his side, his other hand gripping a staff.

Nathan seemed almost to have disappeared since he gripped the sword. He clearly was in the full grip of the Bleeding Effect, and Cal was glad of it. The memories of his ancestor fueled him, and there was steel in the boy's eyes as well as his hand.

And Lin—she grasped the crossbow she had taken from a guard during the flight to the Animus Room. At her hip, she wore a short, double-edged sword. And on her feet... her unique blade.

The enemy had been steadily banging on the door with no success.

Then, all at once, the doors slid open.

Emir had fallen.

The first two guards who rushed in, yelling, joined him in death, each felled by a different style of bow. Once Cal had released the arrow, he used the bow itself as a weapon, knocking one charging guard off balance with a smooth sweep and bringing the bow up to block the downward stab of a second.

He turned, drawing another arrow in the same motion, fitted it to the string, and let it fly. It pierced a third guard through the eye. He dropped like a stone.

Cal turned on the next assailant, kicking, punching, ducking, his body moving with an almost joyful ease.

He had spent his whole life preparing for this moment, fighting alongside his brothers. And he was only now realizing it.

* * *

Lin utilized both her traditional weapons with deadly grace and speed. She leaped and executed a kick, the motion activating the blade in her boot. Her foot struck a guard under the chin, knocking him back and impaling him in the same efficient, single strike.

She landed, drawing her jian, and began beating back attacks from all sides, darting, springing up, and dodging like a demon. It felt so good to be wielding it. It was an extension of her arm, as was the blade on her boot, and she finally felt she was *home*.

One guard got his skull split. Another staggered back, his hand to his throat as he impotently tried to stop the spurting crimson. A third came at her with one of the baton blades, and she lopped off his hand with a single, almost bored, motion.

Lin knew about the scientific reasons for the Bleeding Effect. But for her, in this moment, it felt more like an ancestor's spirit was dwelling in her body, sharing it for their common purpose.

At this moment, Shao Jun was happy.

She was doing the thing she loved to do best: killing Templars, and fighting alongside her brothers.

* * *

There was a lot of rage inside Moussa. Pure, cold, precise rage. Rage at injustices personal and not, at things that had pained his ancestor, at things that had broken his own heart. Like Lin, he, too, darted and dived, using his staff as familiarly as if he'd been practicing with the weapon his whole life.

It felt so easy, so natural. He would bring it sweeping down low, knocking his foe off his feet, then dart forward for a quick swipe of the claw-gauntlet. Moussa didn't need to slice open an artery. Baptiste had said once, "a little nick will do the trick."

And if that little nick put a Templar out of commission, and that little trick was that the man suffered agonizing torment as he spat froth and died in convulsions... well, that was just a little extra something that made the whole thing better.

He whirled in anticipation of a blow, cracking a skull, and laughed.

* * *

Nathan easily blocked a baton strike with his own edged steel, then deftly twisted his wrist to send the guard's weapon soaring uselessly across the room. The guard's side was left open for just an instant. Nathan was there, stabbing forward with his left hand. Eight inches of steel pierced the guard's heart and he fell as Nathan dodged the blow of another guard, coming upward with a cruel grin on his boyish face.

Damn, but he was good. His sword was an extension of his arm, slicing clearly across another guard's throat. Nathan turned with military precision, seized another guard by the shoulder, and held him there as he ran him through.

A sudden white-hot pain shot through his right shoulder and the grip on his sword loosened. A crossbow bolt protruded from his arm. Furious, Nathan grabbed the bolt and yanked it out. A guard charged him and managed to knock the sword out of his hands, sending it spinning through the air out of reach.

He paid for it, though. Nathan used the bloody bolt as a weapon himself, stabbing it down into the man's shoulder and kicking him backwards. When the guard turned, Nathan fired his hidden blade and took great satisfaction in seeing its slim shape pierce the guard's throat.

That was more like it. Despite the searing pain in his arm, Nathan seized another guard and, using the man's own baton as leverage, snapped his neck.

He paused to catch his breath, staring down at the man, taking just a moment to congratulate himself. Even without weapons, a gentleman was always superior to—

The blade piercing him from behind took him by surprise.

It struck deep and true, and almost at once Nathan felt his body grow weak. He staggered, turning in all directions, took a couple of steps, and then fell.

Damn you, Duncan, you arrogant prick, Nathan thought, then knew nothing more.

* * *

Cal punched a guard, sending him staggering back, then snapped his wrists. The twin blades sprang free. He brought them slashing across the man's chest in an X motion. As the man fell to his knees, Cal plunged both blades into either side of his neck. Blood spurted, and the guard toppled to the floor.

Cal looked up for his next target, and saw a gray-clad form sprawled limply on the stone. Nathan's eyes were still wide. In death, he looked so young.

But there would be time to mourn him later. At least Nathan had died fighting the real enemies.

He took a precious moment to assess what the other two remaining Assassins were doing. Cal's torso was glistening with sweat, and he could see that Moussa—implacably slicing with his clawed gauntlet or seizing his enemies and apparently effortlessly snapping their necks—was sweating as well.

Lin, however, seemed to have not been

physically affected by any of the battle. She had gotten hold of a thin, weighted rope, and was now almost literally dancing through the fight, looking calm and in control, minimizing effort and maximizing kills as her rope tripped opponents, whipped around throats, or simply crushed skulls with the heavy ball at its end.

The floor was littered with bodies. Cal did not waste time counting, but there were easily a dozen, perhaps twice as many fallen Templars. No doubt more living ones would be coming to replace them soon—unless the other prisoners had assisted Cal and the others by dispatching them.

As he caught his breath, he heard a distinctive sound from high above him. The battle-focus left him. He had been transfixed earlier, when somehow he had found himself surrounded by so many Assassins from bygone centuries. But part of him had also been aware of what else was going on around him.

He had heard Alan Rikkin say that he had gotten what he needed, and order that the facility be purged. He had seen Sofia offer up resistance—and been dragged away.

They knew where the Apple was hidden.

And the sound coming from above him was the sound of helicopters about to depart for

Seville Cathedral to claim the Apple of Eden.

Cal sprang before he even consciously chose to do so, leaping onto the great mechanical arm that had been the source of so much torment and so many blessings at once, climbing up it with monkey-like agility. Below him, Lin took out a final guard and then jumped up onto the arm as well, following him.

Rikkin had to be stopped. The fate of the world quite literally depended on it.

He reached the top, his progress stymied by the enormous circle of the skylight. Furious, fearful, Cal activated the blade on his right hand and punched the glass of the central circle. It shattered, falling in glinting pieces around him, decorating his body with tiny scarlet slices.

Cal ignored the pain, leaping upward and balancing on the large, gently curving dome. The helicopters had already left.

Cal gave chase, leaping from the dome onto another part of the roof, running as fast as he could, but he was too late. A minute more— perhaps even twenty seconds—and he could have caught them.

Instead, alone on the rooftop of the Abstergo Foundation Rehabilitation Center, Callum Lynch watched the helicopters full of Templars angle off into the cloud-filled sky.

CHAPTER 25

Sofia had never been to the Cathedral of Saint Mary of the See, better known as Seville Cathedral, before. She had seldom ventured forth from the Madrid facility, and then only when it was pertinent to her research. Hitherto, the Cathedral had not been.

She knew about it, of course. One could not be a Templar without being aware of the role played by the major medieval cathedrals.

Once, religion had been an important part in the Templars' quest for control and direction of humanity's destiny. Rumor had it that in 1401, when it was decided to build a church to replace the mosque that had stood on the site the cathedral now occupied, the members of the cathedral chapter vowed, "Let us build a church so beautiful and so grand that those who see it finished will think we are mad."

Sofia suspected if they had lived to see that day when it was completed in 1506, they would have deemed their request met. Seville Cathedral remained one of the largest in the world, and it was breathtakingly beautiful.

The central nave rose to a staggering height of forty-two meters. Its lavish gilding and the large stained glass windows bathed the interior in a warm, color-spotted glow. Sofia supposed that many would find a sense of peace here, in the quiet beauty with the scent of old incense permeating the wood. But she found none. Her heart was heavy and aching, with guilt and fear and anger.

She had not said a word to her father since they had departed the rooftop of the Abstergo Foundation Rehabilitation Center. She had watched as the rest of her team also piled into helicopters, choppered to safety. Sofia knew better than to think it was an act of kindness on her father's part to include them in the evacuation. She had heard him order McGowen to secure the Animus; for him, the people that operated it were part and parcel of a machine that had proven singularly valuable and would continue to be so. Retraining new people would take time, and money.

Things were as simple as that in Alan Rikkin's world.

They flew straight from the facility to the cathedral, radioing ahead and explaining that yes, it was indeed absolutely imperative that the location be closed down upon their arrival and that the tomb of Christopher Columbus be opened. And no, it could not wait for the archbishop to return to oversee the process, one of the bishops already on site would have to suffice, and by the way Her Excellency would also be arriving, could she please be accommodated as was appropriate to her position.

In silence the Doctors Rikkin had traveled, and now in silence they walked along the marble flooring. Sofia followed several paces behind her father. No one noticed, or cared. It was Alan Rikkin whom they knew and respected. Sofia was little more than an afterthought to the bishops as her father was greeted and shown inside.

Columbus's body had traveled almost as much in death as it had in life. His remains had been moved from Valladolid, Spain, where he died in 1506, to Seville. In 1542, they were relocated to colonial Santo Domingo—the future Dominican Republic—and rested there until 1795, when they were transferred to Havana, Cuba.

It wasn't until 1899 that Columbus was interred here, in a tomb as splendid and ornate as the rest of the cathedral. It was held aloft not by angels or pillars, but by allegorical figures representing the kingdoms of Spain during his life—Castile, Aragon, Navarre, and Leon. Sofia halted, letting her father go up to speak with the bishop.

It did not escape Sofia that although he lay in the most extravagant surroundings imaginable, Christopher Columbus had died in poverty—a fate he could so easily have escaped by selling the Apple to the Templars.

They were precisely on time. One of the bishops was climbing down from the tomb, carefully cradling a small, ornate metal box next to his body.

Sofia inhaled swiftly.

This was not the same box she had seen in the simulation.

Was it possible that the Apple she had spent her life pursuing had vanished—or been stolen—during Columbus's post-life adventuring?

Part of her—absurdly, madly, traitorously—

hoped it had.

The bishop handed the box to her father, who stared at it for a long moment without touching it.

I should be the one opening it, Sofia thought.

It was like ashes in her mouth. She had spent her life working toward this moment, had permitted her father to perform an atrocity in the name of this Apple. She had told Cal she was his protector, but in the end, she had abandoned him.

Her father's callous words floated back to her: *We've merely abandoned them to their own inexorable fate.*

And her father, who had forced her to abandon Cal, would be the one granted all the honor.

Sofia heard the click-click of high heels behind her, the sound echoing in the vast space. She turned to see Chairwoman Ellen Kaye standing beside her.

"Your Excellency," Sofia said, inclining her head slightly in respect.

Kaye did not initially acknowledge the greeting. The two women stood watching as Alan Rikkin slowly opened the small metal casket.

"The glory will go to your father," Kaye said unexpectedly. "But we both know who found it."

Sofia turned to look at her, surprised and gratified. She had met the chairwoman before, but Kaye had never seemed to take any interest in her. Now, the older woman graced her with a smile—reserved, as Ellen Kaye ever was, but sincere.

"Your time will come, my child."

Then the chairwoman of the Council of Elders of the Templar Order walked up to stand beside the CEO of Abstergo Industries. And together, they looked upon the Apple of Eden while Sofia Rikkin, scientist and discoverer, looked on from a distance: unwelcome, unacknowledged, and unwanted.

And as she stood there, solitary and ignored, her thoughts crept back, unbidden, to the woman in the hood who wore her face.

* * *

Sofia was nominally English, having been born in England and living there for the first few years of her life, but in her adulthood she had seldom returned. It was too damp and cloudy for her liking.

When she was a little girl, she often asked why the sky cried so much, and if it was because it had lost its mama, too. She never shook that association. As far as she was concerned, it was either raining there, about to rain, or had just finished raining.

Tonight, it was the latter. The road, black and wet, glistened in the lights of the busy night street as her car pulled up directly across from the future scene of her father's performance—Templar Hall.

Many similar cars were doing likewise. Templars from all over the world would be gathering here, for the momentous occasion. Politicians, religious figures, captains of industry; nearly two thousand would be present.

Father will have a full house tonight, Sofia thought sourly.

She stepped out of the car, closed the door, and crossed the street to the huge stone building, which exuded power in its strong lines, but was still beautiful. In one hand, she clutched a sheaf of paper, crumpled from her tight grip.

She wore a conservative dress, high heels, and a cape—all black.

It seemed appropriate.

Security, of course, was out in full force. There were cameras everywhere, metal detectors, sniffer dogs, pat-down stations. Sofia was greeted immediately. After a cursory and apologetic inspection, she was ushered inside.

She located her father in one of the side cloakrooms. He was busy donning traditional

Templar robes over his smart Savile Row suit, examining himself in the mirror.

He caught her reflection, and smiled fleetingly at her as he adjusted his impressive cravat.

"How do I look?"

As always, he was fiddling with his cufflinks. She did not offer to help.

Sofia took in the perfect graying hair, the distinguished lines in his face, the crisp fold of the maroon and black of his hooded robe, the classic, square red cross on the medallion on his chest.

"Like a Templar," she replied.

He either did not catch the ice in her voice or, more likely, did not care.

"A world without crime," he said. "They'll give you a Nobel Peace Prize for this. You'd better start writing your speech."

"I've read yours."

This time, he did catch it. His motions slowed and his eyes met hers in the mirror.

"And?"

Sofia lowered her eyes to the sheaf of pages she had clutched so tightly, repulsed all over again at the words in front of her, and read aloud.

"'If we eradicate free will, we eradicate the Assassins. A cancer that has menaced society for centuries.'"

Her voice caught on the word "cancer." *Violence is a disease, like cancer,* she had told Cal. *And like cancer, we hope to control it one day.*

For her, the cancer was violence. For her father, it was the Assassins themselves.

She flipped through the rest of the speech angrily. "'Mongrels... *vermin...*'"

"It's not my best work, but it gets the point across," he answered.

"Your point is *genocide!*" Sofia snapped.

"It's a new beginning."

His voice was calm, rational, and his mien was pleasant as he turned to regard her.

"You've done a remarkable thing, Sofia. You don't see it now, but you will, one day. All these centuries, we've been looking for *solutions.* You, my child... you've eliminated the *problem.*"

She had known he despised the Assassins. They had taken her mother; she, too, had grown up abhorring their Brotherhood. She never wanted another family to suffer as her family had—or as Cal's family had.

It was strange, how the child of Templars and the child of Assassins had so much suffering in common.

Perhaps more than Sofia had ever realized.

Sofia had longed to end that suffering. Been desperate to end it. So desperate that she hadn't seen—or had refused to see—what had been right in front of her for her entire life.

"We... I... did this to save lives," she whispered, so choked by the horror of the revelation she could barely speak.

"Not everything deserves to live," her father said. She flinched, thinking of the last Assassin face she had seen.

He glanced at his watch and headed for the door. He paused and quirked an eyebrow when she didn't follow.

In a daze, she forced herself to move, forced herself to walk beside him as they went down the hall. Robed Templars, some with their hoods up, most with them down, brushed past her.

She tried to work through it, unable to quite understand how twisted her dream had become.

"So my program...."

"Has brought order to society for the first time," her father said, completing her sentence for her in a way she never would have done. "We are witnessing the birth of a golden era."

Bought with blood of untold millions. Nothing good can come of such a birth.

The guilt was so profound Sofia almost stumbled. "I'm accountable for this."

"You've already been accounted for. Our work belongs to the Elders. This is *their* finest hour."

Sofia couldn't believe it. Had he actually misunderstood her? Or was this yet another dismissal?

I've been so stupid, she thought. *So very blind.*

"You lied to me." It wasn't an angry retort, flung by a rebellious teenager against a controlling parent. It was the simple truth.

He had lied—not just about how her decades of passionate research would be utilized, but about everything. About what it meant to be an Assassin. And what it meant to be a Templar.

There was the faintest hint of softening in his patrician face as he gazed down at her. His voice was kinder than she had heard it in years, but the words were sharper than an Assassin's hidden blades.

"I've always known that in your heart, you were a scientist first, a Templar second."

And for him, that justified every single thing he had done to her since his wife and her mother had been taken from them both.

Sofia stared up at him, sick. "Your recent work has impressed us much," he said, "but it has confirmed our belief that mankind cannot be redeemed."

And there it was.

"So." Her voice was ice cold and steel hard. "You've thought of everything."

"Not quite. My speech... it could do with one of your elegant openings."

For a moment, she simply stared, aghast that he was occupied with something so trivial when they were discussing the absolute elimination of not just the Assassins, but of free will itself.

Then she understood. He wanted her *with* him.

Not just as an asset; he already had that, he could—and had—used her and her brilliance as it suited him. He didn't need that. He didn't need her editorial skills, her "elegant words."

The comment was an olive branch. Alan Rikkin wanted his little girl truly on his side. As an ally, a believer.

She recalled his comment to her a few days ago. *Do I look old to you?* No one lived forever, not even Grand Masters, and he wanted his only child beside him to carry on his legacy with a willing heart.

He had never been a demonstrative father, and whatever warmth and paternal affection had once existed had all but vanished when her mother gasped out her last breath.

This was how he showed regard. This was how he showed love.

But he had shown her something else tonight as well; had been showing her something else time after time after time. It had taken his endorsement of genocide for her to fully grasp the depths of Alan Rikkin's inhumanity. He was now offering what he could, and she could see it in the slight look of wary hope on his face.

But it was much too little, and far, far too late.

She had the perfect eloquent opening, spoken by the perfect person. Sofia looked her father full in the face and quoted, "'Now I am become Death, the destroyer of worlds.'"

A muscle twitched in his cheek. That was all.

"Not sure I could make that work."

A voice floated to them through the closed doors, interrupting the spell that held them captive in their dysfunctional, intimate connection. "It is with great pleasure tonight that I introduce the architect of our ancient Order's future: Please welcome Grand Master Templar, and CEO of Abstergo Industries and Foundation—Doctor Alan Rikkin!"

The doors swung open and light streamed into the dim corridor. Her father did not give her another glance, but turned and strode in, walking to the podium as if nothing, absolutely nothing, had occurred while he was waiting outside to be introduced.

CHAPTER 26

Thunderous applause and cheers filled the room, issuing from nearly two thousand Templar throats. The spotlights followed him as he strode to the podium as if he were a rock star. Sofia supposed he was.

Her father's pleasant voice flowed out as the crowd's cheering died down and they leaned in, eager for his words.

"For centuries," Rikkin said, "we have been at war with an enemy who believes that individual needs are more important than the peace of mankind. With the recovery of the Apple, the time is upon us when we may eliminate the Assassin threat forever."

More applause. More excitement. Sofia had thought she could not feel more wretched, but now, she realized that what she despised in her father's attitude was not the exception among the Templars. It was the rule.

"We are now in possession of a genetic road-map to humanity's instincts...."

Sofia squinted against the light, suddenly feeling nauseous. It was too harsh, too white; she felt exposed and vulnerable. Like a wounded animal, all she wanted was to seek darkness, stillness, and solitude. To lick her wounds and perhaps, some day, recover, if such a thing were even possible.

"Any impulse towards independence, resistance, or rebellion, will be crushed. Any predisposition that might oppose our march of progress can now be eradicated," Rikkin went on.

Sofia went out into the main entrance area, the droning voice of her father and the click of her heels on the floor the only sounds. Up ahead, against the stained glass, movement caught her eye. Sofia thought it was another Templar in his traditional robes; perhaps a latecomer.

Then she realized that the shape did not move like a Templar.

Her father's speech of hatred and genocide couched in comfortable platitudes fluttered to the floor.

Sofia froze in her tracks as he approached her. She couldn't see his face beneath the cowl of the hood, but she didn't need to. She had watched him move, had learned to recognize the lithe, rhythmic flow of his limbs, like a big cat. She had seen it in the Animus Room. And she was seeing it here, now, in a place where it was the least likely—and those most dangerous—to be.

She knew she ought to be terrified to see him. This was a man she had captured and imprisoned, to whom she had exposed all manner of torment. But all that was going through her mind was how unspeakably relieved she was that he had survived.

He stopped three feet away. Now, she could see him; see the blonde-red growth of beard on his strong jaw, his unblinking eyes that, even as a prisoner helpless before her, always seemed to stare straight into her.

Sofia was having trouble breathing. From fear, grief, or desire, or all of the emotions striking at once in a heart that had been guarded against them since earliest childhood; she wasn't sure.

There were a thousand things she wanted to say to him. What came out was: "All I have to do is shout."

She could not tell if it was a threat or a warning. Once, everything had been so clear, so straightforward in her life. So *orderly*.

And this man and all he had taught her—about himself, about the Assassins, about Sofia Rikkin—plunged everything into unknowable, beautiful, terrifying chaos.

Still, she did not shout. And he knew she wouldn't. He trusted her, despite everything.

Cal's eyes were full of what looked like sympathy. He should hate her, but he didn't. He spoke, softly, as he always did.

"I'm here to help you. And you're here to help me."

Sofia flinched. Tears stung her eyes, but she refused to let them spill. Once, she had said those words to him. Once, she had meant them.

"I can't help you anymore." Not him, not humanity... she couldn't even help herself.

"What about those great plans? Cure violence. Combat aggression." Was he making fun of her? Tormenting her, trying to shame her? No. That was not Cal's way. That was her father's way.

"That's not going to happen." Sofia's voice

and heart both broke at the truth and despair in the words.

He continued to regard her steadily, almost sadly. Then, he stepped closer, closing the distance between them. Her heart leaped in her chest. Again, she could not name the emotion. She had been disconnected from them for too long. Was he going to kiss her—or kill her?

And which did she want him to do?

But he did nothing. He did not even touch her. "You started this, Sofie. You don't get to walk away."

How did he know? How did he know that was the nickname her mother had given her? Wildly, she again thought of the woman who looked exactly like her, wearing an Assassin's hood.

What are we to each other, Cal?

"We both know what happens next," he whispered, adding, echoing her father's words, "Not everything deserves to live."

And she did. She knew exactly what he would do, and why. He would be justified in it. The Assassins did not deserve the fate about which her father pontificated in the next room to a gleeful, unnaturally detached audience. Cal did not deserve to have been abandoned like an old shirt that no longer fit. She could not blame him for wanting revenge—but yet, his expression was not that of a man obsessed and hungering for vengeance.

Callum Lynch wanted something quite different. He wanted justice—something that, somehow, the Assassins, thralls to their emotions in a way the Templars found so repugnant, understood better than their age-old enemy.

Her father. His contempt, his casual dismissal of millions of lives. Alan Rikkin could die a thousand times, and it would still not be justice for that.

She and Cal had been far too similar despite their differences not to have sensed a connection when had first arrived. Like her father, Cal wanted Sofia with him. But he wanted her for all the things her father and the Templar Order he represented would desire to see crushed in Sofia's spirit. Her fire, her curiosity, her compassion.

"I can't do this," she whispered. Something inside her shattered at the words. *I have been broken all my life. I can live with being a little more broken.*

Cal's gaze remained kind, as his eyes flickered down to her lips and then back up to her eyes.

"Yes... you can." Slowly, slowly, he leaned forward.

Sofia closed her eyes.

Cal did not smell of cologne and starch and fine wool suits, as her father did. He smelled of sweat, and leather, and the cleanliness of the evening's rain. And for a moment, Sofia wanted nothing more than to run away from the Templars, and their Order, and their lies; from her father, who embodied the very worst of them. To find out who the woman was who had gazed at her, surrounded by images of Assassins, at the base of a broken Animus.

But that gulf was too wide too cross. Not even an Assassin's Leap could clear it. Her father was a monster; but he was her father, the only one Sofia had. Her Order was horrifyingly wrong; but it was all she had known.

Cal sensed it, moving past her, silent but for a faint rustle of fabric, and she was left alone, shaking, and more lost than ever.

Sofia tried to calm herself, to breathe deeply. Her father's voice floated out to her.

"It is not to ourselves but to the future that we must give glory. A future purged of the Assassin's Creed."

Purged. The same word he had used when he had forsaken the Foundation facility, and

instructed the guards there to kill the prisoners—the patients—in cold blood. Sofia
blinked, feeling dazed, drugged, as if she
were swimming toward wakefulness out of
the drugged sleep of grief and disillusionment
and shattered dreams almost too great to be
borne. Still she could not move as the cheering continued.

Her father had taught her chess when she
was young. The game did not call to her with
the same tug as did probing the mysteries of
science, so she had not played in years. But a
German term floated back to her now: *Zugzwang*. The direct translation was "compulsion
to move." It described a situation where a player
was compelled to move, even though a move
would put them at a disadvantage. Sofia now
was compelled to move—to either warn her
father, or choose to remain silent and let what
would, unfold.

Assassin... or Templar.

The tears that had threatened all evening finally spilled down her flushed cheeks.
As they slipped down, she made no effort to
stop them, and was not even sure why—or for
whom—she wept.

"Ladies and gentleman," her father said, and
she had heard that tone in his voice before—

the grandeur of it, the booming resonance tinged just so with excitement—"I give you... the Apple!"

The crowd exploded. Sofia had never heard so reserved an audience give vent to so furious, so thrilled, an expression of approval.

Still she stood as if she was carved of the same stone as the building. She couldn't move to join Cal. She couldn't move to stop him.

And then the screaming started.

Time slowed to a bizarre crawl, the sounds of panic about her muffled and distant. She did not scream; there was nothing to be gained by it. Templars shoved past her in their maddened crush to escape, their glee at the thought of killing Assassins in a craven fashion completely erased by the terror caused by a single Assassin boldly striking in their very midst.

She moved, still dazed, into the auditorium, against the flood of fleeing, hooded Templars, their robes flapping as they stampeded toward safety, shoving past Sofia. She felt one of them brush her arm, smelled sweat and leather, and then he was gone.

He could have killed indiscriminately, taken down several others of the ancient enemy, but he had come only for one man.

And one thing.

Sofia ascended the stage, now empty of everything save the corpse of her father. His killer was skilled, and had known exactly how to cut so that death would be as swift as possible. It was more mercy, more restraint, than Rikkin himself had ever displayed.

Blood was still flowing, forming a puddle beneath her father's cooling body. Sofia's vision was blurred by tears, but her gaze traveled from his face to his right hand.

The Apple was gone. In its place, her father's dead hand cupped a small green apple.

Zugzwang.

Something snapped inside Sofia.

"I did this," she said. It was not brow-beating. It was the simple truth. She had been complicit, even willing, in every inexorable step that had led to this moment, with her father bleeding out on the blue carpet of the auditorium. She had burned to impress this man, to win his love with her intelligence and her discoveries. She had pushed to locate the Apple for him, and had succeeded. She had been too weak to defy her father when he had revealed his true nature to her.

And she had failed to warn him when she knew an Assassin was coming for him.

"I will retrieve the Apple for the Elders,"

she heard herself saying as McGowen stepped beside her. She couldn't tear her eyes from the sight before her; not her father's dead face, or surprised eyes, but the apple he held.

It had not been necessary. It had been a message to the Templars... one Cal had known Sofia would likely be the first to discover.

Whatever Rikkin had done in the past, he was her father—the only parent she had. She was an orphan, now. Cal had taken not just the man as he was in that moment when he died, but all that Alan Rikkin might possibly ever become. He had taken away any chance Sofia might have for closeness, for understanding, for respect for the man whose DNA flowed through her. There would be no chance, either, for her to question her father about the Assassin who looked so very like his daughter.

Callum Lynch had ended Rikkin's present, and his future had disappeared along with it, vanishing like one of the holographic images in an Animus simulation.

And that, his daughter could not forgive.

"Lynch," she said, "I want for me."

Sofia felt a prickle along her spine. Others were watching her. The tears presently flooding her eyes spilled over onto her ashen face, but no more were coming. Her grief was slowing, congealing, turning cold, like her father's spilled blood. She turned slowly, knowing what—who—she would see.

Ellen Kaye stood, gazing down at Sofia. With her stood several of the Elders. Kaye's hands were clasped calmly in front of her. Sofia thought about the day when the older woman had stood beside her as they regarded Rikkin gazing down at the Apple.

Your time will come, child.

"It is not to ourselves, but to the future, that we must give glory," Kaye said.

***

No one stopped Sofia as she moved through the crowd, with McGowen glowering at anyone who might try.

Outside, the world still went on as usual. It did not know, yet, how enormously it had changed. But it would. Soon.

Sofia heard the wail of approaching sirens and steeled herself. There would be much to do, going forward. Everyone would be questioned, the incident examined. A plausible story would be fabricated and released to the press about the tragic demise of CEO Alan Rikkin.

She raised her eyes to the night sky, not seeing the clouds or the shy stars trying to peep through the soft gray. She saw the tops of buildings, and knew that the man who might have been her love but who was now her enemy, was out there among them.

But that was all right. The Templars would find him.

They would find them *all*.

EPILOGUE

The Assassin stood upon the roof of a building. Below him spread the River Thames. Night embraced him. He had discarded the Templar formal robe once it had no longer served as camouflage, and now wore a long overcoat of dark blue wool that protected against the chill of a London late autumn.

He was not alone. His brothers and sisters stood beside him on the roof. There were more out there. As if in solidarity with him, the Assassin caught the dark silhouette of a raptor against the gray-clouded sky. An eagle? He did not know. Perhaps; perhaps.

But he could see with its eyes.

And in his own way, as he had believed he could as a boy, he could fly.

Callum Lynch took a deep breath, spread out his arms, and leaped.

◪REGRESSIONS

✖ SUBJECT: NATHAN

Nathan had vomited, twice, in his room earlier. With every fiber of his being, he did not want to return to the *machine*, to the *arm*, to see the hauntingly beautiful, slightly sad, yet implacable visage of Sofia Rikkin staring up at him before he was plunged into the maelstrom of violence, passion, and contemptibleness that was the Assassin Duncan Walpole.

But he wanted even less to become like those poor lost things in the Infinity Room, so he had agreed to go this time. Sofia smiled and said she was glad he was there, that he had decided to come of his *own free will*, that she was sure that there would only be a few more regressions before he'd be done.

Tears had poured down his face as he nodded sickly at her.

I hate him. I hate Duncan Walpole. I hate how he treats people, and his awful arrogance and greed.

I hate him because he's too much like me.

And I want to be better than that.

REGRESSION: LONDON, 1714

Duncan Walpole's head felt like someone was using it for an anvil, but that in and of itself was nothing new. He tended to experience the sensation most mornings. He had learned that a visit to Blake's Coffee House as soon as he— sometimes literally—rolled out of bed was usually a wise idea. All the rage, coffee was a thick and sludgy beverage, and Walpole had said more than once to anyone who would listen that he never knew whether to drink it, dip a pen in it and write a letter, or pour the stuff in a chamber pot. But it was hot, and reviving, and addictive, and it cleared his head sufficiently that he could then attend to whatever business was required by either of his masters—the East India Company or the Assassins.

London boasted over three thousand of the shops, and every one of them had their own personalities and clientele, and more than once Duncan had learned something that would be to the benefit to either or both of the organizations he worked for. And with that done, he could then turn his attention back to drinking and patronizing the local brothel.

Sometimes, conveniently, the two businesses operated out of the same site. He fancied both the ale and the whores offered by the Rose of

England tavern in Covent Garden. It had a leg up, as it were, as far as Duncan was concerned, in that it had a separate room belowground where cockfighting was conducted. Not nearly as satisfactory a pastime as bull-baiting, of course, but at least *some* blood sport was to be had while one held an ale in one hand and a wench in the other.

The knock on his door sent spikes through his temples and he hissed. "Go away!" he shouted, then winced afresh at how loud his own voice sounded.

"Your pardon, sir, but I've a message," came a youthful voice from the other side of the door. Duncan groaned in recognition. He propped himself up, blinking, finding the light to be too intense even with the shutters closed. He sat for a moment on the edge of the bed, observing that he'd forgotten to remove his breeches before unconsciousness last night. He reached for one of the coins he'd dumped on the small, elegant table, then got to his feet, padded to the door with one hand pressed to his pounding head, and pulled it open.

Geoffrey was more than likely ignorant of the true nature of his employers. It was safer for the boy that way. All he needed to know was that he was well paid, and the only services asked of him were those of a courier delivering messages and packages.

He was eight, with bright blue eyes and locks of curly blond hair. The oft-overused word "cherubic" was, in this case, most definitely applicable. Duncan wondered idly if Geoffrey realized that the generous pay the Assassins gave him kept him from falling in with other more unscrupulous men who might take advantage of the angelic child.

Stay your blade from the flesh of the innocent was one of the Creed's tenets, and once, it had been one Walpole cherished. Now, less idealistic than he had been over a decade ago when he'd joined them, he was still glad of that as he looked at the boy. Children didn't deserve what London—indeed, the world—sometimes offered them.

"Sorry to wake you, sir, but I've a message and was told it was important."

Randall thinks it's important to know when one of his Assassins takes a piss, Walpole thought, but did not say. Speaking took energy he didn't possess right now, so he simply nodded, leaned against the door frame and waved for the boy to continue.

"He says, you are to meet him to dine on fish at

one o'clock," the boy said, adding with obvious reluctance, "... and, ah... you're to be sober." At the expression on Walpole's face, he added hastily, "If it please you, sir."

Duncan let out an exasperated sound. Like Randall himself, the message was clear and to the point.

"I don't think he actually said that last part, did he?"

"Erm... well, no, sir. Not the 'if it please you' part, at any rate."

"Good lad. Don't lie. At least not to me, eh?" Duncan tossed the boy a coin and started to close the door.

"Pardon, sir, but I was particularly instructed to wait for a reply."

Duncan swore colorfully.

"Should I tell him that, then, sir?"

Ah, wouldn't that be nice, Duncan thought. "No, you probably shouldn't. Tell him I'll be there."

"Yes, sir, thank you, sir!" And the boy scurried off down the stairs.

Duncan leaned against the door. His London lodgings were small but elegant, located on Tottenham Court Road, although he seldom spent much time here. *Conscious* time, at least. Nonetheless, whether it was consciously appreciated or not, the lavishness was not inexpensive. He trudged to the table and picked up his pocket watch, a gift from his second cousin, Robert Walpole, upon his twenty-first birthday. The two had never been particularly close, but Duncan was fond of the watch.

He had no other meetings at East India House until the afternoon, and it was only seventeen past ten now.

Plenty of time to call for a hot bath and visit the coffeehouse before his meeting with the Assassin Mentor.

"Dine on fish" meant to meet outside Mrs. Salmon's Waxworks in Fleet Street. It was an extraordinarily popular attraction. For a ha'penny or thereabouts, one could stand in the presence of wax versions of royalty, from King Charles I upon the scaffold to the warrior queen Boadicea, and experience such lurid scenes as Canaanite women sacrificing children to the god Moloch or the inside of a Turkish harem. A fairly realistic figure of a crippled child greeted visitors outside the door. Duncan was peering at it, grinning, when he sensed the Mentor's presence behind him, followed by the familiar cool, clipped voice.

"You're late."

"Damn you, I'm here now," Walpole said, standing and turning to face the Mentor. "And I'm sober. That should count for something at least."

Randall's hair was iron gray, his eyes pale blue. Never known for his sense of humor, his lips were usually little more than a thin line. Now, they were pressed together so tightly his mouth almost disappeared until he spoke.

"It counts for less every time, Duncan. And if you address me like that again, it will be the *last* time."

Duncan stepped away from the lines thronging to get in as he spoke. "You wouldn't kill a Master Assassin for having colorful language," he said.

"No," Randall replied, "but one who is also unreliable, erratic, disrespectful, and drunk half the time?"

"Even so."

Randall sighed, clasping his hands behind him and looking out at the busy street. "What happened to you, man? Thirteen years ago when we met, you were all on fire to make a difference. To make things better. You despised the exclusivity the Templars stood for and their desire to control everyone and everything. You believed in *freedom*." His blue eyes were melancholy.

"I still do," Duncan snapped. "But thirteen years can change a man. The Brotherhood is no different from the army. You say pretty things, Randall, but in the end, there's a rank, and everybody has to answer to it."

"Of course we do." Only someone who had known Randall as long as Walpole had would have noticed the man was distressed. His voice, always calm and precise, was even more so now. "Duncan, you're one of the smartest people I know. You understand what we're up against. You know that we need good coordination. I must be able to rely on my people to carry out their missions as planned, not turn them into spur of the moment tavern brawls. We, all of us, work in the dark to serve the Light. We don't get our names engraved on plaques, or statues erected in our honor. Those trappings are for the Templars, and well do we know such frippery is transient and hollow."

He sighed slightly, and shook his head. "The work we do is our legacy," Randall continued in a gentler tone. "Our names aren't important. All that matters is what we leave behind."

Duncan felt a hot wave of fury surge through him and he tamped it down. Calmly, carefully, he said, "Did you send Geoffrey to bring me here to scold me? He's the one who's eight years old, not I. I," and he took a step forward, towering over the smaller man, "will not be spoken so in such a way. I am a Master Assassin."

"Yes, you are. And *I* am your *Mentor*."

Oh, and that was a warning if there ever was one. Their eyes met and for a fraction of a heartbeat, Duncan actually considered taking him down right there.

It was the same everywhere Duncan went. The navy was like this. The aristocracy was like this. One was stuck where one was, no matter what one did.

Even the Assassins, who extolled individuality, were hypocrites in the end.

"My apologies, Mentor," he said, placing a hand on his heart and bowing. "I am here, and I am sober. Why did you summon me?"

Summon. It was an accurate word. Like a dog to heel.

Phillip's cool gaze seemed to bore into him as he spoke. "I have a new assignment for you. We've received word from Ah Tabai in Tulum. There are rumors that another Sage has appeared, and Ah Tabai has reached out to us and others for aid in tracking him down."

No, Walpole thought. *He can't be saying what I think he's saying.*

Ah Tabai was a Mayan Assassin, Mentor of the Brotherhood in the Caribbean. He was the son of an Assassin and had grown up in the Brotherhood, and all reports of him and his instruction had been excellent. Randall had spoken ere now of trying to strengthen ties with the Caribbean Brotherhood, feeling that the aptly named New World, still quite new, would eventually become a seat of power for the Templars. And, therefore, would need Assassins to keep them in check.

But Tulum was five thousand miles away, in the jungle and set amid ruins, and there were no coffeehouses, no taverns, no whores, and, as Walpole well knew from his days in the Royal Navy, if there was any grog to be had, it would be horrible. There would be no fame, and no fortune, and if Randall wanted him to go there—

"We don't have a strong presence in the New World yet—at least not as strong as we'd like. Ah Tabai can help us change that. I'd like you to assist him in the hunt for the Sage, and continue your training under him."

Duncan blinked. "I'm sorry... I must be misunderstanding you. Because I could have sworn that you just told a *Master Assassin* to go get more training from a primitive—"

Randall's hand shot out so fast Duncan didn't even see it coming, and he was reminded just why this mild-seeming, unprepossessing man was the Mentor. He felt his cheeks flame with embarrassment and anger as Randall gripped his arm tightly, strong fingers pressing in at precisely the right spots to cause extreme pain without causing damage.

"You will take the missions you are given, and you will give them your best," that Mentor said. His voice was as calm and conversational as ever. "If the Templars find this Sage before we do, they will have a terrible weapon to use against us and humanity. Ah Tabai knows things the rest of us could *all* stand to learn... and I believe he could teach you how to control that temper of yours as well."

The term "Sage" referred to an individual who was a particularly powerful descendant of the Precursors, the creators of the artifacts like Apples of Eden that could give an individual—or an organization—a great deal of power.

Randall was right. This was important.

But the implication that Walpole needed training after almost a decade and a half as an Assassin....

"The East India Company values me," Walpole said, a touch too harshly. "They won't be happy if I suddenly disappear."

"That's another reason I'm sending you. We believe that you have attracted unwanted notice, and you—and we—may be in danger. Tender your resignation and tell them you need more adventure and independence. They'll believe you."

That got Walpole's attention. The East India Company, with its de facto monopoly on imports of spices, silks and other textiles, and tea, unsurprisingly attracted its share of Templars. For years, Duncan had been watching its employees, trying to determine who was and who wasn't a Templar. He had narrowed it down to a few suspects, but it was a man he had never considered whom Randall had recently confirmed as member of the hated Order: Henry Spencer, Esquire, one of the newest members of the EIC's powerful Court of Directors.

Duncan knew the man only in passing, of course. Walpole had started out as a sailor, but even though he'd risen in the company, he seldom had cause to interact with one of the Directors. Spencer was a soft, doughy man, with pink cheeks and a small red mouth seemingly permanently set in a jovial smile. He seemed utterly harmless. Duncan wondered how it was that Spencer had deduced his association with the Assassins, and he was vexed that not once had the man's name floated in his consciousness as a member of the domineering and selfish Templar Order.

Although all the points Randall raised had validity, they also emphasized one cold and unpleasant fact: As long as Walpole operated within the tenets of the Brotherhood, he would never achieve the honors and wealth that he felt were his due. And he knew that despite Randall's words about "all" of them standing to benefit from training with the Mayan mentor, he was the only one of "all" of them Randall felt could use it.

On some level, it was a rebuke.

He would have none of it. "I'm not going."

"Of course you're not," Randall said affably, surprising him. "You're angry with me. You feel slighted. You and I have danced this gavotte before, Duncan. But you're a good man, and I think you still believe in the goals and philosophy of the Brotherhood." His thin lips curled in the rarest of smiles. "Why else do you think we've put up with you as long as we have? You'll come around. You always do."

"You are lucky we are in a public place, old man," Duncan hissed. "Or you'd be dead where you stand."

"Indeed, this spot was chosen deliberately. You don't acquire the rank of Mentor without wisdom," Randall said wryly. "Take some time to cool that hot head of yours, Duncan, and we'll talk again when you're ready. This could be an enormous opportunity for you, if you'll just step out of your own way long enough to see it."

"You're about to see my arse, and you may kiss it if you like," Duncan shot back as he turned and stalked off, seething with fury and wounded pride.

He spent the day sulking at India House, where, as luck would have it, the weekly meeting of the Court of Directors was occurring, and the rotund Henry Spencer, Esquire, was in attendance. As the man departed, Duncan decided to go on the offense.

He followed Spencer's carriage through the streets of London, waiting patiently as he stopped at his inn before leaving again to dine with other members of the Court of Directors, and then finally presumably settling in for the evening at one of the more respectable taverns.

Walpole feigned a double take as he spotted Spencer sitting alone, puffing on a long-stemmed clay pipe and reading one of the seemingly hundreds of pamphlets that littered the city.

"Henry Spencer, Esquire, isn't it?" He gave a little bow as the man looked up. "Duncan Walpole, at your service. I have the honor of working for your fine company."

"Ah, yes," Spencer exclaimed, his pink face beaming as if this was the nicest thing in the world. "Your name's been bandied about, Mr. Walpole. Have a seat, have a seat. Care for some sherry?" Without waiting for an answer, he made eye contact with one of the servers and she brought over an extra glass, blushing prettily as she set it down before Duncan.

He was more than a little disappointed that he wasn't simply tavern crawling tonight, but made a note of her for the future.

"There goes a pretty piece," he said. "Too bad she's not on the menu."

"Oh, I'm sure for the right fellow, everything is permitted," Spencer said, and let his gaze linger on Walpole's just a moment too long before taking another pull on his pipe. And all of a sudden, he didn't look quite so harmless.

Nothing is true; everything is permitted.

Part of the Assassin's Creed.

Walpole didn't react, but his pulse quick-ened. So—Randall had been right. He *had* been sniffed out.

Most of the time, Duncan was a hothead, and he had never denied it. But sometimes, he went cold, as if that hot head had been plunged into an icy pool, and he knew that aspect of his personality was even more frightening.

The cold settled into him now as he regarded Spencer and he gave the Templar a pleasant grin.

"Good thing too, eh? I won't tell if you won't."

"Of course not," Spencer said, "We're gentle-men and employees of Britain's finest company. I'm certain we'll both take any indiscretions we observe to the grave."

Oh, how right you are.

"Well, in that case, I highly recommend Rose of England. Ask for Jessamine."

They talked idly of the price of silk and tea, and whether it would ever become quite as popular as coffee. "Perhaps," Spencer said. "Although I rather hope it may remain the pre-ferred beverage of gentlemen. Let the riffraff continue to swill the vile concoction."

It was ludicrous, but that was that offhand comment which cemented Henry Spencer's fate in Duncan's eyes.

Spencer would die tonight.

Walpole bided his time, playing cards and drinking, until Spencer got up to leave. His eyes on his cards, Duncan heard the Templar declining the offer of a carriage ride home, saying his lodgings were not far and it was a pleasant night.

Duncan gave him enough of a head start so that the bastard wouldn't suspect, then cashed in his cards and followed.

Although it had been ten years since Michael Cole's patented globular lights had been first lit outside of St. James's Coffeehouse, the lamps were still not widely implemented, and the London streets were dark. But the half-full moon provided more than enough illumination for Duncan to observe Spencer trundling up ahead along the street, lantern in hand. Walpole followed on the street for a bit, then ducked into an alley, shinnied easily up the stone side of another tavern, and leapt lightly on the slate roof to continue the pursuit from above.

His quarry was enveloped in a faint scarlet nimbus, and Duncan grinned. Why had he not done this before? It was far too easy. He ran lightly along the roof, springing from one to the next as chimneys from the taverns, gaming houses, and whorehouses sent black smoke up into the air.

Then he paused.

Far too easy. Damn it.

Was he walking into a trap? For a moment, he thought about abandoning his pursuit of the pudgy, solitary figure huffing purposefully along. Perhaps he should go back to Randall and accept the mission. It might not be that bad.

But of course it *would* be that bad. A long, difficult, unpleasant sea voyage, with nothing but jungle, ruined temples, and lots and lots of "training."

No. He would not go slinking back to Randall like a dog with its tail between his legs. Grimly, he continued on.

Spencer turned a corner and vanished into an alleyway. Unless the fellow was about to unbutton and take a piss, this really was a bad idea for a wealthy gentleman.

Which, of course, meant that this really *was* a trap. Duncan wasn't sure how, as the man was alone. But if he *knew* it was a trap, then it ceased to be one. *In for a penny, in for a pound,* he thought, flicked his wrists to activate his hidden blades, and sprang.

Ordinarily, Walpole would have impaled the man's throat upon contact. But not this time, especially as he realized that Henry Spencer, Esquire, was standing, trousers quite properly buttoned, looking up expectantly and making no move to escape as the Assassin sprang upon him.

Such confidence was impressive, and as he landed squarely upon the fleshy Templar, Duncan merely pressed the blade to the man's throat.

"You knew I'd follow you," he said.

"I certainly hoped you would," Spencer answered.

Duncan blinked. Keeping his blades to the man's throat, he looked about. They were completely alone. Intrigued, he said, "You don't strike me as one eager to die."

"Oh, no indeed."

"And yet, I am going to kill you, Templar,"

Spencer smiled. "Not quite yet, I think. You're a smart fellow, Walpole. I'm offering you a proposition that might interest you."

Abruptly, Walpole laughed. "I'm not moving my blades," he said, "but I'll let you speak before I cut your throat."

"This is trifle uncomfortable, but as you wish. I wasn't the only Templar in that tavern. We *know* you're an Assassin. And we have for some time. You may kill me right here and now, but you wouldn't get far."

"Leaping from rooftop to rooftop, are the Templars, now?"

"No, but we do have eyes everywhere. And you'd never dare approach anyone in the Company again. Quite the loss."

Duncan scowled. "Go on."

"We've been watching you for some time. I don't know how the Assassins treat you, but I know that you've been passed over for promotion within the Company. And if you were truly content with the Brotherhood, you'd never have hesitated to kill me just now—suspected trap or no."

Damn the man's eyes, he was right.

Duncan made a decision. He swung himself off the man, getting to his feet and extending his hand to help Spencer to his. The man's grip was strong, though his hands were soft and damp.

I can easily take him if I don't like what he says, Duncan reasoned. "Are you offering me a... *position*?"

"At the East India Company? No. You'll fare better and rise higher if you join the Templars.

Pride in one's work and recognition and advancement for it are not flaws in one's character, to our way of thinking."

The wording took Duncan aback. He realized that the Assassins did, indeed, look upon his ambition as a flaw, and the revelation was surprisingly painful. He said nothing for a moment. Spencer held his tongue, not pressing him.

At last, Duncan Walpole said quietly, "The Mentor of the Caribbean Brotherhood has heard rumors of a Sage."

Spencer inhaled quickly. "That information is indeed... extraordinarily helpful."

Walpole took the next step. "That could be just the beginning."

Duncan looked up at the coffeehouse's sign: a golden pot of the beverage against a red background, with two long-stemmed clay pipes crossing one another on below it. He gazed down the street; the day was clear enough that he could see the Tower of London which gave the cobbled street its name.

He peered through the wavy glass of Lloyd's Coffee House. Randall was inside, as was his wont at this hour, listening to the news brought by the executives of shipping companies, their sailors, and the merchants who sold the goods they brought.

For a moment, Walpole stood outside, hesitating. His head hurt, and the coffee would help it, and it was time to finish what he'd begun last night.

Time to stick a different kind of hidden blade into the Mentor's heart—one the man would, if Duncan Walpole played his cards right, never feel until it was far too late.

Randall looked up as he entered, one gray eyebrow quirking in mild surprise. "Good morrow, Duncan," he said. "You look sober."

"I am," he said, "but I am in want of coffee. I've thought about what you said, and you're right. One should never settle for being 'good enough.' One should strive to become the best, and if I can learn from Ah Tabai and help the Brotherhood... then I should do so."

Something that looked like real affection flickered across Phillip Randall's aquiline features.

"I know how difficult it is for you to swallow your pride, Duncan," he said, almost kindly. He waved down a server, who brought an extra cup, and filled the empty receptacle with the steamy hot, thick black liquid.

As he accepted the beverage, the traitor to the Creed said to his Mentor, smiling, "It goes down easier with coffee."

⊠SUBJECT: _____
EMIR

REGRESSION: CONSTANTINOPLE, 1475

Yusuf Tazim, eight years old, stared out at the port of Constantinople, his eyes as big as two full moons and his mouth a perfect circle of astonishment.

It had already been a journey bursting with wonders, traveling from Bursa, where he had been born, to this ferry, and then over a vast expanse of water. He had never been more than a mile from home before in his life.

His mother, Nalan, stood beside him, smiling as she placed a hand on her son's narrow shoulder.

"Do you see? I told you that Constantinople had something Bursa didn't have."

She had come into their rooms three nights ago, her slender, strong body awkward with tension as she told him they needed travel to Constantinople, right away. It was odd, and frightening, and he had not wanted to leave.

It had been just the two of them all Yusuf's young life. He had never known his father, and all the asking in the world about what had happened to him served the boy little, save for the reassurance that his father had not wanted to leave his wife or his son and was, more than likely, not going to be able to return to them.

There were stories, though, that his mother would share with him; tales of his laughter and kindness, and the warmth in his smile. "You are much like him, my child," Nalan would say, and her eyes would somehow be happy while still haunted by sorrow.

Now, however, there were no shadows in his mother's eyes. Whatever it was that had caused her to want to depart Bursa so quickly had, it seemed, been left behind in that city.

"Are you glad you came, my little lion?"

Looking out at the approaching harbor and the buildings that crowded behind it, tall and proud and colorful against the blue of the sky, Yusuf considered the question. It was not so far away that he could not return one day should he so desire, his mother had pointed out while she packed their meager belongings.

He did not like to think of how they had left, or wonder why. His usual good nature asserted itself and as the vessel drew closer to port, with the sounds of the ropes slapping against the ship's hull and the sight of small figures scurrying to greet it and bring it in safely, Yusuf nodded.

"Yes," he announced. "I am."

The voice penetrated Emir's consciousness. It was female, cool, in complete control. Kind, but with no true compassion. But the more he focused on it, the more his head hurt.

"This tells us nothing of import. We know he was a troublemaker as a child, but this seems to be too young to get into much mischief."

"I wouldn't count on that." A male voice this time. Clipped, dry, to the point. "Apparently something significant happened within his first year here."

Emir didn't want to hear this. Somehow he knew it was dangerous, knew it could lead to—

"Can you narrow it down to a specific date?"

"Yes, hang on. There, that's got it."

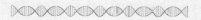

Bursa was the second largest city in the Ottoman empire, so Constantinople, or Konstantinyye, or Istanbul—a recent, local name for the great port city—did not dazzle the boy quite so much as it might have if he been born in a distant village. He knew his way around street corners, alleyways, tunnels, and areas that he knew his mother would not like to know he visited. But while Bursa had certainly been large and bustling, Istanbul was the capital city of the Ottoman Empire, and offered much more.

It was a hub of commerce and activity, where merchants and sailors and travelers, innkeepers and mercenaries, soldiers and beggars all intersected in a noisy, colorful, fragrant, and vibrant collage. People of all walks of life, of all cultures and religions were welcome—indeed, encouraged—to come to the city.

Yusuf had always felt that his mother prepared the best sweets anyone had ever tasted. In Bursa, where she worked in the market, her kemalpasa—a dessert made with unsalted sheep's cheese, flour, eggs, and butter rolled into walnut-sized pieces and then cooked in lemon syrup—was unrivaled. So he was not at all surprised that once a local vendor, a jovial, corpulent man named Bekir bin Salih, had tasted it, he hired her after the first bite.

Yusuf's tasks initially were what they had been in Bursa—to help his mother obtain the ingredients needed to prepare the kemalpasa, to draw customers to the stall, and to deliver cloth-wrapped packages of the delicious treats to customers all over the city. He sometimes took... different routes than most people would, choosing to go over-or under—rather than through the city.

On one such adventure, as he climbed like a monkey onto a rooftop to get an absolutely glorious view of the city, he observed something strange. Certain roofs had poles erected on them. Attached to the poles were ropes that stretched from higher buildings to lower ones. What were these for? Sometimes cords were strung to dry clothing, or to hang banners. But these were thick and solid. They could easily support a man's weight, and he discovered it certainly supported his as he went, carefully, hand over hand from one rooftop to another. Who had put them up? What were they for? He wondered about them every time he looked up.

But there was a more pressing problem than who had erected the rooftop ropes. As the months stretched on, it became apparent to Yusuf that although his mother was able to feed them, she did not come home with the same amount of coins she had earned in Bursa, and what money she was able to make did not go quite as far. The ingredients for the kemalpasa were more expensive here, and the cheese much harder to find. He had already outgrown the clothing they had brought with them, and he knew that replacing them was an expense they could not afford.

Despite the growth spurt, Yusuf was still small for his age and thin as a rail, so he slipped easily among the crowds in the Grand Bazaar and elsewhere. Too many careless people wore their funds either tucked in their sleeves or in small pouches with leather lacings that were the work of a heartbeat to cut and abscond with. Each night, he presented his mother with a handful of coins he had "earned" while supposedly performing acrobatics in the street to draw attention to Bekir's stall, or had "been given" as tokens of appreciation for particularly fast deliveries.

At first his mother was pleasantly surprised, praising him for earning extra income. But as it happened more and more regularly, she grew concerned. One night, she said to him, "Yusuf, tell me, and do not lie... you have not been *hurting* anyone to get these, have you?"

Relieved at the phrasing, which enabled Yusuf to deftly sidestep the real issue and answer quite honestly, "I would never hurt anyone for money, Mama!" She seemed to take him at his word, and didn't press further.

One night, when the Bazaar was lit with torches and several musicians were pounding nagaras and plucking sazes for coins, Yusuf wound his way through the crowd. He stood next to a tall woman dressed in a colorful, well-crafted kaftan and ferace—clearly a woman of means. One hand, soft and clearly unused to physical labor, held tightly to that of a small child of perhaps three or four. In her other arm, she cradled a baby. The older child stared raptly, then giggled and started stamping her feet and jumping up and down. Her mother's face shone brightly, and she swung her arm along with her daughter's capering.

Thus distracted, she was the easiest target Yusuf had encountered all day, and he was in and out in the span of a breath. The purse was surprisingly heavy as he stashed it inside his shirt and maneuvered to the edge of the crowd. A quick scamper and he was out of the bustling major thoroughfare into a side street. He took a look around and, satisfied that he was alone, opened the pouch.

It was too dark to see clearly, but Yusuf had taught himself how to recognize the coins by size and feel, and grinned. This would last him for weeks! He had just started to place the purse back in his shirt when a figure launched itself at him.

Instinct caused him to whirl, and he almost struck a blow of his own before his much larger adversary knocked him to the ground. He landed hard with an *ooof* as the wind rushed out of his lungs.

Yusuf was pinned and couldn't see his attacker's face in the darkness of the alley, but that didn't stop him from struggling and flailing and trying to bite. *Oh, if I were older...!*

"What did you think you were *doing* out there?"

The voice belonged to a boy, older than he and definitely bigger and heavier, but not yet an adult. Yusuf took the opportunity to attempt to knee the older boy in the groin. The other youth twisted out of the way, swearing, and the fight was on.

Yusuf punched hard on the inside of the other boy's elbow, forcing it to bend and the boy to lurch even further to the side. He then pounced atop him like a cat on a rat. Yusuf had not done much fighting; his size did not predispose him to it. But he was angry now, and he began to pummel the other boy with clenched fists. He felt one blow crunch the other's nose and was rewarded with a sharp yelp... before the much larger adversary decided to quit toying with him. One big hand came up, closed around Yusuf's throat, and squeezed as the boy forced him over on his back.

"You idiot, I'm trying to *help* you!" the boy

said, his voice thick from his bloodied nose. "I'm going to let go of you now, all right?"

He was as good as his word, releasing Yusuf and moving quickly out of striking distance. Surprised curiosity chased away anger as Yusuf sat up, touching his neck experimentally. It didn't even hurt much.

The two stared at each other in the dim light, panting. "You're Yusuf Tazim," the other said at last. "I'm Davud bin Hassan."

"How—" began Yusuf, but the other interrupted him.

"I've been watching you," Davud said. "That was a lucky blow. Do you have any cloth?"

Yusuf did; it had been used throughout the day to carry deliveries of kemalpasa and smelled faintly of the sweet as he passed it over to Davud, who, he realized, wouldn't be smelling much of anything anytime soon.

"Well, you attacked me first," Yusuf said, though he wanted to apologize, and knew as well as Davud did that it was, indeed, a lucky blow.

"I was only trying to pin you." Davud accepted the cloth and started to gingerly blot his bloody face.

"And why did you want to pin me if not to attack me or steal my money?"

"Because it's not your money, is it?"

Yusuf had no response to that. It *wasn't* his money. But... "I give it to my mother," he said quietly. "We need it."

"And the woman watching the dancing didn't?" Kemal retorted. "Her children didn't?"

"She looked like she could spare some coins," Yusuf answered, somewhat defensively, as he recalled her well-made, attractive clothes.

"Just like you, Selime's children have no father. I don't know what happened to yours, but I know what happened to theirs. He was violent and cruel to them, and Selime fled in the night to escape. You took everything she had. You could see her fine clothes, but not the bruises on her face, eh?"

Shame washed through Yusuf and he felt his face heat up. The purse *was* unusually heavy; generally those who went out in the market didn't carry quite so much money with them, as thefts weren't uncommon.

"I suppose you want me to give you the money I took from her. But how do I know you're not lying?"

"I don't want you to give me the money. I want you to give it back to her. What *I* want from you is just you."

"I don't understand."

"The Bazaar, Istanbul itself... it can be a difficult place if you are not wealthy or powerful. And it can be particularly dangerous for children. We all look out for each other."

His nose had stopped bleeding, but even in the faint light Yusuf could see it was a mess. Davud started to hand the cloth back to him but he waved it away. He was afraid he had broken the other boy's nose. He thought about the happy little girl dancing gracelessly but joyously to the music. He wondered if the story Davud was telling was true, and if so, how long had it been since that girl had laughed.

"Obviously, you're already a fine cutpurse. I can teach you how to fight. Well, fight even better." Through the mask of blood on his face, Davud smiled. "There are things, and people, that are worth getting a bloody nose—and more—for. And those who aren't. You need to be able to tell which is which, or else one day those light fingers of yours will steal from the wrong person."

The whole thing sounded very strange... and very suspicious. But it also made a lot of sense. Yusuf was well aware that Davud could have killed him just now, and the boy had released him.

Davud got to his feet, towering over Yusuf by about a foot. Yusuf guessed he was about thirteen. "Come on. I'll introduce you to Selime and her family and you can give the money back. Or," he said, "you can leave right now."

Yusuf made up his mind. "Show me."

An hour later, Yusuf walked home alone. His shirt was empty of coin, but his heart was full of satisfaction and his head was full of ideas. He was excited to learn everything that Davud could teach him.

"Cross reference this Davud bin Hassam with our database," came the soft, modulated female voice.

"Nothing. No ties to the Assassins, at least none that we can determine."

"How odd. I had thought, given the significance of this memory, it might be when Yusuf was recruited."

"Too young at age eight even for Assassins, I suppose."

"Formally, perhaps. Still... this was enlightening. What's the next date?"

"April 23, 1480."

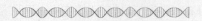

REGRESSION: CONSTANTINOPLE, 1480

It was the bayram of Hidirellez, the festival

that marked the beginning of the spring and summer, and everyone in the city was happy. Though it specifically honored the meeting of two prophets, Hizir and Ilyas, all members of the diverse population of Istanbul found something to celebrate in this bayram that was all about making wishes, letting go of the old and welcoming the new, good health and fortune, and plenty of eating, dancing, and music.

Nalan had been working harder than ever to prepare enough kemalpasa for the celebrating throngs that crowded the Bazaar, and the always genial Bekir bin Salih, the vendor who oversaw several stalls and spaces in the Bazaar, was practically radiating goodwill at the turnout. For once, Yusuf was kept too busy with legitimate deliveries to cut purses, but he would not have done so anyway.

"Hidirellez is about community," the now eighteen-year-old Davud had told his group of young thieves, scouts, spies, and vigilantes. "We won't start our new beginnings by making them bad for others." Yusuf agreed wholeheartedly. There was enough legitimate business going on in the Bazaar anyway.

The festivities went on well into the night. It was the small hours before the last few celebrants headed to their homes, sleepy with full bellies and perhaps a little the worse—or better—for alcohol. After Yusuf and his mother had retired to their modest lodgings, she surprised him by placing something wrapped in cloth on the small table.

"Today is a day for wishes and new beginnings," she said, "and your father had a wish for you... when you were ready. I think it is time."

Yusuf's heart leaped. He sat down on the single bench, eyeing the mysterious bundle. "A wish... what was it, Mother?"

"That I tell you what I could of him, without betraying any oaths he made. And that I gift you with something that once belonged to him."

Yusuf trembled with excitement, and as his mother spoke, he listened with not just his ears, but with every part of himself.

"I have always done what I do," she began. "I prepare kemalpasa and sell it. Your father helped me, as you do now, but he did other things as well."

Her dark eyes watched the small candle flame on the table, obviously wrestling with what she felt she could reveal to their only child, and what needed to remain secret.

Exasperated, Yusuf grabbed his hair and pretended to tear at it. "Mama, I am going to die of anticipation! Tell me before my hair goes gray, will you?"

She laughed then and, sitting down next to him, tousled his hair fondly. "You are barely thirteen, still my little boy in so many ways. But," she added as he rolled his eyes, "also not... in so many ways."

"You were saying he did other things," Yusuf prompted helpfully.

"He was no friend to the Ottomans, or... to others who seek to dominate and control the people." She gave him a sly smile. "My sweet little lion, do you think I do not know what you do when you are not in my sight?"

Yusuf blanched. How did she....

"You could not possibly earn what you do by simple deliveries or entertaining customers. I have seen you with Davud and the others. You explore, you climb, you run along the rooftops. You give what you can to those you can. So did your father."

"What happened to him, Mama?"

She looked away, back at the leaping flames. "He is dead, Yusuf. I have only a few things that were returned—" she caught herself and clucked her tongue. "I say too much. But these things are yours, now that you are of an age where they will fit you. You are not a little boy anymore."

Far from it, Yusuf thought, his pride slightly wounded. But any offense he felt was washed away by the look of pride commingled with sorrow on his mother's strong, beautiful face. He accepted the outstretched bundle, noting the length of teal-colored silk cloth in which it was wrapped.

"Be careful as you unwrap it," his mother warned.

"Why, is there a scorpion or viper hiding inside?"

"No... but it might bite you, nonetheless."

He turned the last fold of cloth and stared at what was revealed. It seemed to be a bracer, or gauntlet of some sort. The leatherworking was beautiful, and Yusuf picked it up carefully, mindful of his mother's warning. Turning it over, he saw that there was something attached to the underside.

"What is it?"

"Your father called it a hookblade," his mother answered. "There is a mechanism in it that will—"

Yusuf started as with a sharp sound, a piece of metal shot out from the end of the gauntlet.

"Ah, I see you found it," his mother finished wryly. "There is a hook, as you can see, and there is a simple blade as well."

"How do I use it?"

Nalan's smile faded. "I never saw them in use," she said. "You know as much as I do, now. But... I think you were meant to know more."

He looked up at her, the question in his dark gray eyes. Her own suddenly glinted in the candlelight, bright with unshed tears.

"I was selfish, and somehow hoped that you would be content to live an ordinary life, with me, and one day with a wife and children. I knew who and what your father was when we wed; and I cannot love you and deny the parts of him I see in you. You were not meant to stay with me, selling kemalpasa and working in the Bazaar, any more than he was. Go, and discover your father's legacy, my darling boy who is now a man."

He wanted to promise her he would be safe, that he wouldn't add the grief of his own death to that which she had already borne. But he couldn't lie to her. The night, the dark alleys, the looks on the faces of those who helped— and those he harmed—drew him too powerfully.

So he did the best that he could to be a dutiful son in this moment. He rose and embraced her, realizing as he did so that somehow in the last year he had shot up to become a half a head taller than her. Holding her so tightly he feared he might crush her, he whispered in her ear, "I will be wise."

It was all the reassurance he could offer.

The night called, and he was anxious to learn.

And... to show off to Davud.

Very, very carefully, he experimented with how the hookblade functioned. Unlike the blade, it was a tool, not a weapon, and his quick mind starting wondering just exactly how it worked. He was able to snag things off the ground as he wandered in the streets, mostly deserted now. It added almost a foot to his reach, so handholds that were impossible suddenly became so, and he found he could ascend much more quickly.

Ascend... and perhaps descend as well....

He made for one of the buildings where he remembered seeing the mysterious ropes, using the hookblade to climb swiftly atop the roof. His heart pounded in his chest and he extended the new tool toward the rope.

It fit over it exactly... as if the rope's thickness had been selected specifically to accommodate the curve of the hook.

Yusuf's mouth was dry with excitement. This couldn't be coincidence. This was deliberate—and he wondered if, perhaps, his father had stood on this very roof years ago, using the blade his son now wore.

He had to know what it was like. But it was a long fall. A very long fall.

Gingerly, he reached out with the hookblade and snagged the rope. It took him a moment to work up his courage, but then he took a deep breath, and stepped off the roof.

Smoothly, swiftly, he sped along the rope. Several yards below, stone streets lay ready to break his bones should the hook slip or give way. The ride was dizzying, exhilarating, and far too brief. Before he knew it, his feet touched the roof of the shorter building.

Yusuf struggled not to let out a whoop of sheer exultation. What a sensation! He had to feel it again. Grinning from ear to ear, this time he didn't fasten the hook on the rope slowly and carefully. He sprang, caught the line, and soared.

He hoped that somehow, his father could see him, and was proud.

"This is unusual," the woman said as Emir drifted, caught between his present and Yusuf's past. "Using an Assassin's weapon at thirteen so efficiently with no training. Remarkable."

"This weapon and this little gang he's running with—all the evidence we've gathered suggests they're extremely important to who he will become."

"And who he becomes has an effect on one of the most important Assassins we know of to date," mused the woman. "Ezio Auditore. Is there anything else we should see before we go to their first encounter?"

"There does seem to be something important about two years on. Hang on... let me get the exact date."

REGRESSION: CONSTANTINOPLE, 1482

Yusuf was both tremendously excited and terribly nervous. In the seven years since he had first met Davud in the alley and learned of the older boy's odd organization of the Bazaar's children, they had had many adventures and close calls.

Davud—whose nose had never healed quite right after that memorable first encounter—had kept his word. He had taught Yusuf how to fight, both fairly and sneakily. He had introduced him to the other members of the group—

children all at the time, though some of them, like Davud and Yusuf himself—who was now second only to Davud—had grown up. Some of them had left the city, or moved to other areas of it. But he and Davud stayed, to look out for the interests of the Bazaar community in ways that the merchants themselves could not.

Tonight, they would perform that duty in a way they had never done before. They would not be throwing small smoke bombs to cause distractions, or stealing coins in a crowd, or even defacing property. Tonight, they would be breaking into a private residence, and stealing whatever they could smuggle out.

Their hands had been forced. Vendors, like the kindly Bekir, rented their stalls from others who owned the spaces. Rent was steep, but that was understood—it was a prime place to sell in the greatest city in the world. But in the last week, a stranger, riding in a palanquin and wearing the finest silks, had made his way through the Bazaar, turning cold, appraising eyes on certain stalls.

And the next thing the stunned merchants learned was that their rent was about to quadruple.

There was nothing they could do, a heartbroken Nalan had told her distraught and furious son. "Poor Bekir is sobbing. He has run his business out of that stall for a dozen years. And now, he has to leave."

"What if we could meet the price?" Yusuf had asked.

She'd laughed, bitterly. "Even if you could cut that many purses, my light-fingered boy, you would not have time to do so. We will need to be out in five days." At the thunder in his face, she added, "We are luckier than most. There are other souks in the city, and everyone likes kemalpasa. We'll be all right."

They might land on their feet, but not everyone else would. What would become of friendly Bekir, and the others who could not readily ply their trades elsewhere?

Fortunately, Davud agreed with Yusuf, and they hatched the scheme they were now about to enact.

They had sent some of the younger children to act as beggars in the area near the new owner's lodgings, and to follow him unobtrusively as he went about his business. That night, one of them reported that the owner, who was obviously not Turkish, would be dining out and not returning until well into the small hours.

He was staying, unsurprisingly, in the best part of town, an area near to the Topkapi Palace, though not, thankfully, within its walls. It was a private residence, and there were a pair of guards out front and a few servants within. As planned, a group of children began to distract the guards long enough for the pair of young robbers to maneuver toward the back and hide themselves amid the flowering trees of a private garden.

While the guards tried to chase away the children, it was the work of a moment for Yusuf to activate his hookblade, ascend to an upper story window, open it, and lower a rope down for his friend. Once Davud had climbed up, they pulled the rope into the room and closed the shutters, so that no passing guard below would notice anything amiss.

Voices floated up from the rooms below; idle conversations from servants who were taking advantage of the fact that their master was not home to gossip and relax. Any theft would have to be conducted upstairs, and Yusuf, who had the ability to do many things at the same, listened with half an ear to the chatter below while he and Davud searched the upstairs rooms.

Yusuf tried to be nonchalant about what he beheld, although he had never seen such luxuries in his short life. Silks and furs decorated the rooms. There were carved, heavy chairs, not benches, and drawers filled jewelry and with ornate clothes with gems sewn into them. He went right to work, using his blade to separate the gems from the fabric while Davud scoured the rooms for coins and other smaller, portable riches. They had several merchants who "knew people" and would be able to liquidate the gems and small valuables quickly.

"This is unbelievable," Yusuf murmured as he picked up a small alabaster carving and thrust it into his sack. His eye fell on a small, wickedly sharp dagger. The hilt was covered with gold and dotted with rubies, and the sheath was made of buttery soft leather. He tossed it to Davud, who caught it deftly. "Here, for you for now," he said. "You are so jealous of my hookblade."

Davud grinned. For the next several minutes, they scoured the large room, shaking their heads at the vast amount of wealth. "We should think about doing this more frequently," Yusuf said. "I have enough in my bag alone to cover the increased rent for a year. Maybe two or three."

"No," Davud said. "It would attract too much attention. We had to do it, this time. But it's best if we keep to the shadows. Don't get greedy, Yusuf. It'll get you every—"

The word died on his lips as they heard the door open below and conversation floated up. Their gazes locked, and their eyes flew open wide. Yusuf turned at once toward the window, cracking the shutters and peering down into the garden below.

Where a guard, dressed like none he had ever seen before, stood. There would be no chance of escaping via rope until he moved.

"We're stuck here," he whispered, "at least for now."

Davud nodded. "Keep watch. Maybe they won't come upstairs right away."

"I am glad all is proceeding well," came a voice. It was a thick accent, and though Yusuf couldn't place it, he took an immediate dislike to it. "The Templars have always had eyes in the Bazaar, of course. The Assassins are not the only ones who can hide in plain sight if need be. But now, we have permanent stalls."

Raucous laughter floated up. Davud and Yusuf stared at each other, horrified. Was the cold-eyed new owner of the stalls setting up some kind of spy ring? Assassins? Templars? He had never heard the terms before.

But they did seem to mean something to Davud. The older youth paled, and he was trembling.

"Davud?" Yusuf said, but Davud lifted a finger to his lips. He touched his ear, indicating that Yusuf should keep listening, then went to the window to peer at the guard for himself. What he saw seemed to shake him even more.

The conversation continued. "You are poised to become one of the wealthiest men in the city," the first speaker continued.

"*One* of?" said the new stall owner.

"I think the sultan might have just a few more coins," the first speaker said. "Regardless, this calls for a celebration."

"Well, since I am about to become at least one of the richest men in Constantinople, let me share a vintage I have kept for this occasion. It is upstairs, in my room. I lock it in there because one can never trust servants. A moment while I fetch it."

"Go," said Davud, suddenly.

He turned to face the door, slipping the sheath off the narrow dagger Yusuf had jokingly handed to him. "Take the bags. You're much quicker than I am, and you have your blade. You can get away. I can't. I'll stall them as long as I can."

"Davud—"

They both heard booted feet coming up the stairs.

"The merchants are counting on you," Davud hissed. "So much I wish I had time to tell you, but—go. Stay alive, keep to the shadows, protect the Bazaar!"

Yusuf stood, rooted to the spot.

The door opened, and everything seemed to happen at once.

With a cry, Davud launched himself on the new owner, raising the dagger and plunging it downward. Despite his surprise, the hard-eyed man pivoted just in time, so that the blade went into his shoulder instead of his chest. Grimly, he pulled out the dagger with his right hand, impossibly seizing Davud's hair with his left despite his wound, and pulling down hard, turning the boy so he faced Yusuf.

Horrified, Yusuf stared into his friend's eyes as Davud shouted, "Run!"

The stall owner lifted the dagger and brought it plunging down.

Crimson. All Yusuf saw was crimson.

The blood spurting from his friend's pierced throat.

The red cross on the ring that adorned a murderer's hand.

Yusuf wanted more than anything to stay and fight, to die alongside his friend. But that choice had been taken from him. Davud had bought him for the merchants and their families with his own life.

Sobbing, Yusuf did as Davud wanted—he fled, taking both bags, leaping out into the night and using the blade bequeathed to him by his father to escape to safety, while his friend bled out on the beautiful rug.

The next day, the hard-eyed man was found dead, and the deal to purchase the stalls mysteriously fell through.

Yusuf didn't know what happened. All he knew was that he would spend his life doing what his friend had died for.

He would stay in the shadows, and protect those who could not protect themselves.

And he would watch, and wait, for other men wearing the red cross.

◼SUBJECT:
MOUSSA

"He's always difficult," a male voice said.

"Moussa or Baptiste?" the calm, almost-caring female voice inquired.

"Both."

"I don't disagree with you. They are both complex individuals."

"Baptiste will make the regression even *more* complicated if his memories are affected by certain toxins."

"Memories are always tricky, even without chemical alterations," the female voice said. "We know that. They're never entirely accurate. We don't see what's *really* there. We only see what he sees."

"As I said... he's always difficult."

"Begin regression," the woman said.

REGRESSION: SAINT-DOMINGUE, 1758

Drumming.

The sound of drumming, forbidden to them when they were property owned by others, was the sound of liberty to the Maroons of Saint-

Domingue. François Mackandal had known this well, and he had taught this truth to those he had trained and liberated.

Had taught that and so much more to the man who now surveyed the dozens of Mackandal's followers, who danced and drank before him in their base deep in the jungle.

Baptiste took another swig of rum as he watched. There were three bonfires, one in the center of the clearing and two smaller ones over to the sides. The dark, sweat-glistened skin of the dancers gleamed as it caught the light. Baptiste had known many of the dancers since he was thirteen, when he and Agaté had run away from their lives as slaves to join Mackandal in his passionate, angry search for liberty and vengeance.

When they had become full members of the Assassin Brotherhood.

Agaté. Agaté, with whom he had grown up on the plantation, and had fought beside. Baptiste had always expected that they would die beside one another. Never had he thought he would witness what Agaté had done earlier today.

The recollection knotted his stomach and he made a sour face. He took another drink, deeper this time, trying and failing to dull the combination of shock, white-hot fury, and, shamefully, pain that stirred in his heart at the thought of the other man.

Agaté. The two men had been as close as brothers, once.

But the third plantation slave Mackandal had selected for training... *she* had ruined that closeness.

Mackandal had come to the plantation in secret, by night, and no one had betrayed him. Those who could—those who dared—managed to sneak away to meetings where he taught them about the life they could have away from the plantation, away from slavery.

At first, he only spoke. Told them about his own life, free, to do as he pleased. Then he taught the eager slaves how to read and write. "Much I will share with those who are worthy," he had promised, "but this may be the most powerful weapon I give you."

She had liked that, skittish little Jeanne. And she had liked Agaté, too. Baptiste had caught them holding hands once, and he had laughed at them, warning that Mackandal would not be pleased.

"You're not strong enough," he had told Jeanne scornfully. "All you do is keep Agaté from his training."

"Training?" she had asked, looking at them both. "For what?"

Baptiste had scowled and dragged his "brother" off to their private meeting with Mackandal. "She will never be an Assassin," he told Agaté. "She is not one of us. Not really. Not in her heart."

Mackandal realized it, too, after a time. She learned how to read and write, but nothing more. He never invited Jeanne to participate in the *real* training. It filled Baptiste with pride to realize that Mackandal—a former slave, one who was even missing an arm due to a childhood accident with a sugarcane press—had not only managed to escape, but could lead others. And win.

In this special training, Baptiste and Agaté learned how to use weapons—and how to attack without them. How to mix poisons—and how to deliver them, as powder in drinks, as a thick coating on darts.

The pair of boys learned how to kill, openly and from the shadows; even, as Mackandal demonstrated, how to do so with only one arm. And when at last they escaped the plantation, leaving the cowardly Jeanne behind, they *did* kill.

The drums grew louder, drawing Baptiste's thoughts from the happy past to the solemn present. Tonight, he, Baptiste, would lead the ritual. This, too, Mackandal had taught him.

Vodou.

Not the true ritual of it, no, but the trappings. The power of symbol, and the power of what was not magic, but appeared to be.

"Let them fear you," Mackandal said, "those who hate you. Even those who love you. *Especially* those who love you."

Tonight's ceremony would change everything. It had to, or all that Mackandal had fought for—all Baptiste and, once upon a time, Agaté, had fought for—would fall apart.

The celebrants had drunk deeply of the rum he had handed out, unaware that there was more in their cups than alcohol. Soon, they would be ready for the ritual; ready to see things they would not otherwise see.

To believe things they would otherwise question.

To do things they would otherwise not do.

The drumming increased, climbing to an almost frantic crescendo, and there was a bawling, bellowing sound off to one side. The bull that was led out had a wreath of flowers around his massive neck. He was drugged and calm, and would not struggle.

Baptiste rose, his powerful fingers curling around the hilt of his machete. He was a large, well-muscled man, and he had done this before, for Mackandal's rites. He leaped lithely down from the platform and strode to the beast. Earlier, by his command, it had been bathed and anointed with perfumes stolen from former masters. Now it turned its horned head, peering at him with wide, dilated eyes. He patted its shoulder and it grunted, as placid as an old cow.

Gripping his machete, Baptiste turned to his people.

"It is time to begin the rite! We will make an offering to the *loa*, and invite them to come to us, to tell us what the Brotherhood must do to go forward!"

The words hurt as they left his lips. Mackandal. For twenty years, from age thirteen to thirty-three, Baptiste and Agaté had fought at his side. They had learned their Mentor's version of the Assassin's Creed—one, he had assured them as they listened to him raptly, that was *not* watered down with misplaced ideals like mercy and compassion. These were weaknesses, not strengths. No one was really innocent; everyone was either with you, or they were against you.

Everyone was a Templar or an Assassin, in one way or another.

A master who did not beat a slave was still a master. An *owner*. And even those who did not own slaves could still do so, by law. Therefore, they were guilty. They served the Templars, even if they were unaware of it. They had no place in Mackandal's world, nor in Baptiste's.

And so it was that Baptiste—and the others who had now stopped their dancing and had turned to face him—had attempted a few nights ago to poison the colonists with whom they were forced to share this island.

But they had failed, and their leader had paid the price for them.

"François Mackandal was our Mentor. Our brother. He inspired us and led by example. And he died without betraying us—died in torment, his body taken by the fire!"

Roars went up. They were drunk, and drugged, and angry, but they were listening to him. That was good. It was Baptiste's plan that soon, they would do even more.

He continued. "And in this time of grief and anger, one who was my brother—your brother—has left us as well. He was not killed in a struggle, nor did he suffer the flames. He simply left us. Left us! Agaté has fled like a coward instead of carrying on the legacy François Mackandal bought with his life!"

More roaring. Oh, yes, they were angry. They were almost as angry as Baptiste.

"But I am here, as your *houngan,* your priest, to plead to the loa for their wisdom. I have not abandoned you! I will *never* abandon you!"

He drew his hand back. The long, steel blade of the machete caught the firelight. And then Baptiste brought it down, quickly, cleanly, putting all the strength of his body into the blow.

Blood fountained from the creature's slashed throat. It tried to make sounds, but could not. The earth beneath it turned red and spongy with the bull's life fluid, but it died quickly. Probably more swiftly than it would have in a plantation owner's abattoir, Baptiste thought; certainly in less pain due to the drug.

He wiped the blade on the beast's hide, then dipped his fingers into the hot blood, marking his face with it. He raised his hands in invitation, and they surged forward now, Mackandal's people, anointing themselves with crimson, placing death on their bodies as it had touched their souls.

Later, the corpse would be roasted at the central large bonfire. Machetes would be used to carve off hunks of delicious, juicy meat. The living would continue to live through death.

But before then, Baptiste had a plan.

Once everyone assembled had bloodied themselves with the sacrifice, Baptiste announced, "I will drink of the potion, and ask the loa to come to me. They will, as they have done before."

They had not, of course, nor had they come to Mackandal, although both men had experienced some interesting hallucinations. The mixture he prepared was lethal at a certain dose; unsettling but harmless when lower amounts were ingested.

And Baptiste was a master at knowing exactly how much to use for what purpose.

Now, he crushed some fragrant herbs between his hands, smelling the clean, fresh scent mingled with blood, and then produced, seemingly out of nowhere, a small bottle of the toxin. Gasps rippled through the crowd. Baptiste hid a smile. He was a master at sleight of hand.

He brandished it and cried, "Tonight, with death so close to our memory, I offer the death of this powerful bull to the *Ghede loa*! Who will come to speak through me to offer wisdom tonight? Who will tell us what Mackandal's people should do?" And he downed the bitter draft in a gulp.

It was but three breaths later that the world began to change.

Colors shifted, seemed to shimmer. There was drumming, drumming, but no one was striking the drums, and the sound was distorted and mixed with what might have been screams of ecstasy or torment. The noise increased, became overwhelming, and Baptiste grunted in pain and clapped his hand to his ears.

Then he realized where the sound was coming from.

It was his own heart, slamming against his ribs, crying out to break loose.

And then it *did* break loose, tearing through his chest, lying on the earth in front of him, red and pulsing and reeking of hot blood. Baptiste stared down at the hole it had torn in his body, aghast.

It's the poison. I took too much. I'm going to die.

Fear surged through him. Stupidly, knowing this all to be an illusion, he reached out and grabbed his still-beating heart. It slipped through his bloody hands like a fish, flopping about, eluding him as he raced for it.

It's never been like this. The dream state—

"That's because this isn't a dream," came a voice, smooth and thick with humor that might or might not be cruel.

Baptiste lifted his eyes to see the skeleton laughing at him.

And screamed.

He clawed at his eyes, forcing himself to see clearly, but even as his vision sharpened, the images didn't depart. The skeleton's body slowly transformed, putting on flesh and formal clothing, looking like one of the fine, wealthy plantation owners—if a plantation owner had black skin and a skull for a head.

"Baron Samedi," breathed Baptiste.

"You asked to be ridden by a loa, my friend," the Baron replied in a silky voice. "You need to be careful who you invite to the party."

In vodou, the loa were the intermediary spirits between humans and the distant god Bondye. The Ghede loa were spirits of the dead. And their leader was the lord of the graveyard—Baron Samedi. Now that loa strode up to the kneeling, shivering Assassin and reached out a hand. "I think you look better with my face rather than bull blood," he said. "You wear it from now on, yes?"

Baptiste reached up his bloodied hands to touch his face.

He felt no warm, living flesh... only dry bone.

The skull peering down at him grinned.

Baptiste closed his eyes and rubbed at them frantically, whimpering as his fingers dug into empty sockets. His face—Baron Samedi had taken his *face*—

Don't be a child, Baptiste! You know better! You made this potion yourself! This is only a hallucination! Open your eyes!

He did.

The Baron was still there, grinning, *grinning*. And beside him stood Mackandal.

Baptiste's Mentor looked as he did in life— tall, muscular, proud and strong, a decade or so older than Baptiste. As in life, he was missing his left arm.

"Mackandal," breathed Baptiste. Tears sprung to his eyes—joy, relief, and wonder. Still on his knees on the bloody earth, he reached out a hand to his Mentor, to grasp at the robes he wore. His hands touched something soft— not fabric—and *passed through it*.

Baptiste fell backward, staring, shocked, at a hand covered with soot.

"I died, burned by those who should have died by my hand," Mackandal said. It was his voice, and his mouth moved, but the words seemed to float in the air around the mentor, like smoke, twisting around Baptiste's head, into his ears, his mouth, his nostrils—

I am breathing his ashes, Baptiste thought

His stomach churned, as it had done earlier, and he began to retch.

A snake emerged from his mouth—thick as

his arm, black and glistening with Baptiste's saliva, undulating as it emerged from his body. When at last he had vomited forth the serpent's tail, the reptile slithered over to the specter of Mackandal. He reached down and picked it up, placing it across his shoulders. Its tongue flickered and its small eyes watched Baptiste.

"The serpent is wise, not evil," Baron Samedi said. "It knows when it is time to change its skin, so that it might grow larger and stronger than it was before. Are you ready to change your skin, Baptiste?"

"No!" he cried, but he knew it was useless. Baron Samedi stepped back, doffing his formal hat to Mackandal to reveal that his skull was as devoid of hair as his face was of flesh.

"You summoned us, Baptiste," Mackandal said. "You told our people you would never abandon them. Now that I am dead, they need a leader."

"I—I will lead them, Mackandal, I swear," Baptiste stammered. "I will not flee from whatever you would have me do. I'm not Agaté."

"No, you are not," Mackandal replied. "But neither will you lead them. *I* will lead them."

"But you are...."

Mackandal began to dissolve into smoke, the snake around his shoulders vanishing with him. The smoke hovered, like mist, then formed itself into tendrils and began to waft toward Baptiste.

Suddenly, Baptiste understood what was about to happen and he tried to get to his feet. Abruptly the Baron appeared behind him. Strong hands—flesh, not bone, but even so, as cold as the grave—clamped down on Baptiste's shoulders and he couldn't move. The thin wisps of smoke drifted to his ears and nostrils, seeking entrance. Baptiste clenched his jaw shut, but Baron Samedi clucked his tongue.

"Ah, ah," he chided, and tapped Baptiste's tightly pressed lips with his skull-headed cane.

Baptiste's mouth opened, and the smoke entered.

And he was both himself... and Mackandal.

Three more tasks, then we shall lead them.

Baptiste stared at the machete he had dropped. It lay beside his still-beating heart. With a strange detachment, he understood that he did not need his heart. It was better, to not care. To not feel love or hope for others. Only his own desires, his own needs, mattered. And so, he left his heart where it was.

But he picked up the machete.

He lifted it slowly in his right hand, and extended his left arm. Part of him screamed not to do this, that he could lead just as well as himself. But another part of him—of him, not Mackandal, not Baron Samedi, wanted this.

Besides, the drug would help with the pain.

Baptiste lifted the machete, took a deep breath, and with a single blow severed his left arm just above the elbow.

Blood seemed to explode from the wound, spurting wildly, but he was right. It didn't hurt. His amputated limb fell to the earth and turned into a serpent, this one crawling toward the skull-faced loa.

Inside his head, Mackandal whispered, "Very good. Now, you are like me. You are no longer Baptiste. You will be François Mackandal. They have seen your gesture. They know I ride you, like they might ride a horse. Usually, the loas leave when they are done.

"I'm not leaving."

Calmly, Baptiste tugged at the sash tied around his waist. By himself, he tied off the spurting wound before the lack of blood could kill him. After all, unlike the Baron, he was still alive.

Baron Samedi nodded in approval. "Good. He is with you, now and always. I will be, too." He tapped his jawbone. "Wear my face, Mackandal."

Baptiste nodded. He understood.

And he agreed.

From this moment on, the rumors would spread. Mackandal was not dead, people would whisper. He had escaped burning at the stake. He was here, and he was full of hatred and vengeance.

And from this moment on, Baptiste would never be seen again. He was still himself, yes; but his name would be Mackandal, and his face would wear, painted in white that would stand out starkly against his black skin, the bony visage of the grinning Baron Samedi.

⊠SUBJECT: ___
LIN

Lin listened to Dr. Sofia Rikkin as she explained patiently, for the third time, that Lin needed to go into the Animus of her own free will. Lin folded her arms, staring, not answering.

"I know what happened to you last time was... traumatic," Sofia said. Her wide blue eyes were kind, but distant. There was compassion in their depths, but not true empathy.

"You know nothing," Lin replied.

Traumatic was a thoroughly inadequate term; a bloodless, clinical word for what Lin's ancestor, a concubine-turned-Assassin named Shao Jun, had been forced to witness five hundred years ago, and what Lin had been forced to witness in the present day.

Five years old. Shao Jun had been *five years old* when the then-new emperor, born Zhu Houzhao and later known as the Zhengde Emperor, had ordered the execution of a eunuch who had conspired against him. Liu Jin had been the leader of a powerful group of eunuchs in the court known as the Eight Tigers, but he had been betrayed by them, as he had betrayed his emperor.

For the dreadful act of treason, Zhengde had ordered that Liu be made to suffer a fate equally dreadful—the Death by a Thousand Cuts.

There had been, in actuality, well over three thousand cuts made by the time it was all over. The gruesome event had lasted for three days. Fortunately for Liu, he had died on the second day, after only about three or four hundred cuts. Onlookers could purchase a piece of the man's flesh for a mere qian, to be eaten with rice wine.

Lin could not get the image out of her mind for days. Sofia's concerned face hovering over her as Lin spasmed and screamed on the floor of the Animus Room became inextricably entwined with the horror. Even now, as Lin looked at the woman, she wanted to vomit.

"I hope you understand that much of the time, we're as ignorant about what you'll experience as you are," Sofia continued.

"How reassuring."

"The reports say that you're doing well," Sofia said warmly. "I'd like you to go back in. After the last regression, we've scoured through as many other sources as are available to us, and I believe this time we've found a memory that's important for us to know, but not quite so..." She groped for the word, then, in a moment of sincerity, blurted, "horrifying."

Lin didn't respond. Her captors—for that was the only way she could think of them—knew more about Shao Jun than she did at this point. More than anything, Lin did not want to back into that poor girl's body; a child who was a concubine to one of the worst playboys in Chinese history.

No. That wasn't entirely correct

More than anything, Lin wanted to keep her sanity. And she knew that they would send her in, regardless of whether she wanted to go, regardless of whether the memory was horrifying.

Sofia Rikkin might want to believe she was inviting Lin to reenter the horrible machine, but both women knew she wasn't. She was *telling* Lin.

The only choice Lin had was how she would comply—willingly or not.

After a long moment, she said, "I will go."

REGRESSION: BEIJING, 1517

Summer was coming to Beijing, but it was not yet time for the court to relocate to the summer palace.

Dim lanterns cast flickering light over the forms of dozens of women, none of them older than thirty, who slumbered fitfully in the nigh-stifling heat. The ornately carved wooden ceiling of the vast room, the largest of nine in the 1,400-square-yard Palace of Heavenly Purity, was lost to view in the darkness, but the light still caught glimmers of dragons painted in gold leaf, and the gleam of locked ornate doorknobs.

Twelve-year-old Shao Jun eased open the massive door and moved quietly over the black marble floor. The palace was the largest of the three located in the Forbidden City's inner court; the residence of the Zhengde Emperor, his empress, and his favored concubines.

Shao Jun had been born here, to another concubine who had not survived the ordeal. If any place was her home, this was, with its exquisite carved ceilings, large, comfortable beds, and the murmur of women as they learned the fine arts of their station: dancing, playing instruments, embroidery, and even how to walk, move, and laugh appealingly.

She had learned these, too. But early on, her talent for almost unnaturally beautiful dance and phenomenal acrobatic skills had attracted the attention of the young Zhengde Emperor, who had had at once put her to good use spying on his enemies and playing amusing tricks on his friends.

Shao Jun tried very hard not to wake Zhang as she climbed carefully into the large bed they shared with two others, but she failed. Zhang murmured sleepily, "One day you will come to bed with the rest of us and we will all die from astonishment."

Jun laughed softly. "No, I do not think that will happen."

Yawning, Zhang made room for her and sleepily pillowed her head on her friend's shoulder. In the lantern-lit darkness, Jun smiled.

Singled out for her tumbling and put to work by Zhengde as early as she had been—three years old—Shao Jun had always been the object of hostility, veiled and otherwise, from her fellow concubines. She'd risen swiftly, despite a comparatively low-class birth, whereas many of the hundreds Zhengde kept in the three harem buildings had only seen the Son of Heaven from a distance.

So when Zhang, the daughter of a palace guard, had been brought into the harem a year ago—the epitome of womanly Chinese perfection with her small, bound breasts and feet, demure manners, shell-pale skin, and large, soft eyes—Jun had assumed she would be just like the others.

Instead, once she heard about Shao Jun, Zhang had sought out the other girl. Due to her experience as the emperor's favorite spy, Jun was particularly mindful of the false faces the court—and other concubines—could display. At first, she had been cautious and close-mouthed.

Zhang seemed to understand and did not press. But gradually, something strange happened. Even though they were in competition for the attention of the emperor—whose approval could, quite literally, mean a life of luxury and comfort or a horrifically brutal death—Zhang never seemed to see it as such. Once, she made an offhand comment that struck Jun poignantly.

"There is no one who moves as you do, Shao Jun," she had said admiringly after Jun had bested her for the court's approval of the Ribbon Dance. "That is why I simply watch and enjoy, like everyone else."

"But you are so beautiful, Zhang!" Jun had exclaimed, gesturing at her own feet and chest, which had never been bound. Zhengde had forbidden it: *You are too good at hiding and climbing,* he had said. Without the binding, Jun knew, men would never think of her as attractive. 'I could never be like you, either!"

Zhang had laughed. "Your tumbling and my smile are like a rabbit and a butterfly," she said, referring to two creatures particularly loved by the Chinese. Both were valued, and neither was better than the other. They were simply different.

She understands, Shao Jun thought, and had to turn away lest anyone see the quick tears of joy that sprang to her eyes.

They had become like sisters since then, and now, as Zhang lay next to her, she said, as she always did, "Tell me."

It was both pleasure and pain for Jun to tell the stories, because she knew, as Zhang did, that they would never happen for the older girl. This butterfly was in a cage, like a cricket; but the rabbit was free.

Once, Jun had tried to show Zhang her world. It had been a few months ago, before the third watch, when soldiers in the Drum Tower would strike the thirteen kettle drums to rouse the household in preparation for the daily audience. The concubines, of course, did not need to rise, but the eunuchs, the court officials, and their staffs all had to be ready to meet with the emperor at four A.M., and this audience would be repeated twice more during the day.

Zhengde hated it, of course. He had proposed a single audience at night, with a banquet afterward. But even an emperor, it seemed, could not have all his desires met; the idea was met with vehement opposition.

It was the optimal time, Jun knew, to sneak out of the quarters and explore. And so she and Zhang had. Many of the eunuchs were asleep at their posts, and Jun was easily able to trick or distract the others. They had slipped outside into the streets, where Zhang stared up at the star-crowded night sky—something she had never seen. Always before, if the concubines were permitted at to be out at night for a festival or other event, the lanterns around them hid the shyest of the stars.

They pressed on. Jun had discovered many hidden passages over the years, but Zhang was too nervous to crawl through them, laden with cobwebs and dust as they were. Jun pressed, promising to help her, but Zhang blushed and simply said, "My feet."

Jun felt as though she had been struck a blow in the stomach. She had forgotten the other reason why concubines and high-born women of the court had their feet bound: so they would never run away with another man.

Sick, she looked at her friend, seeing her own sorrow reflected in Zhang's soft eyes.

They had returned, and Jun had never suggested it again. But Zhang was determined to escape her gilded cage, if only vicariously through Shao Jun's adventures, and, as now, often asked her friend to tell her stories.

Jun listened carefully, but the other girls in the bed appeared to be sleeping deeply. One of them was even snoring lightly. Jun began to whisper, for Zhang's ears alone.

"Tonight," she said, "I performed in the Bao Fang."

"Were there leopards?" Zhang asked.

The name meant Leopard's Chamber, and Zhengde had ordered it built outside the Forbidden City to house exotic animals and for acrobatic and dance performances. It was also a good place to eavesdrop, but Jun withheld that bit of information. It might put Zhang in danger, and Jun would never do that.

"Not tonight," Jun replied, "but there were two lions and seven tigers."

Zhang giggled, covering her mouth with her hand to stifle the sound.

"There are seven Tigers here, too," she said.

Jun did not smile. The most important and

powerful eunuchs in court had been known as the Eight Tigers. As Zhang noted, they were seven, now. Jun had been forced to watch their leader, Liu Jin, die an excruciatingly painful death.

Zhang didn't know that, either.

"There are," Jun simply agreed, and continued describing in detail the powerful muscles of the big cats and the gold and orange-black beauty of their coats, how frightening they were to the court, and how exciting it had been for Jun to perform a routine right above their cages, where she could fall at any minute.

"And last night?" Zhang had been asleep last night. So Jun obligingly told her that last night, Zhengde had indulged in one of his favorite pastimes.

"I know you heard about it," she teased.

Zhang punched her playfully. "But I wasn't there."

"All right. He had the market set up again last night, and this time he pretended to be a commoner from outside Nanjing. He had Ma Yongcheng be a mushroom farmer, while Wei Bin sold silk."

The idea of these powerful men pretending to be ordinary farmers and merchants while he, himself, was a humble customer amused Zhengde greatly. It did not, however, amuse those members of the court forced to perform such roles—especially not any of the Eight Tigers.

"What about Gao Feng?"

"He sold snails."

Zhang buried her face in the pillow to stifle her laughter. Jun grinned, too. She had to admit, watching these proud men gritting their teeth through their performance was a sight to behold.

"And you?"

"Me? I helped cook noodles."

"Tell me more," sighed Zhang happily. Her lids were closing again. Jun did, describing more of the silliness, speaking softly and steadily until Zhang's breathing became slow and regular.

Sleep did not come so easily for Jun. Zhengde had told her he was curious about the fighting going on in the north to repel some of the raiding expeditions led by the Mongol warlord Dayan Khan.

"Maybe I will visit in secret," he had said, warming to the idea the more he spoke about it. "I need another name—just like I do for the market! What do you think of 'Zhu Shou'?"

"As my emperor wishes, I am sure it is a fine name!" she had answered promptly.

But he wasn't done. "I will need my clever little kitten Shao Jun to wander around the campsites and listen for me," he had told her.

Although it could be argued that by following her emperor to battle Jun would be in a more dangerous position than Zhang, Jun couldn't help but think the opposite. Zhang wasn't stupid, but there was an innocence, a vulnerability inherent in her nature that Jun thought she herself had never had. Like the cat Zhengde sometimes called her, she always seemed to land on her feet.

There was plotting afoot with the Eight Tigers, and cunning and deception among the concubines. She did not like the thought of abandoning Zhang to that. But she did not have a choice—not this time.

If the Son of Heaven wanted her to accompany him while he attacked the Mongols, she would have to go.

A fierce protectiveness rose in Shao Jun as she watched her friend sleep peacefully.

This I vow, Zhang, my best friend, my only friend. If you need me, I will come. No matter what, no matter where—I will come for you, and keep you safe. No threat, no Imperial order, nothing will keep me from you if ever you need me.

Ever.

And as if she somehow could hear the words that Shao Jun spoke only in her heart, Zhang smiled in her sleep.

ACKNOWLEDGMENTS

Many thanks must go out, as always, to my hardworking agent, Lucienne Diver. I'm also grateful to the terrific team at Ubisoft: Caroline Lamache, Anthony Marcantonio, Anouk Bachman, Richard Farrese, and especially Aymar Azaïzia, whom I pestered mercilessly and who always replied promptly and cheerfully.

I must also acknowledge the talents of director Justin Kurzel and actors Michael Fassbender, Marion Cotillard, and Jeremy Irons, who provided so much inspiration during the writing of this book.

**TURN THE PAGE FOR
AN EXCERPT FROM**

**ASSASSIN'S CREED®
HERESY**

BY CHRISTIE GOLDEN

**AVAILABLE WHEREVER
BOOKS ARE SOLD**

The autumnal night's chill sliced through the man's thin shirt as he fled, feet flying over first the concrete pathway, then the manicured grass of the rooftop's park. Why did I come up here? he thought, wildly and far too late. I'm a bloody rat in a trap.

The Templars were behind him.

They knew where he had fled. And they knew, as he did, that other than the lift and the two stairways from which they now emerged with grim and silent purpose, there was no way off this roof.

Think. Think!

Thinking had saved him before, many a time. He'd always relied on logic, on rationality, on analysis, to solve every predicament that life in all its sadistic whimsy had thrown him, but now it was of no use to him at all.

The deadly percussion of gunfire exploded

behind him. Trees, his rational mind shouted, and the logic saved him. He altered his path, zigzagging to make himself an unpredictable target, careening erratically like a drunken man toward the trees and shrubberies, statuary and now-vacant ice cream and beverage stalls that would shield him from the hail of bullets.

But it would only delay the inevitable.

He knew very well what the Templars were capable of. And he knew what they wanted. They were not coming to question him, or capture him. They were intent on killing him, and therefore, very, very soon, he would be dead.

He was not without a weapon himself, one that was ancient and powerful. A Sword of Eden, which had known the grip of both Templars and Assassins through the centuries. He had used it earlier. It was strapped to his back, its weight calming and reassuring, and he would leave it there. It would not serve him now.

The Templars were single-minded of purpose, dedicated only to dominance and death—his. There was only one way out, and it would be a bloody miracle if it worked.

His heart was slamming against his chest, his lungs heaving, his body taxed to its limit because in the end, he was only human, wasn't he, no matter what kind of training he had, no matter what sort of DNA was floating about in his blood. And he didn't slow, couldn't slow, couldn't allow that logical, analytical, rational brain of his to interrupt the signals from the deep primal instinct of survival. Couldn't let his brain overrule his body.

Because his body knew what was called for. And it knew how to do it.

A tree branch exploded right beside him. Splinters grazed his face, drawing blood.

The fate offered by the Templars behind him was one of heartless certainty. The stone roof that encircled the edge of the rooftop garden of the London office of Abstergo Industries offered a wild, desperate chance.

If he had the faith to take it.

He didn't slow. As he approached the wall, he surged forward, clearing it like runner would a hurdle, his long legs pedaling in the air as he arched his back, spread his arms—

—and leaped.

ABOUT CHRISTIE GOLDEN

Award-winning and eight-time New York Times bestselling author Christie Golden has written fifty-one novels and several short stories in the fields of science fiction, fantasy, and horror. She has earned wide critical acclaim and a devoted fan base for both her original work and her authentic and skillful literary treatment of many beloved film, television, and gaming franchises.

Golden has written more than a dozen Star Trek novels, and about the same number of World of Warcraft and StarCraft novels. She has written three books in the Star Wars series Fate of the Jedi, which she co-wrote with Troy Denning and the late and greatly missed Aaron Allston, as well as *Star Wars: Dark Disciple*, the novelization of the unaired episodes of *Star Wars: The Clone Wars*, cited as one of the best of the new canon novels.

Golden has been an aficionado of the Assassin's Creed universe since 2014, and has already written two books for the franchise: *Blackbeard: The Lost Journal*, a companion book to the video game *Assassin's Creed IV: Black Flag*; *Assassin's Creed Unity: The Abstergo Employee Handbook* and *Assassin's Creed: Heresy*, which published in November 2016.

Christie Golden has been publishing books for twenty-five years. The TSR Ravenloft line in 1991 was launched with her first novel, the bestselling *Vampire of the Mists*, which introduced elven vampire Jander Sunstar. To the best of her knowledge, she is the creator of the elven vampire archetype in fantasy fiction. Among her original fantasy novels are *On Fire's Wings*, *In Stone's Clasp*, and *Under Sea's Shadow*, the first three in her multi-book fantasy series The Final Dance. Her very first original novels, *Instrument of Fate* and *In Stone's Clasp*, are currently available in digital form nearly fifteen years after their original publication.

Born in Atlanta, Georgia, Christie Golden currently lives in Virginia. You can find her online at christiegolden.com, on Facebook as Christie Golden, and on Twitter @ChristieGolden

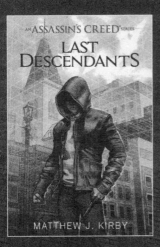
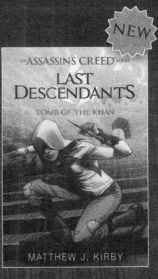

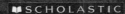